Watch for More

Deep Indigo Books

From Michael Rose

www.indigoseapress.com

Gracie of Hobbs County

By

Michael Rose

Deep Indigo Books
Published by Indigo Sea Press
Winston-Salem

Deep Indigo Books
Indigo Sea Press
302 Ricks Drive
Winston-Salem, NC 27103

This book is a work of fiction Any resemblance to any event,
locale or person, living or dead, is purely coincidental. All
characters in this book are either fictional or are tall, beautiful and
live with happy dogs in green meadows.

First Deep Indigo Books edition published
December, 2015
Deep Indigo Books, Moon Sailor, and all production design
are trademarks of Indigo Sea Press, used under license.

For information regarding bulk purchases of this book,
digital purchase and special discounts, please contact the publisher
at indigoseapress@gmail.com

Cover design by Cynthia O'Neill
Photography by Michael Campbell
Manufactured in the United States of America
ISBN 978-1-63066-357-5

ACKNOWLEDGMENTS

My heartfelt thanks to the following individuals, whose ideas and encouragement helped make this book possible: Lorraine Ahearn, Laura Baker, Christina Bartolomeo, Jennie Blackton, John Coates, Bill Morris, Amy Rose, Howard Rose, Jeannette Rose, Jessica Rose, Lawrence Rose, Matthew Rose and Stephen Rose.

For Amy, Jessica, Matthew and Rocky

Part I

Chapter One

At the base of Burnside Mountain, a stray dog rested in the cool crawlspace of an abandoned farmhouse. His last and only owner called him "Vick," a name inspired by the dogfighting NFL quarterback, and, more importantly, by the unshakable belief in Hobbs County that what a man does with his own property, canine or otherwise, was his own damn business.

The farmer who once owned Vick had no intention of fighting him, however. No Friday-night barn mauler, Vick was a mix of retriever and spaniel. He was a gun dog, a flusher, cagey and finely tuned to detect the twitch of prey, even in the thickest brush. He never spooked at the crack of buckshot whistling over his shoulder. And he displayed the type of level-headedness and even temperament that hunters praise as "steady to wing and shot."

In an easier world, Vick would have spent his days on Burnside Mountain, rousting dove, turkey and pheasant from the upland mountain laurel. But things rarely worked out easy in Hobbs County for man or for beast.

One night, Vick's farmer left his lights on late into the evening. There was only one other time the dog saw him do that, the night the old grandmother died. This night was something different, however. There was a steady slam of screen doors in the dead of night, people walking from the house to the car and back again. The man was packing up his family and blowing out of state, leaving behind a house in arrears, ten thousand dollars in unpaid medical bills for the old dead woman, and a dog who was too late to answer the whistle.

"Vick! Dammit, git back here!" the man yelled, forking two fingers against a curled tongue and blasting three high notes into the thick night air. Nothing. The dog often roamed at night and

1

could be anywhere in the valley at this late hour. For 15 minutes, the man shouted and cussed and whistled until his wife rolled down the car window.

"Leave it. If we're going, then let's go," she hissed in a low voice, careful not to wake three kids curled up in the back seat. "That dog don't matter. You got no place for him now, anyways."

Vick trotted into the backyard just in time to hear the crackle of tires along the gravel. He ran to the front yard and gave chase— loping along on three good legs, his right forepaw shriveled and deformed since birth. Instinct made the little foot keep the rhythm, flapping uselessly by Vick's side as the black-and-copper dog ran faster. Finally, the taillights grew small, faint and disappeared over a hill for good.

Just like that, Vick was a stray, and he adjusted to the new life with ease. He was, after all, one of the most notorious rovers in Hobbs County, so the life of a stray wasn't much of a stretch. Only a few times did hunger, cold and curiosity get the best of him. Vick would hobble back through the frosted fields of late winter, back to the old house where he was once a family pet and valued gun dog, even with only three good legs.

It had been more than a year now since there was light in the windows, smoke from the chimney or scraps in the dish by the back stoop. The only sign of life in the old five-room rambler was a "No Trespassing" sign the sheriff had nailed to the front door.

In those early days, Vick would slink to the edge of the old lawn and stare for a few seconds, peering through the overgrown weeds, chewing on a dry sheaf of grain out of hunger. His ears stood foxy and upright as he searched the windows for the man, the woman and the kids. All was cold and dark. Finally, the dog would turn and trot away, looking for a barn, a shed or a car with a warm engine block to hide under.

By spring, the farmer's house was just one of many the dog would visit in a constant search for game birds, rabbits, chickens or bitches for the taking. The routine was set once the long, hot days of summer arrived. Vick would bide his time in the daylight, hiding and sleeping in shade and cool patches of dirt, waiting for Burnside Mountain to swallow the hot, red sun. Once the dim arrived and the cool balm of twilight spread across the land, Vick was out and on the prowl. Every night he loped west to east, hugging the weedy fringe of Route 23, the only highway in Hobbs County.

Vick followed the road until he reached a flashing traffic light in Cochrane, the county seat. It was the only signal in the small town, the only light in all of Hobbs County, the point where Route 23 spurred onto Main Street for a few desperate yards of ailing retail. More than half of the stores on Main Street were now boarded and padlocked. The ones out of business for a long time looked like overgrown terrariums, their roofs caved in, their walls corralling the rain and snow inside. Weeds took hold in the wet and rotting floorboards and snaked to sunlight through broken foundations and shattered glass.

Vick peered in a few uncovered trashcans for fresh garbage and glanced up at the traffic light, pulsing yellow. There were no hard signals at this hour—it was pushing 9 p.m. and the only stores doing business this late were the minimart in the BP station and a bar called The Watering Hole.

Inside the bar, a few men in farmer's caps and flannel stooped at the counter to nurse beers in the blue glow of ESPN Sports Center highlights. They grunted at good plays but exchanged few words. Sips from their frosted mugs were well spaced, almost dainty. Drinking slow meant going home late. Going home late meant less bitching they'd have to endure about unpaid bills, the kids' ratty shoes, and other assorted failures to provide.

A metal sign was bolted to the traffic light outside the bar. It read, "No cruising, No loitering, 8pm-6am" and was signed by the Hobbs County Sheriff's office. Below the advisory, some cutup had spray-painted "No meth hos" in watery red letters.

The sign was ignored by a handful of girls on the street, some as young as 16 and a couple in their 40s. Most were skinny and wore dingy wife-beater T-shirts or tube tops. They were tight enough to make a showy display of tits that covered the entire spectrum: the good, the bad and the droopy. Many of the girls wore sweatpants with easy-on, easy-off elastic waists. They were loose and rode low, showing off diamond tramp-stamp tattoos centered above thongs, G-strings or just the bare cleft of their pale asses. Most had bad skin and teeth that were rotten if they weren't missing.

After 20 minutes, a slow-roller pulled onto Main Street and two girls peered in to chat with the stranger. The younger of the two girls leaned halfway through the open window while the older one stood behind her, scouring the street for the sheriff's prowler. Through the negotiations, the older one kept hold of her partner's red tube top, ready to yank her out of the Accord if things went wrong. The meeting ended abruptly, with the young blonde shaking her head and the driver pulling off alone. The road was empty again, and the girls walked to the minimart for L&M cigarettes, chips and Colgate travel-sized mouthwash.

"Hey, it's gimpy!" the young blonde cried after spotting Vick on the sidewalk.

Vick limped over, slowly and suspiciously, and the girl reached into a bag of Cheetos to offer him a morsel. The dog took his time, inching toward the girl and backing off as fear and hunger took their turns. Finally, Vick snatched the curl from her hand and shot down the street, heading east again.

"You'll be back. All you dogs come back!" the girl called with a cackle, orange paste filling in the gaps in her smile.

The dog hit a comfortable trot. In a few minutes, he was passing the new rail station at the edge of town. The depot was three planks of plywood nailed together, an open-air shed, just enough roof to keep a handful of commuters dry. Across the street sat the county office building with a two-story mural painted on its side: Daniel Boone blazing a trail through the wilderness.

It had been years since the mural was painted, and ol' Dan'l clearly had seen better days. The artist had done him up Walt Disney style, putting him in one of those coonskin caps that Fess Parker made famous, a hat the real pioneer detested and refused to wear. Adding insult to injury, the snow, rain and ice had rubbed out the tail, transforming the cap into a Turkish fez. And someone had retouched Daniel's musket to look like a semiautomatic, unloading a stream of bullets (or possibly rabbit pellets) into the hills. Boone seemed to take it all in stride—unfazed even by the fact that the artist had put his back to Burnside Mountain. Rather than blazing a trail, the frontiersman was turning tail for the coast.

Vick pissed on the wall and trotted on.

Dark claimed the landscape, and Virgo lounged on the horizon as a glow appeared ahead. It was the dull gleam of lights illuminating the work of the night cleaning crew at Burnside

Overlook School. The modern, two-story school was lined with cobblestone paths and trimmed with tiered landscaping. Elaborate and expensive playground equipment was swaddled in wood chips and painted in fresh, cheerful pastels. At Burnside Overlook, overtime was never an issue; maintenance worked till the job was done. By morning, every bathroom would have soap, every stall would have paper, every urinal would work, with no tile left unshined.

Behind him, Vick heard tires coming up the road. The pitch of the engine was low and growly, like the sound of the dogcatcher truck. Vick darted into the brush, watching as the vehicle passed by. It was a Ford F-150, a dually—two wheels in front, four in back, and a heavy pair of pink rubber testicles dangling from the rear bumper. They hung just below the license plate, decked on the margins with two chrome girls on all fours. Rodney Atkins sang "Take a Back Road" through the tinny truck stereo. Vick hunkered down as the truck slowly rolled by. Through the open window, the dog spied the Cheetos girl riding shotgun.

Only a few hundred yards now separated Vick from Burnside Overlook School. It sat by the bank of the river on the county's eastern flats. Beside it was the only gated community in Hobbs County. It was a nest of McMansions that hill folk called "Snottytown," and later, when talk radio turned a gaffe into dog-whistle politics, "Arugula Acres."

Vick was searching for a hole in the development's brick wall when something caught his eye: two golden circles no bigger than quarters, peering through the rows of corn in the farm next door.

Vick froze. The copper fur on his shoulders stood tall. Somewhere a screen door slammed but the glowing circles in the corn never moved.

"Ruth! Come here, sweetness!" a woman yelled.

For a second, the golden circles went dark and the inky profile of another dog's head snapped into focus under the full moon. A dog was turning toward the woman's call.

Vick flared his nose and filled his lungs. The scent of heat, a smell like blood and iron, was mixing with the musky aromas of the farm. Vick's belly was gnawing. In truth, a stray chicken would have won the dog's best effort that night, but the earthy call of the dark retriever was a clear second best.

5

Vick squatted low on his forepaws and raised his haunches, ready to spring at the mark's slightest move. He was frozen except for the slow deliberate wag of his bushy tail.

The golden lights reappeared, the eyes turning back to measure Vick coolly through the corn. Then the lights took off.

Vick broke for the female. The scratch of dry stalks tracked his progress through the night. The retriever was powerful and fast, with four good legs to Vick's three. But her flight was halfhearted and Vick was cagey, cutting her off at every turn.

The two dogs pulled even, panting and sparring with playful open jaws as they loped along in the open field. Vick, the smaller, hopped on and off the retriever's flanks like she was a show pony in a circus ring. The woman threw open the screen door again to call the dog's name, but Ruth paid her no mind. She bounded for the shadows with Vick prodding her along.

They ducked behind a barn, and the minutes that followed were nasty, brutish and short. They were also fruitful.

*****

Nine weeks later, Ruth was lying behind the same barn—five squirming pups pressed to her belly. They were good-looking dogs. All had the sleek, broad skull of their mother, along with her golden eyes and a hint of midnight color; all had Vick's high, foxy ears, and traces of his copper coat. The pups were even-tempered but hardly mild. They jockeyed hard for the nipples while their mother panted behind the barn and stared into space.

Something appeared at the corner of the barn. It was the woman, the woman at the screen door, and she sighed mightily as she gathered the whelps into a cardboard box before walking them inside with Ruth on her heels.

All nursed eagerly and grew—all save Gracie, the runt. She alone had inherited Vick's short forepaw and it cost her dearly in the fight for feeding rights with her marauding brothers and sisters.

The woman was forced to take matters into her own hands. She scooped the runt into her palm twice a day and fixed her on a bottle. Gracie took it eagerly and nursed with a look that pups get—sweet, almost cross-eyed, a gaze both vacant and alert. The woman smiled, stroking the shriveled right forepaw between thumb and finger. She cooed at the dog, bringing the tiny face close to hers, grazing noses and looking into the whelp's small, puffy eyes. Gracie would have none of it. Her small jaws worked the bottle methodically with her golden stare fixed somewhere else.

Soon, fliers were up on telephone poles around Hobbs County, "Five pups, free to take," and it wasn't hard to place the litter. The pups were chubby and playful and alert. All had the makings of good gun dogs, and they were snatched up by local farmers always eager for the right dog at the right price. Two of the pups went to families in the gated community, two-paycheck couples who wanted a mild-mannered dog that wouldn't bark all day while the kids were in school and the adults were working.

All were taken, except Gracie.

Ruth, the mother, returned to her old life. The mild-mannered Labrador loved nothing more than to nestle her boxy, black head into any lap seated at the kitchen table. For hours, she would pad back and forth on the checkered linoleum, weaving between the legs of the woman and her husband, nuzzling for strokes and pats under the table. It was something that always seemed to soothe anxious discussions about overdue feed bills, busted fences and broken equipment (which were most of the topics these days). Gracie watched her mother closely and saw how Ruth loved every moment. She had the talent—the makings of a true therapy dog, a Zen-like warrior against anxiety, a hound keeping human heebie-jeebies at bay.

There was only one conversation that Ruth couldn't soothe: What to do about Gracie, the only pup left in the cardboard litter box.

People had looked into the box and quickly passed on the last of the litter. It wasn't hard to understand why. There was the shriveled paw. She was puny, and her gaze never engaged when people peered over the cardboard. Soon, the doorbell stopped ringing; the phone went silent. Word was out that there were no good dogs left.

"It's time to shelter that last pup," the man told this wife one morning.

"Take her to county? Forget it! They run a kill shop," the woman replied, stroking Ruth's head as she spoke.

7

"Well, we're not keeping her," the man snapped. "Do something this week or I'll be taking her myself."

The woman sighed and leaned down to Ruth, who rewarded her face with gentle kisses and nuzzles.

"You!" the woman gently scolded, stroking the dog's head. "See what happens when I call and you don't come?"

Chapter Two

Gracie showed up in a cardboard box dropped at the back door of Ellen Blair, the owner and lead trainer at the Kozy Kennel & Comfort Dog Training Academy.

This backwoods operation often received mysterious packages from Hobbs County locals. Most of them waited for night to fall. Then they would fill Blair's back porch with their boxes, sly presents wrapped only in a mountain fog so thick that it muffled the sound of the getaway cars. The boxes came from the kindhearted sorts. These were the ones who refused to deliver pets to Animal Control, where they would get 10 days behind the wire, dogs pacing the concrete floors until a final needle stick put an end to it all.

Kozy Kennel didn't kill. The policy was firm. And it was sinking the business, although folks nearby said that the renegade kennel-academy was never much of a going concern even in its best days.

Ellen almost stepped on the dog before she saw the box on her back porch. The old woman's knees crackled in the early hours as she stooped to pick it up. She carried it to the kitchen table, still half-bent, and brushed back a shock of wild, white hair for a better look. The deep creases around her mouth softened a bit once she peered inside. Her green eyes, usually so absent and angry, suddenly flashed into focus.

Inside was a pup, gold and black, not much bigger than the saucer under the old woman's morning coffee. The dog's right forepaw looked shriveled, and she was sucking on it like an oversized pacifier. Ellen reached in and stroked the velvet of each ear, slyly folding back the little triangles to check for red flesh and the scatter of critters. Then she slid a thin, weathered finger under the pup's lip and gently tugged back, revealing white teeth and gums that were pink and firm. Satisfied, Ellen spread the dog's eyes wide. The iris glowed bright and gold, unscored by stress, surrounded by clear whites.

"Someone's took care of you," Blair whispered to herself.

"Guess they weren't entirely fixed on giving you up."

Gracie ignored the old woman's words and stared at the wallpaper: little Dutch boys beside blue windmills.

The kennel owner turned her attention to the dog's frame. She rubbed the tiny paws between thumb and forefinger, kneading the bones, gauging how big the dog might grow. Medium, 25 pounds tops, she guessed. That would make her small enough for apartment living. Then Blair wiggled the pup's hips, checking for tenderness. None. Through it all, the dog stayed still and sweet, just staring at the wall. Inside the box was a note, and Ellen fished it out.

This is Gracie. Good dog, but runty. Sceared of noise and chews herself some. We give the others away. This one never took. Thanks.

"Thanks," Ellen huffed. "Least you got manners."

The note didn't lie. Gaps in the copper fur showed a little anxious chewing going on. That could be broken easily enough. The short paw would be a problem, too, but mostly for those looking for a hunting dog. It wouldn't matter much to any shut-in wanting to adopt for company.

The important thing was temperament, and Gracie seemed to have it in spades.

The little dog stayed sweet and still throughout the inspection, fixing the walls in a gaze that was calm and keen. The first dog Ellen ever owned had that look, too. He was a placid spaniel with bright eyes and a tail that swept high and friendly for everyone he saw. They named him Lucky. He was run over and killed by a truck 10 years ago.

Lucky was the first dog Ellen trained to be a therapy pet. In his gaze was a loving calm, and Ellen could call it up like it was yesterday. It was a special look, almost otherwldly. Ellen had not seen it since the old dog died, not in the dozens of canines that Kozy Kennel had taken in and trained over the years. She was sure she would never again see that Lucky look. Until now.

"Just might have something here," Ellen whispered as she cradled the new pup. Gracie turned for a moment and locked on the woman's face. Then the dog turned back to the blue windmills and Dutch boys on the wall. Ellen smirked.

"Can't fool me, young'un. I saw what I saw."

Wisps of smoke began to fill the kitchen. They came from a pan on the stove, boiled dry, glowing and forgotten on the range's red coils. Eggs that were supposed to be breakfast sat smoking in the bottom of the pan. Gracie, this little echo of Lucky, had chased them from the old woman's mind.

"Cap, get in here! We got another one," Ellen called over her shoulder, still rocking the pup.

A tall, thin boy rubbed his eyes as he stumbled into the kitchen. Two whiffs of smoky air sent him dashing to the stove, where he grabbed the glowing pan to douse under cold water. The eggs cracked open with a pop.

"Mamaw, set the timer! That's three times this month," the boy said as he walked back to switch off the burner. "You're going to kill us for sure."

The boy moved toward the box, still rubbing the sleep out of green eyes that grew narrow and hard once he peered inside. Great, another dog ditched on their porch! And a puny, three-legged one at that.

"OK, I see her. So what?" Cap said flatly. The teenager had the same green eyes and narrow face as Ellen. His auburn hair was as thick and wild as hers, too, and even now a little salted with the gray that would claim it all in 40 years. Anyone would know he was kin to her.

"Look at the face, Cap. If that's not Lucky—"

"Lucky?!"

"You don't see it?" Ellen pressed, holding the pup up for her grandson to inspect. "She's got that look. See it? Gold and sweet, just like Lucky."

"What I'm looking at is a castoff on three good legs," Cap snapped. "What I see, Grandmother, is another dog that's going to stay at this broke-down kennel, probably forever, and we're gonna be running feed and vet bills on her because there's no way anyone'll want to adopt something like that."

Ellen huffed again and turned away. Grandmother! Cap only used those high tones when he was being difficult. Gracie squirmed and craned her neck over the old woman's shoulder. The dog was riveted on this young, new face in the room, the boy seething with fury.

"What I see," Cap continued, "is that you're gonna dote on this

11

dog all day long. In case you forgot, it's supposed to be about the biggest day of my life. And we're supposed to be getting ready for it—not fussing over some mangy new arrival!"

"I ain't forgot and she ain't mangy," Ellen snapped. "She's took care of. Any fool can see that. You just put her in back and get her fixed with the others."

"Common, Mamaw! Don't the folks around here know we got a shelter in this county and it ain't us?"

"Course they know we got a shelter and they also know what kind of shelter we got," Ellen said. "If they were set on that, it'd be easier to touch a gun to the back of her head."

She put Gracie back in the box and handed it to Cap, leaving before her grandson could reply.

The kennel dogs began to yip the moment Cap appeared through the fog with Gracie in his arms. They lost all interest in the new arrivals when the boy pulled a handful of scorched eggs from his coat and tossed them into the corner of the pen. Squeals filled the kennel, and dogs stampeded across the dirt floor to get to the treats.

Cap set Gracie's box in the corner, away from all the commotion, but the pup didn't move. She'd barely noticed the big scramble; all of her attention was glued on the boy. They eyed each other for a long time before Cap heaved a sigh and ended the standoff by storming out of the pen.

The teenager retrieved a crumpled pack of Marlboros from his coat and lit one close to his chest, so his grandmother couldn't see from the house. The fog was beginning to lift and, in the distance, low-slung Burnside Mountain was creeping into view. Mamaw and the old folks always talked about how beautiful it was, at least back before the coal company flat-topped her. Cap was too young to remember. To him, the mountain always looked like the Merrimack, that grim old gunboat from the Civil War. She was one of the first ironclads, the Merrimack, with sides that rose sharply and a top that was hard and flat, just like Burnside Mountain. They had a picture in Cap's history textbook, "The sinking of the Merrimack."

A screen door creaked and Ellen called into the yard. The dogs behind Cap were yelping for more eggs, but there was nothing left to toss into the little compound of corrugated steel and chicken wire. Cap squinted at Burnside again and fired a plume of pale blue smoke in its direction. Then he flicked the coal off his cigarette, saving the rest for later, and started back for the house.

*****

Inside, his grandmother was already busy, ironing the white shirt and navy slacks he would need that day.

"They'll be hanging on your door by the time you're washed," she said quietly, avoiding mention of the new dog. Cap nodded and headed for the bathroom, the spring back in his step.

It was the day of the Senior Summit. Hobbs County Public Schools held it every year, a chance to bus in state officials and foundation executives for a show, a series of rapid-fire testimonials that talked up the dollars these honchos were dropping on local schools.

That sell job fell to six high school seniors hand-picked for the Summit. They were trooped into the high school auditorium to wax nostalgic about their lives, their hopes and dreams, the ways their schooling had always, always helped them along the way—all of it captured on local access cable TV. The kids were arranged alphabetically, and each had a flat 90 seconds to tell the story. The TV camera mowed them down, one by one. Cap had attended the Summit in previous years. Attendance was mandatory, and kids not picked for the front table sat on the dark bleachers in back.

This year was different. Cap was a senior, and his good school record had landed him one of those spots in the lights.

Washed and dressed in a flash, Cap sat in the driver's seat and blasted the horn for Ellen while the family truck idled in the driveway. In his pocket were a few scribbled notes, mostly the names of teachers he'd liked over the years and wanted to mention when the Senior Summit camera came his way. After a few seconds, Ellen walked down the path and glared when she saw her grandson behind the wheel. She slid into the passenger's seat and immediately began putting on lipstick, making it plain she'd rather stare in the fold-down mirror than look at the boy.

"Guess you're driving," she muttered at last.

"Guess so," Cap said, matching her ice with some of his own.

The school was on the other side of town, and traffic was heavy

13

on Main Street. The problem was the VIP tour buses. Every Summit, they rode them into town, big monsters with dark-tinted windows, TV monitors above the headrests and climate control. Ahead of him, Cap could see the convoy of buses had already hit town, crowding traffic in both directions. Inside the buses were murky faces, peering at him and Ellen through tinted glass. They were looking at everyone, all the people on the rough roads and cracked sidewalks of Cochrane, soaking it in like it was Lion Country Safari for hill folk. Most of the people on the street kept their heads bowed when the buses rolled past. Only a few peeked back, angry and suspicious.

Cap punched the gas, darting through the lone traffic light, squeezing past the line of buses.

"Quit," Ellen said. "You know we can't afford the ticket."

It was the first thing she'd said since they left home. He knew she was still sore about the new dog, but Cap figured she'd be over it by now. After all, the Senior Summit was a big deal for both of them. To sit at the front table, a kid needed great grades and recommendations, but you only got those things when there was someone at home who gave a damn about you every single day. Ellen filled that bill. She had done it since Cap was four, when meth did his real mother in. Nobody knew what became of her, not exactly. Christmas cards still came, arriving from far-off places like Knoxville and St. Louis, but they never gave details and usually arrived around March.

"A tough row" was all Ellen had to say when the boy asked about his real mother. "She give herself a tough row to hoe, and I reckon that's how you come by it, too."

It hung over Ellen more than she let on, though, and Cap knew it. What happened to his mom explained a lot of things. It was the reason why Ellen rousted Cap every cold, dark morning to wait for the school bus. It was the reason why he wasn't allowed to hang out in Cochrane. It was the reason why he sat in the quiet kitchen every night with homework spread over the table. Ellen couldn't help with lessons, her own schooling never got her that far, but she could make a quiet space at that table for her grandson every evening.

She did it without fail, and that, as much as anything, explained why Cap was picked for the Senior Summit. The first time he ever saw his grandmother dance was the day the letter arrived, the one announcing that a seat at the Summit's front table was reserved for her grandson. Ellen did a silly clog on the front porch, the letter from school fluttering in her hand, and Cap laughed and clapped time. He was happy to give her that moment, that chance to feel like she'd somehow made amends.

*****

Most of the school board was seated when Cap and Ellen entered the auditorium. The cable TV guy was doing microphone checks, and teachers were herding the students onto the bleachers. Ellen took her seat with the other relatives and Cap walked to the front table, where the other five seniors were already in place. The out-of-county honchos soon arrived and took their seats in the roped-off section. Then the TV lights began to blaze.

Cap didn't hear much of what the first kids said. Every now and then, he'd pick up the name of a teacher who was also on his list of those to thank. He mostly kept his head down, studying his own list while the others spoke. He could see the school board seated in front of him, and after each kid spoke, they smiled and nodded and sometimes glanced sideways at the VIPs behind the ropes. From the corner of his eye, Cap also saw Ellen. She was beaming now, the new dog forgotten, and her eyes sparkled and never left her grandson.

Suddenly, Cap heard his own name and he glanced up. Everyone was staring at him. The camera was pointed his way, too, with the red light on. The buzz of the Summit had ground to a halt. The long silence made a few of the bleacher kids snicker in back. The school board president was looking straight at Cap, nodding in his direction like a bobble-head doll.

There must have been a question, his question, and Cap had missed it. One thing was certain: Everyone expected something from him. Cap decided to gamble, and he launched into his prepared bit, figuring that the question posed to the other seniors had finally come his way.

"Well, uh, we've been lucky to have great teachers all through school," Cap started. His voice sounded squeaky in the big room, and he coughed, trying to modulate it down to a manly bass.

15

"Some of the other students mentioned a lot of them already. Miss Anderson was great. So was Miss Praul and Mr. Smith and Mr. Nash . . . I learned a lot . . . They were all, uh, great."

There was a twitter in the room. Something was off. Cap tried to rush through the rest.

"So, umm, I'm hoping to go to college and maybe study engineering. So, like I said, my teachers were all great . . . all the other teachers, too . . . just great. Thanks."

Cap put down his notes and looked around. There were puzzled expressions on all the faces, including Ellen's. The kids in back were snickering hard now.

"Well that's just fine, son," the school board president said at last, "but what I asked, Cap, was what you might like to do with all that learning. How about coming back to Hobbs County and putting some of that knowledge to work? Maybe even build some bridges and houses in these parts. We could sure use 'em. Think you might want to do that?"

Cap blushed. That wasn't what they asked the others!

"Well, uh, I got accepted to Pitt, and that's where I'll probably go if a scholarship comes through. I might want to stick around after I graduate, too, I guess. In Pittsburgh. At least for a bit."

It was clearly not the answer they wanted. The little buzz in the room began to build. The kids in back began to laugh out loud and elbow each other.

"I see, well," the school board president said, clearing his throat to stall for time and glancing nervously at the roped-off section. "How about all you others? After your fine educations, which ones want to come back and start exciting new lives here?"

Students at the table exchanged sheepish glances, like somebody just asked who left the lid off the jelly jar. Cap thought he saw Jennie Slough's hand start to rise but she dropped it just as quickly. Every other arm was pinned to the table, and every chin was tucked low. The school board president's face turned crimson, and the VIPs squirmed in their seats. Then, suddenly, the bright lights went out as Cable TV cut abruptly to the midday news.

The Senior Summit was over.

"You should have just told him you'd come back," hissed Dwight Tillis, the student seated next to Cap. "It's not like they're gonna hold you to anything."

Cap barely heard him. All his attention was on Ellen, who hadn't moved since the camera went off. She sat frozen in place while the others slid past her to get to the aisle. She was still staring at Cap, a pained expression painted over the glow from a few minutes before.

*****

The drive home was just as tense as the drive up. To ease the strain, Cap turned the radio on and dialed up the country station that Ellen liked best. It was playing "Readin', Rightin', Route 23," Dwight Yoakam's cautionary tale about escaping the hills, and Ellen snatched it off.

The truck had barely come to a stop before she was out of the cab, making her usual beeline to see how the dogs were faring in her absence. Cap knew she'd be out back for a long time, and not just because of that new pup. Until now, until the Summit, Cap had never told her that he wanted to go so far off to college, and maybe even stay after he'd graduated.

The boy flicked the ignition off and sighed in disgust. He was going to tell her when the time was right. And he might have found it if that jackass school board president hadn't gone off the script like that. Nobody ever asks rich kids those types of questions! Nobody ever tells them, "come home after college and fix up everything." Those kids go where they choose, because they can. If they end up back in Manhattan or Beverly Hills, that's only because it's a great place to live. Only kids in places like Hobbs County get told they're expected to come home and set things right. Cap slammed his hand on the steering wheel. They should be glad if we're able to make it out!

He started inside to change clothes. Something made him change course and slink to the back yard. The sun was setting, and the kennel lights were on. Ellen was standing in the light, her back to him, and against her shoulder was Gracie, who wasn't paying the old woman any mind. Cap could see that the glow of Gracie's eyes had locked on him, just a boy in the dark more than 30 yards away.

Chapter Three

Rush Rudling was twirling his whistle and barking at the sleepy, doughy kids in first-period calisthenics. He was the physical education teacher and assistant principal at Burnside Overlook School, the flagship elementary school at the eastern end of Hobbs County. By 8:30, class was over and Rush was back in the school office, donning his assistant principal's hat. It was a new duty and easy enough, since he was already the building's muscle. He scolded the students who mouthed off, showed up late or came to school out of uniform. All of it was piddly stuff, as far as public schools go. Other than that, Rush's school mornings were his own.

A 10 a.m. phone call changed everything.

It was the secretary for the school district's superintendent. She was ringing him on his direct line, wanting to set up an afternoon meeting—not in the posh, well-appointed crib that the county had constructed for the Burnside Overlook community but at Flattop Elementary, that old Title I building for trash in the hills.

"Superintendent Chambers wants to see me? At Flattop?" Rudling repeated, suspicion already creeping into his voice. "Who else is going to be there?"

"Just you and Superintendent Chambers," the woman replied.

"Mind telling me what this is all about?" Rudling pressed, feeling his gut begin to roll at the queasy thought of a one-on-one meeting with the big man.

"I'm not at liberty to say. Dr. Chambers doesn't like tardiness, though, so please make sure you're there on time," the woman replied, cool and overformal in her tone, the way executive assistants sometimes get when they've dialed into the squirms of an underling. Rush would have hated her, but she sounded like she might have great tits. Most of Chambers' girls did.

He signed out of the building and snatched the juice box from a student lunch sitting unattended at the secretary's counter. On the drive over, he'd need something to wash down the Xanax.

Traffic was light through Cochrane on a day when Rush would

18

have been happy for a delay. Soon he was in the hills, forced to switch off his car radio after the search button crapped out for the third straight time. A fourth pass wouldn't have made any difference. He was moving deeper into western Hobbs County. The only signals that filtered through these worn mountain creases were the sandpaper sounds of AM radio: hellfire sermons, mostly, and maybe some old-timey bluegrass and a little NASCAR talk thrown in for good measure.

Whenever he could, Rush avoided the hill country. At least that's what polite people called it. Rudling, like most on the silt-flat east side of Hobbs County, had taken to calling the western hills "Methopotamea" or "Oxywood." Hobbs led the nation in per-capita overdose deaths. It was a high-volume stop along the OxyContin Express, a prescription-drug trafficking route that ran all the way to the pill mills of South Florida. The whole county got the blame, of course, along with the ugly national rankings and press reports. But insiders knew where the fault really lay—in the mountains, all that western trash.

It had gotten so you couldn't say Hobbs County in the grocery store or at a party. People just assumed you were the son of an unemployed coal miner or the father of a meth-tweaking slut. They didn't have time to slice and dice: upwardly mobile technocrats to the east, cousin-banging crystal smokers to the west, and damn little in between.

"You're from Hobbs County? Ever hear the one about the old mountaineer who farmed out his daughter to pay for his family's Oxy tabs?" And you laughed, however weakly.

The afternoon buses were leaving Flattop Elementary at the same time Rudling's black pulled up the long, thin service road that led up the mountain. A few students waved from the window, but Rudling was too lost in thought to see them. He had made a point of arriving at the school 20 minutes early—extra time to help calm his nerves. Even so, Rush could feel sweat beading along his forehead. His chest was heaving as soon as he crested the hill and pulled into the faculty parking lot.

What was this all about?

Rudling had never met the superintendent before, not face-to-face anyway. He usually made a point of sitting in back of the auditorium whenever Chambers popped in for faculty meetings (a vantage point that was less of an option now that Rush was filling in for an assistant principal on medical leave). Chambers was intimidating: a round, little man with a short fuse. He always wore a sour expression, at least when parents and board members weren't around. His 42-inch belly was fitting for a man who fired principals in batches and needed a huge belt for the notches. The PE teacher in Rush despised his soft overlord. But that still didn't stop the newly minted assistant principal from shitting his pants whenever the school system's Little Big Man passed him in the hall.

There were brown-shirted custodians by the fountain guarding the entrance to Flattop Elementary. The water was turned off, and they were shoveling up white mounds of soapsuds with dustpans and dotting the walkways with "Wet Floor/Piso Mojado" signs (curious, Rudling thought, since Flattop wasn't one of the system's bilingual buildings). One of the brown-shirts scowled as the assistant principal inched by.

Rush paused at the front door and took three deep, deliberate breaths. *Calm down!* He studied the dim, worried reflection in the plate-glass door. He centered the dimple in his tie, smoothed his thinning black hair, and brushed his teeth with a finger. He adjusted his face, trying on different expressions to see if they could smooth the worried mannequin lines that bracketed his smile. Finally, he gave up the effort when the school engineer walked by, doing a double take at the suit mugging through his plate-glass door.

Behind the engineer, Rush could see a pretty woman in a purple dress, dark-haired, probably in her late 20s. She wore granny glasses with gold rims, so outdated that they somehow made her prettier. A real Marian the librarian, probably great in the sack as long as the lights were out, Rush thought, his overtaxed brain beginning to take libidinous shelter.

The woman was trying to balance a heavy stack of books in one arm while using her free hand to break up a hallway fight—just two boys, maybe fourth-graders, or second-graders held back a couple of times. They had mullet haircuts with the sides buzzed obscenely short, down to the pink-white scalp. Both wore football jerseys from colleges that would dial security if either of them ever set foot on campus after dark.

Gracie of Hobbs County

Rush walked up to the woman to ask directions. She had one of the little beserkers by the collar and he swung around, slamming her into Rush, spilling her books in the hallway. The little dark beauty bent down to pick them up, still hanging onto the boy's collar, and Rush stooped to help her gather the stack. They reached for the same book of nursery rhymes, and Rush gasped as their hands touched. The last two fingers on the woman's hand were shorn off clean, leaving her with three beautiful, tapered digits that ended without warning, the space where the last two fingers should be just a ribbon of pink and purple at the knuckle line.

Rush pulled back and jumped up like he'd just touched 12,000 volts.

The woman pursed her lips in a weary half-smirk, not even bothering to look at the man. The wound was obviously old. Her face was just tired and impatient, with not the slightest hint of hurt at Rush's reaction. Rush collected himself quickly and stooped down to help her again.

"No, really, I've got this," she said, tugging on the boy's collar sharply with her right hand, letting him know he was still on her radar despite the distraction.

Rudling nodded and inched back to the school's front doors. The spot offered a welcome rush of air conditioning, and it soothed a little. Overhead, there was a banner that read, "Flattop Elementary: Can you dig it!!!!" The extra exclamation points, he thought, were downright annoying. There was the tap of a fingernail on glass, and Rush turned to see a brick-house blonde, smiling and waving to him from the fishbowl of the school office. He waved back weakly.

The woman was in her mid-40s and said her name was Eva Knox, the school secretary. There was a Daughter of Dixie coo in her voice, the sugary twang of the hills. Without asking, she took Rush by the elbow like a prom date, gently leading him into the principal's office and the scheduled showdown with the superintendent. Any other time, Rush would have felt coddled and special, thankful for the flaunt of feminine attention, but there was too much riding on this meeting. Rudling still felt dread every time he walked into a principal's office, even his own, even though he now sat on the side of the desk that got to dish it out.

"Dr. Chambers will be with you shauwt-ly," Eva said in her

21

husky drawl, tilting her head slightly as she spoke, pulling the man's sheepish eyes to hers. The sweetness in her voice walked a balance beam, toeing the line between sexy and matronly, yet it did nothing to soothe Rush, who was too stretched by now to think about sex. He remembered the last time he had heard this much silk in a woman's voice. It was at a local bar called Rumors. Two hours later, someone was getting fucked.

"Would you care for some coffee? I can make a pot," she said.

"No, thanks. Maybe a glass of water?"

The woman smiled and the hard roll of her hips carried her out of the room. A moment later, she returned with a paper cone filled from the water cooler. Rudling waited for her to exit again before he reached into his suit jacket for a little white pill, his second Xanax of the morning.

Rush began to scowl. He didn't need this crap! If he was getting canned—if that's what this was all about—then dragging him to the hillbilly school just added insult to injury. A sulk that faintly resembled courage began to well inside his breast.

The door flew open and a short, fat bald man blew into the room. It was Chambers, jacketless, with a let's-get-down-to-business roll in the sleeves of his white shirt. The high-energy entrance unnerved Rudling, and the newly minted courage of his man-pout flew like a quail flushed from the scrub. He stifled what must have sounded like a girlish squeal.

"There he is!" Chambers called out with a chuckle, slapping his plump palms together. The affection in his voice was a broad and flinty imitation of Eva, who trailed Chambers through the door. Rush stood up and shook the superintendent's hand. No words would come.

"Rushmore? Dwayne Chambers, we finally meet! Uh, may I call you Rushmore?" Chambers asked.

"Yessir. Or Rush. That's what most people call me."

"OK, Rush it is. Have a seat son," the superintendent said, patting Rudling on the shoulder, pushing him down into the "bad student" chair. Rather than taking the chair behind the principal's desk, Chambers nestled his beefy ass on the edge of the furniture just inches from Rush. Rudling sank into his seat, pivoting left and right so that his leg wouldn't touch the hairy white gap between Little Big Man's pants and socks. He prayed for the sweet relief only a second Xanax can bring.

"No doubt you're wondering why you're here, young man," the super continued. "I'm sure you saw maintenance outside the school. They've been scooping up those friggin' soapsuds all day. They're everywhere! It's probably going to set me back $700 in overtime."

Rudling nodded.

"Well, here's the deal. Harry Cray, the principal at Flattop, uh, you know him?"

"I've met him a couple of times, sir."

"Well, we had a little issue with Mister Harry Cray last night," Chambers continued, fluttering his fingers next to his temple, the cuckoo-for-cocoa-puffs motion. The superintendent sighed heavily and launched into an elaborate explanation: how the Flattop Elementary principal, who was on the bubble for consistently failing test scores at the school, had snapped 14 hours earlier.

Cray just quit—no letter, no two weeks' notice, no nothing. Or at least nothing that the superintendent would ever tell the school board about. The Flattop principal was alone in the building the night before and decided to announce his decision to depart from academe in an unconventional way. He stole a carton of industrial-grade dishwashing powder from the school cafeteria and dumped it into the fountain outside the school. After a few hours of steady agitation, the pool was an overflowing mountain of suds, a creamy, white fill that stood four-feet high in some places. Buses pulled up the next morning to a school that looked like it was foaming at the mouth.

"When I gave Harry the job, I told him he was just the man to clean up this school. Guess this was the little bastard's idea of a joke," the superintendent said, shaking his head sadly like a wronged lover.

Rudling just nodded. He still didn't get why he was there.

Chambers walked over to place his short, thick arm on the assistant principal's shoulder. Rush stared at the breast pocket of Chambers' tailored white shirt. It was monogrammed, maroon letters in a boastful serif. Rush looked at his own bare breast pocket. It puffed out with a PE whistle, chrome finish, hanging from a teacher's lanyard stitched with Elmer Fudd, Porky Pig and other cartoon characters.

"Here's the thing, Rush. I need someone to step in as interim principal at Flattop. I believe you're that someone."

"But sir, I'm really not.... Well, I *am* the assistant principal at Burnside Overlook, but..." Rudling stammered, breaking the superintendent's grip on his shoulder. "I stepped in when Johnson went down on a medical, remember? It was two days before school started. I'm really the PE teacher.... See?"

Rush retrieved his whistle and flapped it at the superintendent like a flirty senorita.

"What about Thompson? He's head of our curriculum committee and our data review team. Nights, weekends—you can't get him out of the building. Or Suarez. She sits in for Burnside Overlook at the Common Core Standards meetings? Or . . . or . . . "

"Rush, listen," the superintendent soothed, returning his arm to the underling's shoulder, "don't you think I thought of them? Thompson and Sordo are fine teachers, but—"

"That would be Suarez, sir."

"Suarez," the super repeated, frowning at the interruption. "Thompson and Suarez are fine teachers, but here's the thing, Rush. My principal just flipped out, you follow?"

"I need someone now—a team player. Someone who can put a lid on this mess while I figure out what the hell to do with this school. When the going gets tough, the tough get interims, Rush, and I believe that someone is you!"

Rush tugged at his collar and said nothing. He tried to remember if "I believe that someone is you" was from a song he'd heard but forgotten.

"Listen, curriculum and Common Core are fine things to know, but a principal has to be more than that," Chambers continued. "A principal has got to see the big picture. Pull everyone together! A school is a team—and who knows teamwork better than you?" Chambers said, reaching over to give the PE teacher's whistle a flirty flap of his own.

Behind the superintendent stood Eva, staring and smiling, resting her weight on one hip. She seemed lost in thought as she slid a gold crucifix along a chain around her neck. A section of chain rested between her plump lips and made little clicky-clack noises as she slowly pulled the pendant back and forth. Rush followed it for a bit before her deep cleavage hijacked his eyes. He snapped to when he realized Chambers was still talking.

"I'll have to go to the chair of the school board tomorrow, Rush. I have to tell him that I lost my principal at Flattop. He's already in a mood, getting shown up by some punk kid at the Senior Summit like he did, and he'll want to know I'm getting this Flattop mess under control. You with me? Now, Petrie and I have been talking, and—"

"That would be Brad Petrie, sir? My principal at Burnside Overlook?" Rush stammered.

"Correct. Now I can't replace from inside Flattop. This school is a little nuts right now. It's an emergency replacement, so I need something quick—someone in the system. Petrie says you're just the administrator for the job."

Rush swallowed hard. Petrie hated him! Petrie only put his name out because he wasn't going to let Chambers take anyone good from Burnside Overlook—not to waste on a school stashed in the hills like the crazy aunt you hide in the attic during holiday meals.

"I want to be able to tell my school board chairman to stop worrying," Chambers said, squeezing Rush's shoulder. "I want to say 'Sir, I've got Rush Rudling in the building, and no one runs a tighter ship than Rush!'"

"Dr. Chambers, like I said, sir, the only reason I'm assistant principal now is because—"

Chambers threw up his hand to choke off the reply, and Rush watched as the big man began to pace the room.

"Rush, leave the details to the detail people, guys like Thompson and Sordo," the super said. "I need a tight hand on the tiller of this ship. A school is like a ship, Rush, whether you believe it or not. It doesn't matter if it sits in a valley like Burnside Overview or up on a mountain like Flattop. The point is I need you, here at Flattop Elementary, steering this mountain through troubled waters."

Rush smiled weakly. Simon and Garfunkel cued in his head. The super winked. He was getting through.

"Son, don't overcomplicate things. A principal's job can be boiled down to two words—expect more."

"And pay less?"

"What?"

"That's Target's motto, sir. You know, the department store? 'Expect more, pay less.' That's their slogan."

"Huh. How about that," the super said, eyeing his underling suspiciously. He wasn't sure if Rush was insubordinate or just a little dim. He decided to give him the benefit of the doubt.

"Yes, Rush. 'Expect more, pay less.' That's the job. Except *this* job pays 40k more than your base salary at Burnside Overlook. What do you say?"

Rush cleared his throat to buy a little time. The extra money was great, more than double his salary as a PE teacher. But that didn't make any difference, not if he wasn't around long enough to collect. The churn at Flattop was constant, and principals didn't last more than a year or two. The cruel choreography played out like clockwork: The big test scores came out in early summer, and the *Hilltopper-Sentinel* ran the story under a big freak-out headline announcing Flattop Elementary's unblemished record as one of the state's premier failing schools. That's when Chambers would get to work—firing or reassigning anything he could lay his hands on, beginning with Flattop's principal.

"I really appreciate the vote of confidence, sir," Rush said at last, "but what if . . . what if I just wanted to stay PE instructor at Burnside? After our regular assistant principal recovers, of course."

"We're cutting that PE position at Burnside next year."

Rush swallowed hard. He felt the words fizzing in his skull, bubbling into his tightening throat and demanding release. He felt his quivering lips squeeze, trying to stop the assault, but to no good end.

"I'll take it," Rush told the superintendent.

*****

Only three cars remained in the parking lot when Rush left the school. The sun was sliding off the table. The Flattop crew had finished mopping up the last of the suds, and they were in the utility shed by the side of the road, laughing and riding the overtime clock. Rush sat behind the wheel of his Audi, his hand frozen on the key, staring at the workers. They were probably trading stories about "crazy Harry Cray," he guessed. How long until the stories were about him?

History weighed heavily on Rush Rudling as he drove back down the service road. Debbi, his wife, would be proud of his bump up to principal. They lived in one of the best areas, a gated community on the east side, and too many people still embarrassed his wife by referring to Rush as "the gym teacher." It was well down on the pecking order, even lower than those midlevel technocrats who rode the train to the capital every day.

Rudling knew that his wife's joy wouldn't last. Her heart would sink when he told her that the new position was at the hill school, not at Burnside Overlook. She would steal anxious glances at him, not saying what she knew, what they both knew: Smart and capable men and women, educators much more on the ball than Rush, had tried and failed to turn Flattop around.

The staff at Burnside Overlook had every opportunity to transfer over to this ugly duckling sister, but nobody was that crazy or masochistic. The school system's tight budget was only a minor obstacle for Burnside Overlook, which had the buffer of a well-heeled neighborhood surrounding it. Under the less-than-watchful eye of administrators, the school had transformed its PTA into an ATM—spitting out cash for Chinese enrichment programs, playground equipment, even quilted paper for the toilet stalls. At Burnside Overlook, a kid got sent to the principal's office for playing with his iPhone under the desk.

That wasn't a problem at Flattop Elementary: There was no classroom wireless. Besides, Flattop teachers were supposed to keep their mitts off the discipline referral pads. As long as the kids had pulses and hadn't drawn blood, they stayed in class and out of the principal's office. Too many discipline write-ups cost Flattop a few precious points in the ranking system, points the state's premier failing school could scarcely afford to lose.

Discipline wasn't even the half of it, the differences between the schools ran so much deeper. At Burnside Overlook, parents called in to bitch whenever the county called too many snow days. It meant the family vacation was now screwed because the school year would have to be extended. At Flattop, parents called on snow days to bitch because the system wouldn't throw chains on a few vans to deliver free school eats to the hills. It meant the kids living in those mountain shacks would cry and go hungry till the thaw.

Nobody was going to turn Flattop Elementary around, certainly not Rush, who only wanted to be a PE teacher anyway. It was a job he liked and one he was good at—a job he'd still be doing if the real assistant principal at Burnside Overlook hadn't pulled up lame and scheduled elective hernia surgery at the start of the school year. Now, Rush was head of some shit-out-of-luck school for Title I kids in the hills. That's all Flattop Elementary was, and high-pressure tests were turning the entire school into a clinical population, with crazy Harry Cray leading the way.

*****

Rush could already see Debbi in his imagination, standing in the kitchen and chewing her lip as he told her about the meeting with the superintendent. His wife despised the hills, coal running through the veins of her family, a closeted fact she kept out of conversations at the grocery store. In his mind, Rush watched Debbi narrow her eyes and ask the question that mattered most to her: "You won't expect me to rub shoulders with those hill people at banquets and awards nights and the like, right?"

The bandwidth returned as Rush reached the bottom of the mountain, and his radio caught a megawatt oldies station. He tried to sing along, but the words escaped him.

Day after day
Alone on a hill
The man with the foolish grin
Is feeling perfectly ill

Rush snorted. True dat! He wound up the car's quad speakers and let the Beatles belt it out. Something caught his eye at the turn into town: a beast with high, pointy ears and copper fur. The animal scampered across the gravel and sprang into tall, dark weeds before Rudling's car could mow it down. It was roadkill in the making, whatever it was. All types of critters lived along this miserable mountain scrub. At least it scattered before it splattered, and Rush wouldn't have to spend the night in his garage, digging fur and gristle out of his grill with a screwdriver.

"Probably a fox," Rush muttered to himself. It was the first of many miscalculations the new principal of Flattop Elementary would make.

Chapter Four

Therapy dogs should have been a growth industry in Hobbs County, maybe the last growth industry the region could count on. The potential market showed up daily at the government complex on Main Street. There, they'd cue up to see Dr. Amhir Dewan, a transplant from Bangladesh who the locals had taken to calling "Dr. Denton," the overworked psychiatrist who tried to stem a growing tide of despair in the benzodiazepine mill that doubled as the county mental health office.

A script for benzos, or maybe SSRIs, and five minutes of session chat—that was pretty much all Dr. Denton could spare these days. With no other shrinks, there was no other option and business was just too damn good: returning soldiers with raging PTSD, Alzheimer shut-ins, meth and oxy addicts trying to kick, kids with everything from full-blown autism to borderline Asperger's. And that was just the regulars. Now there was a new class of clients reeling from the grind of hard times. Dr. Denton believed they suffered from "Mortgage-Related Anxiety Complex" and he hoped to write a paper someday.

The 2008 financial meltdown didn't matter to Hobbs County at first. The region had taken center stage in the energy crisis of the disco era, but it wasn't on the front lines of this particular fight. Unhinged and battered mailboxes littered the mountains, but rarely did they contain something as fine and fancy as a brokerage statement with serious money on the line.

Then, as they say, Wall Street hit Main Street. And Main Street responded by filling Dr. Denton's waiting room with clinically depressed, sometimes suicidal, owners of houses in foreclosure and shops on the brink.

They drifted into the clinic every day, taking a number, sparring with the core clientele for the cheap, plastic bucket chairs that furnished the psych office waiting room. Getting a refill at county psych was an all-day event. People put it off as long as they could. Then the drugs wore off, driving the hold-outs back into those plastic bucket chairs to twitch and fidget as they waited their turns.

Dr. Denton didn't like doing medicine this way. He would usually sigh as he wrote the script and then launch into his boilerplate scold. Drugs only get you so far, the doctor warned. Drugs have to be re-evaluated for efficacy and appropriateness. They need to be supported by lifestyle changes, Dr. Denton would add, waving his hand to a side table filled with local business cards. Somewhere in the pile, sitting between Dee-Dee's Yoga and the Book Club for Battered Spouses, was the business card for Kozy Kennel & Comfort Dog Training Academy.

"We got a dog, mister, and he hunts good," one puzzled farmwife with a black eye told the doctor as she fingered the Kozy Kennel card one afternoon.

"This is a therapy dog, a comfort dog," Dr. Denton explained in lilting tones, the legacy of a limey boarding school education. "It is not regular dog, madam."

"So, uh, these dogs is irregular?"

"They're trained to detect panic. You see, dogs know before you do. They sniff it out, madam—they sniff it out! Then, they can settle you down before the full-blown panic episode takes hold."

"Dang!"

"Precisely."

"But my husband says I has to get back on the Lexapro before I drive him crazy and he has to kill me."

"This is better, I can assure you. It's Lexapro on four legs."

"I'll think on it," the woman said, touching the plum-colored shiner under her eye. "Tell you what, though. I'd be pleased to sic a dog on his ass if he ever tries to put another one of these on me. Yessir, that'd bring me a mess of comfort!"

*****

Gracie rounded the circle of dogs and owners, homing in on stress like a heat-seeking missile. She peered through the tangle of legs with that low, steady gaze of her father. Her trot around the circle gradually slowed, like a ball finding its number on the roulette wheel. Then, when the pup targeted the one person in the circle who seemed to be teetering most precariously on the cliffs of panic, the dog would freeze. Slowly, she drew her shriveled paw to her chest, her golden gaze never leaving her sweaty find.

Gracie of Hobbs County

"Cap, what's wrong with you? Settle her down!" Ellen snapped at her grandson, who was tugging on the leash and trying to get Gracie back into formation. It was turning out to be another frustrating morning of busted exercises in the Kozy Kennel training ring, another class where Gracie once again smoked her classmates at finding a cache of owner stress—this time a young boy with Asperger's who had brought his beagle to comfort dog training.

The boy had brought his dog to kennel training as a stress-management strategy, one suggested by his doctor. Now, with Gracie bearing down on him, the boy had lost all composure and began tearing at his hair with both fists. Gracie just watched, riveted, tracking the meltdown.

"Cap! Get Gracie to leave him be," Ellen yelled. "She's not minding you because you're not spending enough time with her."

"Mamaw! I'm feeding her, walking her, letting her sleep in my room. This dog just doesn't connect. There's something really, really wrong with her."

"Did you walk her before class? A tired dog is a good dog," the old woman pressed.

"Walk her? I took her on a freaking four-mile jog," Cap snapped.

His voice was growing shrill. Gracie broke from the boy pounding his head and trotted across the circle. Three feet away, the dog stopped and slowly pointed at Cap. Ellen reached out to stroke Gracie's head but the dog never moved—frozen on three legs, one tucked to her chest, bearing down on the grandson with eyes like armor-piercing bullets.

"See? Nothing! She's more neurotic than . . . than . . . them," Cap whispered to his grandmother, nodding to the circle of owners.

"Quit!" the old woman snapped.

Six months had passed since Gracie showed up at the kennel. There had been dozens of visitors, but no one had showed any interest in adopting a little mixed breed with a withered forepaw and somewhat spacey temperament. And there seemed to be little that Kozy Kennel & Comfort Dog Training Academy could do to sweeten the deal.

Michael Rose

Support dogs and therapy dogs work in the world of human frailty and need. They can give back something as basic as eyes and ears, or restore something as delicate as balance and calm for the mind and soul. Support dogs work one-on-one, therapy dogs work the crowds—but there are qualities that bind them. They get pleasure from devotion, from the praise that comes when they offer openhearted help. Always, there is the quiet alert that shines through the dog's bright eyes. Always, there is the mild, unflappable temperament that can soak up human stress so easily. Just a slow wag of the tail or a gentle nuzzle are all it takes to calm.

Ellen Blair thought Gracie belonged to this world, to a special rung on the assist-dog ladder, and she was right. Or at least half right.

Gracie showed an uncanny and natural talent for sniffing out tension and human stress. In that way, she was the echo of Lucky, Ellen's beloved support pet, the dog she lost years ago. But, like her rover father, Gracie also had a natural talent for flushing prey. Her nature and training had combined to make her good at rooting out human frailty—not to heal it but to give the world a better bead on the target.

It took days for Ellen to persuade her grandson to take Gracie through the paces of therapy dog training—the only dog in the class who wouldn't be there with a real owner or at least a prospective one. The old woman would bring up Gracie at breakfast and carp on it till dinner, but Cap simply nodded and said nothing when the grandmother asked him to train the dog.

The boy knew the checklist for good therapy dogs, too, and knew there was a lot missing in Gracie. The little pup didn't make easy eye contact with humans and still freaked out at loud noises. True, Gracie did seem to outshine all the other dogs at Kozy Kennel when it came to sniffing out stress. But she seemed to have no appetite for bonding with humans, for helping to put it to rest.

Still, Ellen insisted on putting her hunch to the test and inserted Gracie into Kozy Kennel's six-week training course for therapy dogs. The prize at the end of the class was certification through ATPA, the American Therapy Pet Association. It didn't really matter that the association was a shell and a sham, nothing more than a Post Office box in Cochrane. Certification for these animals

32

was never closely monitored. It was a loose confederation of organizations and groups across America, a crazy-quilt of quality, and requirements were as tight or loose as trainers set them in this Wild West climate.

No one seemed to mind too much. What mattered to too many owners was the bright green cape marked "Support Dog" that the animals would don at the end of training. They would parade their pets up to Ellen, who would tack a small ATPA photo ID of the dog on the cape. Then they would return to the line of graduates with a smattering of applause from other owners.

Cap led Gracie through exercises while the rest of the class trained with their owners. The other dogs in training may have been slow on the uptake, but they never failed to respond with a nuzzle or tail wag when panic showed up. Gracie wasn't about that. All she cared about was finding and flushing the worst offender. Around the circle she trotted on leash, dragging the scolding boy in the process, looking for the worst of the worst.

Once she had fixed her mark, Gracie would lock on it like a sharpshooter or an expert archer. She slowly drew her copper paw to her chest in a pointer's stand, her head dropping low and level, her golden eyes fixed on the afflicted.

The freaky attention was insistent, undeniable and often enough to set the target off in cold sweats and swearing, or worse. She was not one of the regular therapy pets, the Zen-like warriors, the dogs that quieted the over-firing amygdalae deep inside afflicted, troubled human skulls. Gracie was a divining rod for human frailty, and she never let go of her find.

Chapter Five

Rush Rudling was lost in thought one spring afternoon, staring through the window of his new mountaintop office, watching a steel-gray battle line of anvil clouds. They were boiling across the Ohio Valley, barreling down on his school at eye level.

It was two hours before final bell. Flattop was deathly silent—a blessing that any building administrator would normally give his left nut for. But this was no normal, nut-giving quiet: It was the week that schools across the state had to administer a battery of standardized tests. The kids were on lockdown for the fourth straight day, kept in their classrooms to fill in the bubbles on answer sheets.

The high-stakes silence at Flattop was suffocating, tense, a quarantine on any and all noise that could distract and cost kids a few points on the exams. Teachers enforced the quiet like prison screws, walking the rows of their classrooms, peering down on answer sheets, denying bathroom passes to all but the hardest of cases. When chatter broke out in the hallways, the teachers would storm out of their rooms, clap their hands sharply and raise a finger to their lips.

The scores would be bad again this year at the school, and Rudling knew it. Flattop Elementary had made the list of failing schools every year since its opening. This academic year would be no different.

All the signs were there. There were endless rounds of interim tests, the dry runs leading up to the state exam at the end. Most of them were time-wasters, but they did give administrators a chance to peek through the keyhole and guess at where the carnage would lie on those big year-end batteries. There were also formative assessments, quizzes and quick drills mostly, tests that offered decent value when a teacher needed real-time information on how kids were doing. Done right, formative assessments are like the nibbles that cooks take in the kitchen before they lay out the big holiday spread. But formatives were of no concern to Rush. He was obsessing over the interims. Good rounds of those would soothe the anxious stomach of any administrator. They are promises that everything will be OK when the big state tests hit and the results are spread out for public consumption. Good interims meant a building would be looking at accolades and blue ribbons rather than corrective action and pink slips.

Pukey. That was the only way to describe Flattop's interims. Rush could see it in the spreadsheets and in the faces of his own faculty. The school might squeeze through on math this year, but there were just too many kids reading below proficiency. Rudling didn't need to wait 12 weeks for the state to tabulate final results and generate a fresh, new list of failures. Flattop Elementary would be there again, in the crosshairs, stuck at the top of the list like some possum treed by howling dogs.

It had been months since the superintendent pushed Rush into the school, and nothing had really changed.

With each day of state exams, the faces of teachers grew more haggard, hateful and dull. The kids would clear out at final bell, the teachers would secure their answer sheets and booklets in the central office and then pack up for the night—slamming supply room doors, offering their principal nothing more than a clipped "goodnight." The Flattop faculty would storm into the parking lot and gun their engines as they squealed down the sawed-off mountain.

Rudling could even see disaster in the faces of students. They had no skin in the game when it came to passing or failing the state exam, of course; these tests were used to grade the schools and didn't really count for these young kids. Yet the students looked numb, weary and miserable after so many unbroken hours of testing. And they were soaking up adult stress at Flattop like sponges.

Rush ran a nervous hand though his thinning hair, unable to move from his corner-office perch as he watched the big clouds roll in. Soon, the stress became too much for the first-year principal to bear. He inched out of his office and moved silently down the corridors, peering through the little glass windows of every classroom.

The principal hoped to see a smile, a nod—some hopeful sign from a few of his teachers. He was denied. Once, he caught the eye of Georgia Minniver in third grade. Rush offered his teacher a crooked smile and a weak thumbs-up through the glass in her door. She turned her back and moved out of view.

At almost every window, the teachers greeted the principal's weak, plaintive face with hard, cold stares. Their looks were not much different from the grim-faced hawks that rode the low thermals over the school every afternoon, scouring the hillside for little, unattended bunnies.

Rudling's heart beat faster. He made for the lunchroom and slipped inside the heavy double doors. It sounded empty from the outside, but fourth-graders filled the foldout tables. Someone had taped five feet of poster paper on the wall. It read "Testing week— Quiet PLEASE!!!" The poster was big and bright and colorful. Its fat, cheerful letters looked down on a silent room full of 9-year-olds hunched over sectioned plastic trays.

The principal hugged the walls as he moved quietly to the back, where Marie Hull monitored the students between bites of a cheese sandwich. Rudling liked Marie. The fourth-grade teacher was one of his team players, a "war horse," one of the few friendly members of the faculty. Marie was smart, dependable and never tried to trip Rush up in curriculum meetings like so many others did, just because he came up through the ranks as a PE teacher.

She was a good sort, a straight shooter, and the principal allowed himself to smile broadly as he circled behind Marie unnoticed. She was working on a laptop beside her lunch tray, and she was seated in one of the few school spaces where a wireless device could pull a couple of shaky bars. A Yahoo Messenger conversation was scrolling down her screen. It caught Rush's attention just as the principal reached out to tap his teacher on the shoulder, and the words on the screen stopped him short.

Dave: UR 2 dramatic

Marie: huh? no way! Worst fail evar!!

Dave: hmmmmmm

Marie: lucky to pass math. forget reading. kids r melting down!

Dave: so what'll happen?

Marie: we

Marie: r

Marie: SCREWED!

The scrawl stopped for a second. Rudling held his breath.

Dave: What'll happen 2 the gym teacher?

Marie: Rudling? he's so DONE!!
Dave: hmmmmmmmm
More silence on the screen.
Dave: What's for dinner?
Marie: FUCK U! GET UR OWN!!!
Marie x'd out of the conversation with an angry snort. Rush felt the blood drain from his head. He stumbled slightly, his broad shoulders hitting the cinderblock wall of the lunchroom. Marie looked back and her mouth gaped in panic at the sight of the administrator's ashen face. How long had he been there?

"Mr. Rudling! You startled me," she stammered, flicking the screen black with a quick tap of her finger.

Rush just stared and fiddled with his nuts. It was a nervous habit, his right hand groping the fly of his pants, something that came out under stress. The "bag tag," the Flattop teachers called it behind his back. It started during Rush's days as a two-sport jock, adjusting his cup as he stepped into the batter's box or up to the foul line, junk in hand. It stuck with him through his days as a PE instructor, where it still seemed forgivable: Nobody thought twice about a gym teacher walking up and down a line of kids, barking rope-climb instructions with one hand jiggling an imaginary jock into place. He was an athlete, for Chrissakes! Now, as a newly minted principal who couldn't resist clutching his sack through a Joseph A. Banks suit, even at the podium on Open House Night, the habit just looked awkward.

"Uh . . . Are you where you're supposed to be?" Rush finally asked Marie. In his fog, the principal was retreating to patter he'd use on kids roaming the school without a pass.

"Fourth-grade lunch ends at 1:15," said Marie, a puzzled look crossing her face.

"Good . . . fine. That's fine," Rush snapped, storming for the door. A scrap of paper on the floor caught his eye and he turned to the nearest kid. "Pick that up and trash it!" he growled.

The walk back to the principal's office was one of the longest of his life, and it didn't take long for survival instinct to kick in. Rush stormed down the hallway, peering through the little classroom windows again. This time, however, Rush was meeting the graveyard stares of his teachers with a hard, level look of his own: If the scores stank and the state slapped Flattop again this

37

year, he wasn't going down alone.

Rush entered his office through the side door, away from the front office staff, and popped another Xanax. His heart was beating hard and his temples throbbed. It was too damned quiet. On a normal day, the junior cheerleading squad's muffled practice would be drifting through the walls from the auditorium next door.

Whenever we've got that Flattop feeling—Boom! Dy-no-mite!
Boom boom! Dy-no-mite!

Rush loved that cheer. He regretted forwarding that memo from the PTA to Ms. Stokes, coach of the squad, asking her to tone down the aggressive shake that the girls gave their asses when they performed it. Rudling liked the way his girls went for it. At least these kids had spirit, like that Honey Boo Boo child.

Rush dropped to the floor of his office for a quick set of pushups, trying to bleed off the tension. Not even Marie, his old war horse, could be trusted! Why couldn't they see? He was a good phys ed teacher, damnit, and he hadn't asked for this job. It was the superintendent's idea—the same guy who was going to can him once the Flattop kids and their rotten reading scores starting popping up in the cells of Excel sheets generated by the state.

The only thing that was going to calm him down today was a little righteous payback. That, and maybe a little time with Eva after the building shut down.

"Eva, get me the attendance printouts for every faculty meeting—August through April," he barked into the intercom of his desk console.

"Yessir. Five minutes."

"Four minutes!"

It was Rudling's ass if the school didn't do better on the state test this year. The teachers clearly knew it, and no tears would be shed if the fourth principal in the last seven years was sent packing. It was the school's best chance for survival. That's what they'd be muttering in the break room after he got deep-sixed. Rudling knew the way they thought. Even a bad principal has eyes and ears among the troops, the suck-asses bartering information for privilege, the climbers who want the better classroom, a reprieve from some bullshit committee or just a real planning period, free from lunchroom duty. Rudling gave them what they wanted—if their dirt was good enough.

Someone wasn't with the program. Rudling wanted names, and he wanted them fast. He had sunk every cent of the school's professional development money into workshops, training that the superintendent swore by in those first crazy days when he took over at Flattop. And he was going to find out which teachers had blown off the enrichment opportunity.

It was called "Calming the Tested Mind," a four-hour guided meditation that teachers could use to help students find their quiet center before the test packets hit their desks. It was mindfulness, a meditation that, if followed to the hilt, was worth a full standard deviation on math and reading.

There actually was some data showing mindfulness might help. The problem, as always, was in the execution.

The facilitator of training just happened to be the superintendent's sister—a gray-haired, dashiki-wearing loon who showed up at his faculty meetings in the hot pre-service days of August with a gong, an audiotape of a babbling brook, and zero experience. Her session was awful, but that wasn't the point. All that mattered was that some of Rudling's teachers were team players and some weren't. Some stayed through the workshops and diligently took notes (even if a few did pitch those scribbles in the auditorium trash on the way out). Rudling could forgive that. He could even forgive the few who fell asleep in the hot auditorium during some of the meditations.

It was the others—the prima donnas who ditched the sessions—they were the ones who needed to pay! They had drifted off to their classrooms during assembly to work on lesson plans and bulletin boards. They had insulted the super's sister, giving Flattop a black eye and a bad name, something that batshit-crazy woman was sure to mention once the crappy test scores came out and her brother started asking why the training hadn't helped.

Rudling wanted the names of the teachers who ditched. They'd get theirs. The principal would see to that.

Rudling flipped the switched marked "Building" on the intercom and barked, "ATTENTION FACULTY. ALL TIER THREE RUBRICS AND REFLECTIONS MUST BE TURNED INTO MY OFFICE BY 3 P.M. FRIDAY. NO EXCEPTIONS!"

A murmur rose up in the building. It was the sound of students talking, the first chance in days to whisper and chatter, relief brought on by Rush's intercom blast. Seconds later, adult voices chimed in, shouting "Shut up!" and "Eyes on tests!" Teachers hated intercom announcements, and a housekeeping PSA during testing week was sure to piss them off royally.

"Fuck 'em. Fuck 'em all," Rudling grumbled. A half-second later, the principal glanced over, wild-eyed, not quite sure if he had killed the connection.

Rudling picked up a baseball he had confiscated from a student that morning and whipped it at the office door. It landed with a loud thud that silenced the chatter in his outer office.

"Eva!" the principal yelled, not bothering with the intercom.

"On my way, Mr. Rudling, sir."

Eva glided into the office, and the principal began to relax the moment he saw her. She had decided to stay on as school secretary when he took the job, and it was the one decent break to come out of this mess.

Eva had managed to keep it together, even after 48 years and four children. Sure, her waist was thicker, and her hips had spread, but she fought back with Pilates three afternoons a week. She had style and guile, often standing with one leg placed in front of the other to narrow her silhouette even more. Her suits were always tailored to catch the roll of her hips just right, and she battled the small sag of her jowls and early crepe on her neck with bright, flouncy silk scarves and heavy umber makeup that Rudling found both tacky and secretly attractive. Then, there was the prim bob of her blond hair and arctic blue of her eyes, impossible to ignore, particularly when they fixed Rush in that sweet look of innocence mixed with feigned obedience.

The thick South in her voice, a little husky and a little motherly, soothed and inflamed Rush at the same time. Most of all, Eva understood him: the man inside, the one who carried the weight at Flattop Elementary, the one who needed her after hours, one or two nights a week, barring family functions.

Eva placed the list of teachers' names on Rudling's desk and stood behind his chair, slowly and secretly grazing his back with her hips. She enjoyed the many ways she could deflect his petulance and turn it into passion.

"That was more than five minutes," said the principal, making his voice hard and decisive, leaning back into the brush of her pelvis.

"I'm sorry, Rushmore," she replied, sweet and low.

Rudling hated when she used his full name, but this time he let it go. It was one of those unfortunate confidences he'd shared with her, just something that slipped out in the wind-down from lovemaking. Such intimacies were diamonds, hard-won and precious. But extramarital sex seemed to turn the lover's confession into something routine, like touching all the bases even though the ball was clearly out of the park.

Still, the principal wished he had shown more foresight four months ago, when the affair with Eva began. He could have offered her something else: how he cried as a boy when his dog got run over; how clowns freaked him out; and spiders—how his wife had to kill them at the house. Instead, Rush told Eva about his name, the seat of so much embarrassment and resentment.

It was his mother's idea. She was on vacation in South Dakota and named him Rushmore after giving birth to her only child painfully and unexpectedly at a scenic stop near Mt. Rushmore. His mother took the premature delivery as a sign. She named him after Mt. Rushmore, the mountain of presidents, over his father's objections and, later, his own.

Rush shared this with Eva that first night, not long after they made love on his office couch for the first time.

"She could have called me Thomas, Teddy, George—even Abe would have been better," Rudling whispered to his secretary. "No, she had to have Rushmore."

"Maybe she didn't want to insult the other presidents, honey. You know, playing favorites?" Eva soothed, wrapping her leg around his. "Besides, Rushmore isn't so bad."

"Rushmore got me beat up at school."

"Well, sugar, it could have been worse. Born under those presidents' noses like that, she could have called you 'Nasal'? Now, how would that sound? 'Hi, guys, I'm Nasal. Wanna play ball?' Goodness, I don't even want to think!"

"Stop."

"I could call you something different if you want. How about Stone—like the mountain? Like 'Stone Cold' Steve Austin?"

"Stop! Get on the radio and make sure the buses are out of the shop," the principal snapped.

Nasal! Rush blew it out of his mind and made himself focus on targets of opportunity revealed by the printout of faculty attendance. That didn't stop him from reaching behind his plush leather chair to toy with Eva's haunches. She rocked back in their well-scripted choreography—her way of accepting a meeting that night in his office once the building went dark. It was a good plan, he thought. There were no extracurriculars during testing week, not for students anyway, and they would have the place to themselves once the custodian cleared out. He flipped up the hem and pressed his hand deeper, between her legs, till his fingertips grew moist.

"Mmmm. Rushmore, honey."

"Call your husband and tell him you'll be late tonight. And don't call me Rushmore anymore."

Eva walked to the door, smoothing and giggling, slightly exaggerating the swing of her hips for his benefit. She turned back with a smoldering look, and a wry curl blossomed on her lips.

"Who knows what I'll be calling you tonight," she whispered as she walked out.

Rudling sat for a moment, sighed heavily and pulled out the bottom drawer, where he stashed the extra gray neckties. Only three left.

"I hope it's not Christian again," the principal muttered.

Chapter Six

It took about 400 million years to carve Burnside Mountain into a graceful rolling breaker on the Appalachian crest. White-capped in winter, emerald green in summer, the old hill was the lush, wild edge of western Hobbs County. It was the place where generations taught their children to hunt, to fish, to keep food on the table even in the hardest of times, which, in Hobbs County, was most of the time.

That was before the 1970s oil crisis sent the nation into a tizzy. The country tore into its domestic energy stores like a drunk on a bender, rummaging through an old pantry of fossil fuels for anything that looked like it had a drop or two left. And it didn't take long for that desperate national grope to settle on Burnside Mountain, which, together with the hundreds of Appalachian hills like it, sat on enough coal to power the country for 200 years—or at least power anyone willing to pay top dollar at a time when buyers around the globe were Jonesing for energy. It was all there for the taking, particularly if you were willing to treat the old Appalachian hills like they were geology's answer to a soft-boiled egg.

In 1977, crews showed up in Hobbs County to flat-top Burnside Mountain. They laced high slopes with dynamite and blew off the top 300 feet, getting at the dark seams of coal underneath. Crews and hungry excavators then moved in to scoop up and cart away the rich Paleozoic yolk. Finally, the leviathan was bulldozed flat at 2,000 feet, and the played-out mountain was permanently tied to the valley with a thin ribbon of asphalt that replaced the coal company's gravel road.

The shock-and-awe excavation went smoothly, without complaints. No one was going to turn up their nose at a good-paying mine, particularly not in western Hobbs County, where jobs were as scarce as bottom land. The community was no stranger to big projects sold as economic revitalization—centuries of it, in fact, failed crusades to fight poverty that stretched back as far as Reconstruction.

Most of these efforts turned out to be empty promises that marinated the locals in cynicism and steely-eyed suspicion. They were onto the outsiders, the do-gooders and the profiteers alike. Now, when the suits showed up in Hobbs County, armed with their slide shows and their rescue fantasies, their glossy plans for the future and their bold promises of "a new day dawning," the locals had only one question: Who was going to cut paychecks and would they clear before folks' Temporary Assistance for Needy Families ran out?

Coal mining was high pay, no doubt about it. And Hobbs County was more than happy to do its part in the '70s energy crisis. The people lined up behind Big Coal, if only to show those A-rabs a thing or two about what the USA was made of (something that really wasn't in dispute once the crews lit those candles on Burnside Mountain and yelled, "Fire in the hole!").

The only real hitch came up at the end of the project.

As part of the coal deal, Hobbs County was promised a new elementary school on top of the mountain once the mine was capped. The new school would be modern and richly appointed, paid for with proceeds from the big dig. It would be an investment in the future, in strong schools and smart kids, in the vaunted "knowledge economy" that had eluded this Appalachian backwater for so long. The new school would be transformative, moving the next generation from cropping shares and colliers' lamps into college degrees and corporate pinstripes.

The soft-boiled egg would become the goose that laid the golden egg.

In no time, the cinderblocks were laid, the boundary maps were redrawn and a small fleet of yellow school buses began to snake its way to the new school.

But what to call it?

Most members of the county council favored Burnside Mountain Elementary. It seemed only fitting to dedicate, to consecrate, to hallow the majestic mountain momma of Hobbs County and the blessings she had so faithfully bestowed over the years on this grateful and God-fearing community. The minority dissented, of course—a public fight over the cosmetics of a new school name being too good an opportunity to pass up—and wanted to call the new school Eagle Elementary, "the school on the mountain where every child can soar."

The dissenters even won a small victory when they collected enough signatures to get the choice of a school name put on the ballot in the next local election. That turned out to be an embarrassing miscalculation. The vote was taken after the mine had played out and closed. By then, layoff notices were tacked to refrigerators in kitchens across the hills. Spending cratered in the county, taking the drive-in movies and bowling alley with it. Soon, the drugstore would go; then the supermarket. The only places doing business now were Hobbs County Social Services, buried under a flood of new claims, and the local U-Haul dealer, swamped by folks looking to hitch up and get the hell out. After a few weeks, even Wal-Mart wouldn't touch it with a 10-foot pole.

Things had turned ugly, and voters were in no mood to mince words. They opted to call a spade a spade and named the new school "Flattop Elementary, Home of the Diggers."

It wasn't as if the public stewards turned their backs on the downward spiral. Decades later, they would build a huge federal lockup on the county line. More than 1,600 six-by-eight cribs, conveniently located in a land without houses and choked with drug-related crime. In business, they'd call that synergy.

*****

Joe Delmar was out in the corridors, buffing the hallways, and Rush put his hand over Eva's mouth as the custodian passed. She was getting it the way she seemed to want it these days, hard and roped-up with those damn neckties, and that meant noise. Rush pumped harder and smacked her ass smartly, trying to bring her off while the whine of the buffer outside his office covered her moans.

She was panting sweet and low, facing the door on all fours, and husky notes began to curl from her open lips. Rush took the cue and looped his forearm under her hips, pulling hard, making the gray silk tie bite gently into her locked wrists. Joe's buffer turned the corner. So did Eva, shuddering and crying out long and loud.

Rushed tuned into the sounds of the corridor, taking the pulse of the building. He would like to think Joe was a cool guy, someone who could keep his mouth shut, but everyone and

45

everything felt risky these days, including Eva.

Someone had given her the wildly popular potboiler at her Tuesday night book club, a book once considered too risqué for full discussion by the ladies of the circle, yet they devoured it on the sly, each and every one. Light bondage became the pistachio nut of passion for the book club women, even the Baptist members who usually clucked whenever one character had both feet off the floor. A few women even went so far as to name their children after the rich rakes and ravaged protégés populating the pages. It was quite the regional obsession.

Eva's new appetite for belts and paddles, tops and bottoms, were putting demands on their affair, however, not to mention Rush's wardrobe. He was spending Saturday afternoons on trumped-up errands, circling a 25-mile radius to buy fistfuls of gray ties that were suddenly swelling the shelves at the Target men's department. The principal kept them stuffed under the floor mat on the driver's side of his car and in the bottom desk drawer at work, anywhere his wife wouldn't find them. She knew Rush preferred blue and gold regimentals, and sometimes cartoon prints for "wacky dress day" at the school.

The gray ones, the ties that bind, only made their appearance on the special days Eva asked for them, which these days was most every day that she and Rush stayed late to screw. Sex unbound was not worth having, it seemed, and Rush couldn't help but wax a little nostalgic for the seedy efficiency of their first encounters.

Still, Rush was determined to make it work. He bookmarked pages on the Internet devoted to dirty passages from her novel. He recited a few lines during foreplay (although his flat voice seemed more suited to a schoolboy's nasty rendering of "The Boy Stood on the Burning Deck"). He even went the extra mile, adding to his knot-tying repertoire by studying a dog-eared copy of the Boy Scouts Field Manual that he found in his home basement.

"See that, bitch?" Rush huffed into Eva's ear one night, doing his best to be the hard-assed dom and a competent top that she obviously needed. He kept a hard, steady pace while yanking Eva's blond bob, making her stare at the knot on her wrists.

"I said, 'see it?'" he hissed again. "It's a half hitch!"

"Sugar, not now! Not so tight and . . . oooh, yeah, just fuck me!"

By the finish, Rush was pouting. You make the effort to be amazing, he thought, and this is what it comes to. "Just fuck me!" He could cry.

The sound of the buffer was gone by now. Lost in thought, Rush didn't even notice that Eva had released herself from the ties and was smoothing and primping in his office mirror. She cocked her head and looked at the man whose sheepish, sorrowful eyes avoided her. It reminded her of the first time they met.

"You're not yourself tonight, honey."

"You came. I felt it."

"It's not that It's just—what's got you so worried and wound up, sugar?"

Rush eyed Eva, wondering if he should double down on confessions after the first-name fiasco. He decided to give it a try. Who else would understand?

"It's the tests," he said in a flat tone. "You know they'll be bad again this year, right? The superintendent is going to call me in a few weeks to ask me why. I'll be damned if I've got an answer that'll satisfy him. At least, not an answer that's good enough to keep me from getting canned."

"You know what you need, Rushmore honey? You need one of those dogs for the kids. The soothing kind."

"Not following you," Rudling said, plucking his boxers off the floor.

"Hang on," Eva said, cracking the door to see if the coast was clear. She had her face on again, but little else. The woman slid out into the central office, grabbed a newspaper from her desk and flew back into the room, a dance of large, dark nipples leading the way.

"See? A soothing dog like this school has," she said, pointing to an article. It was all about a downstate school that was boosting its reading scores by keeping a therapy dog in the media center. The article said that the worst readers at the school had more than doubled their results because of Max, the therapy dog. The school librarian had sacrificed her entire summer to train him.

The "canine counselor" was drawing the little nippers into the library with ease, the story said. Many students who would never go near the stacks were now new regulars in the media center. The dog was the reason.

Reading out loud in the classroom humiliated these struggling students, but reading to Max was different. The chocolate retriever would never giggle or snicker at their mistakes, so the kids felt safe enough to take risks. They could tuck themselves into a library nook with a book of nursery rhymes and feel comfortable, taking as many passes at words as they needed, knowing that Max would always rest quietly beside them, his head on their laps, tranquil and accepting of whatever would come from their lips.

"Read, dog, read!" proclaimed the headline, purloined from Dr. Seuss. The article ran big on the front page, with a huge picture of the therapy dog, the school librarian—and a beaming principal in the background.

"How about that," Rudling said at last. "A therapy dog. My doctor was always on me to get one of those and get off the Xanax. Who would have ever thought?"

"Me, honey, that's who," Eva said, slipping her dress over her head and turning her back to the principal. "Do me up in back?"

"Yeah, but how many kids are we talking about here? Five? Ten? This dog in the paper can't work with more than 15 kids at a time. Flattop has about 150 kids in deep shit right now in reading. They're two and three levels below grade—we'd need a fucking kennel. It's all going to hit the fan when the next round of scores comes out."

"Sugar, that's not the point," Eva said, a painful note entering her voice. She hated the way this man's brain needed spoon-feeding sometimes. "It's all about timing. You get that dog in here now. Get our paper to do the exact same story that ran downstate. Get the story in the paper *before* the scores come out."

"So what? The scores will still stink."

Eva smirked, walked over, and wrapped her arms around Rush's waist. She pressed her lips to his ear, whispering in that low, husky tone.

"Honey, do you really think Superintendent Chambers is going to fire you after that story comes out? After you get him down here to have *his* picture taken with our very own reading dog?" Eva said, touching the photo of the proud principal in the newspaper. "Our super is not going to step on his own story. The test scores will come out and they might be bad, but I'll tell you what: Superintendent Chambers will tell everyone to lay off and give it time. He'll say good things are happening at Flattop. He's not going to take bows for the dog one week and clean house the next."

"Hmmmm," Rush said. Eva was right about one thing. The only thing Chambers loved more than firing principals was good press.

"It's all in the timing, Rushmore, honey," Eva said as she walked out. "What you need to do is to make sure that the new dog is in here soon enough for the paper to write about *before* the test scores come out. You'll see."

Rudling waited five minutes for his secretary to make her way from his office discretely to her car. He tossed that evening's gray cravat into the wastebasket and hid it under a few discarded memos. The tie was too wrinkled and stretched to go back into rotation again, and the one drycleaner in Hobbs wasn't an option. The last thing Rush needed was to have his wife pop in on errands and hear, "You gonna be pickin' up all them ties for your husband today, too?"

It was just past 8 o'clock when Rush left the building. The afternoon storms had passed. The school hallway glowed in that relaxed, creamy illumination of half-lighting that kept custodians going through the night. Around the corner, he again heard the buffer as Janitor Joe gave Flattop a dull shine for the morning.

"Joe! Whatcha know?!" the principal called out, surprising himself at the new chirp in his voice.

"Evening Mr. Rudling," Joe Delmar replied. "School feels funny with no clubs going on at night, huh? Bet you and the teachers will be happy when test week is over."

Even the janitor knew about testing week. If the school bombed badly enough, his job could be on the line, too.

"I wouldn't worry about it, Joe. I've got a hunch things are turning around at Flattop. Yessir, I've just got that feeling!"

Joe watched the principal disappear down the corridor. Just before he hit the door, Rush bent at the knees and then popped into the air, his right hand tracing a delicate arc above his head like he was draining a three-pointer. Then Joe heard the principal exhale heavily, imitating the crowd's roar, and Rush began to belt out a chant that was loud and clear.

Whenever we've got that Flattop feeling—Boom! Dy-no-mite!
Boom boom! Dy-no-mite!

Chapter Seven

On the first Tuesday in spring, Dr. Denton opened his door to see the beaming face of one of his Xanax regulars, the lanky principal from the school on the mountain.

Usually the man looked sheepish, his eyes darting across the waiting room, worried that someone of consequence would mark him in the crowd. It would be easy enough to do—picking a suit out of a sea of grubby T-shirts—and questions would be raised. The only time a professional, someone with real health insurance, was showing up at the clinic these days was to smurf their own stuff: visiting an assortment of doctors around the region for the extra script needed to ramp up prescriptions.

Today, however, the principal looked tall and confident, flashing a row of bright teeth at Dr. Denton. The look startled the doctor, who momentarily allowed himself the luxury of thinking he had something to do with the transformation.

"Mr. Rudling, please come in," Dr. Denton said, returning the smile.

"Thank you. Couldn't ask for a better day, now could you?" Rudling chirped.

"If you say so—and I'm glad you do," Dr. Denton said, settling back behind his desk, rocking a few squeaky springs as he pulled the principal's file and studied it in silence. "So," he said at last, "No problems with the Xanax? No fatigue or drowsiness?"

"Nope. Things are going great."

"Very good," said Dr. Denton, pulling out his pad and scribbling another month's dose.

"Uh, doctor, I did have one question. Remember a couple visits back? You said something about a dog—an anxiety dog, I think."

"Yes, yes, a therapy dog. Go on," Dr. Denton said, a note of enthusiasm coloring his voice. He slid the script across the table and nodded for Rush to continue.

"Well, it's not for me, you understand, but I've got a friend who might be interested."

"Ah, the friend, the friend—I understand," Dr. Denton said with a chuckle, touching his nose and winking like Santa. He walked to the side table to retrieve a Kozy Kennel card. "The friend will benefit greatly. Of this I am sure!"

*****

By the time he pulled into Kozy Kennel, Rudling's black Audi looked like an iced chocolate cake. The dusty afternoon drive around Burnside Mountain was unnerving. It wasn't so much a drive up to the kennel as a drive up, then down, then up again, then around a hairy-ass switchback, then swerving to dodge roadkill on the center strip, then back down a 5 percent grade with the chrome of an 18-wheeler glued to his ass.

The kennel seemed strangely quiet. Rudling had been to the county's shelter before and heard the non-stop baying behind the cinderblock walls. But, here, there was barely a yelp. Rudling checked the kennel's business card against the mailbox number to make sure the little brick rambler before him was, in fact, the place that Dr. Denton had raved about two hours earlier.

There was no answer at the door. He peered through the glass inlay, down the dim entrance hall and straight into what appeared to be the kitchen. At the end of the dim corridor was a screen door. Through it, he could make out gray forms and muffled commands. Someone was back there.

Rush walked around the house and stood quietly, taking in the sight. It was some kind of training. A half-dozen people had dogs on leather leashes, and they were guiding the animals around a triangle-shaped course that was marked by miniature orange highway cones.

At each corner of the triangle was some stereotype of humanity: an old woman balancing on a walker, a child sitting cross-legged reading a book, and a man lying motionless on an army cot with what looked like a fake IV line snaked up his arm. It was a maze Carl Jung could have constructed.

The others in the yard were walking their dogs around the perimeter, allowing the animals to pay short visits to the people at the corners. In the center of the triangle was a gray-haired old woman playing ringmaster, regularly praising and correcting the dogs and their handlers. She turned to the man whose cocker spaniel was now resting his head against the man on the cot. The dog was wagging his tail slowly and gazing at the mark with soft brown eyes, begging for a pat.

"What you need to do, Mr. Darnell, is come at the man on the side opposite the IV line," the woman at the center said. "Also, start by explaining that you're with Kozy Kennel and you've brought Sofia to pay a visit."

"But he's supposed to be in a coma," Darnell said.

"We treat him like anyone else," the old woman replied.

The ringmaster turned to the next station, where a woman had a German shepherd on a slack leash. Next to them was another play actor—a woman done up old and brittle, wrapped in a hospital gown and leaning on a walker tipped with skid-guard tennis balls. The dog handler and the walker woman chatted casually, and the old woman reached through the aluminum tubes to pet the shepherd's big head. The dog pressed back, but gently, so the old woman didn't topple.

"That's just fine, Rocky. You're really gettin' it, Mrs. Hibbert," the ringmaster said.

Rudling only half-listened. His attention was focused on the third station—or, rather, the third station was riveted on him. A small black-and-copper mutt was straddling the child who was reading, half-choking her with the leash and blocking the book in her lap. The dog was locked on Rush, her bushy tail upright and motionless, her golden gaze boring into him as steady as a laser. A skinny boy was holding the leash and tugging back, trying to position the dog's head near the child's lap.

"Oh, for heaven's sake," the ringmaster snapped. "Cap, why is that leash so tight? I want to see a soft, relaxed 'J' in that line. Stop that tugging!"

"Mamaw, this dog wouldn't know a 'J' if she smoked it—Gracie won't relax," Cap muttered. "This is useless!"

"Use your commands," the ringmaster ordered.

"Gracie, lie—lie!" the boy said, dropping down to the dog's level, looking for eye contact.

"Don't repeat commands, Cap. Get her attention and give the order once."

Cap leaned down, but the little mutt just ignored him. She was locked on the stranger, the tall man in the suit, the one in the corner playing with his nuts.

Rudling was fixed, frozen by the dog's stare. Nerves set in. In a flash, the pup was up and tugging her handler across the obstacle course. Along the way, the hyper dog stopped to snatch one of the tennis balls off the walker, almost toppling the old woman, and then trotted over to present it at the feet of the man.

"Mr. Rudling! What are you doing here?" asked Cap, fighting to keep a grip on Gracie.

Rudling studied Cap's face. It registered vaguely from the sea of students past. He looked to be about 18. Rudling was damned if he could recall his name, though.

"Hey! There he is!" Rush said. It was a dodge he often used when students, kids whose name he couldn't recall, ambushed him at grocery stores, restaurants and gas stations. It happened a lot. The students always seemed amazed to discover Rudling had a real life and needed things like foot powder and neckties. Most assumed he and the other teachers lived at the school 24-7.

Cap's forehead wrinkled above the light spray of adolescent freckles that refused to leave his cheeks. His big green eyes narrowed slightly. He was onto Rudling. The man never could remember his name—except that one time, when he got caught passing notes in class and Rudling, the PE teacher, made him run drills after school that were aptly named "gassers."

"That's time, everyone. Good work this week," the ringmaster called to the dog handlers and actors. They began to break down the backyard obstacle course while their dogs sat and stared.

Ellen Blair walked up to her grandson, Rush and Gracie. The little dog was still scampering to get to the man, and her shrunken right forepaw was cocked at her side, like Rush was some bipolar quail she'd just flushed.

"Nice puppy," Rudling obliged. Small beads of sweat formed on his forehead. He patted Gracie's head gingerly, like he was testing a stovetop for heat. The dog never budged, fixing him in that nerve-wracking golden stare. She picked up the tennis ball and offered it again.

"Good morning, Mr. —"

"Rudling. Rush Rudling," the man replied to Ellen, his attention still fixed on the mutt at his feet.

"May I help you?" Ellen said, casting a furtive glance at her grandson, who was trying to pull in Gracie and size up his old PE teacher at the same time.

"Uh . . . Dr. Denton sent me," Rudling blurted out, a sheepish note in his voice, as if Kozy Kennel was a canine speakeasy.

"I see. Well, did you bring your dog?"

Rudling looked even more confused. Gracie, sensing pay dirt, drilled in harder with that gaze.

"Uh, I don't think you understand," Rudling said, nodding to the business card that he was now forcing into Ellen's hand. "Dr. Denton sent me. At the county health clinic? I want to buy a therapy dog."

"I see," Ellen said. "There's been some confusion here. Cap, help them break down the course. Mr. Rudling, will you step into my office please?"

Ellen led the principal through the back door of the modest rambler and into a cramped room, set off from the rest of the house by fake walnut paneling. Stacks of manila folders spilled over the desk and across the floor. There were neat, hand-printed tabs on each of the folders: "Rex/Jones," "Pudge/Anderson" "Duke/O'Hara" and other pet-owner combinations.

A few peeling snapshots were taped to the walls, photos of Ellen on one knee with therapy dogs from sessions past. The pictures featured the trainer and the dog and rarely more than the calf of the owner. Framed prominently behind her office chair was gold-embossed parchment from the mythical American Therapy Pet Association. The document was self-printed and attested to Ellen's standing as a certified trainer in the association she had also fabricated.

The owner of Kozy Kennel settled behind her desk and Rush squeezed into the gray metal folding chair in front of her. The meeting began to feel like a new take on a visit to the principal. Gracie had trailed them both and now sat in the doorway, slimy tennis ball in mouth, her eyes never leaving Rush.

"Mr. Rudling, we don't sell comfort dogs here," Ellen said. "The owners bring in their own dogs and we train both dogs and owners."

"BYOD?"

"Sorry?"

"Bring your own dog?" Rush explained with a crooked smile and a weak laugh.

"Right, therapy dogs are made, not born," the woman said, glancing quickly at Gracie. "Course there are exceptions—some dogs just seem to have a natural knack—but for most it's the six weeks of training we offer that makes the difference. That goes for owners as well as the dogs. Stress runs down the leash, not up."

"So . . . you won't sell me one?"

Ellen pursed her lips and looked at the gangly man whose eyes darted around the room. He seemed slow on the uptake, this middle-aged man who wore suits to dog kennels and couldn't seem to leave his privates alone.

"Mr. Rudling, without getting too personal, do you mind me asking why you want a therapy dog?"

Rudling looked around the room as if the answer was in some corner.

"Dr. Denton sent me," he again offered weakly.

"Yes, we've got that far, and thank you. But what exactly are you hoping a therapy dog can do for you?"

"My test scores are pathetic. I'm going to get tossed out of school if they don't get better fast."

"Oh, I get it. So you're working on your college degree."

"No," Rudling said, a crease of confusion deepening in his forehead. "Third grade, mostly."

Several seconds of silence followed. Gracie's head snapped back and forth, moving from the trainer to the principal, following the volleys of suspicious glances. Ellen broke the silence.

"That your idea of a joke, Mr. Rudling?"

"Joke? No! You don't understand," Rush stammered. He reached into his suit coat to retrieve the news clip that Eva had given him, the one about the downstate school boosting its scores with a therapy dog. The man pushed it across Ellen's desk. "I'm the principal at Flattop and I want to do this at my school."

Ellen grabbed eyeglasses hanging from a chain around her neck. They rode the tip of her nose as she studied the clip in silence. Gracie dropped the ball and waited.

"It says Winter Kennel trained him," Ellen mumbled to herself as she studied the article.

"Yes, and it says the school's test scores went up after they put that dog Max in the media center so kids could read to her," Rudling said. "We really could use something like that at Flattop.

Our scores are in the tank."

"Well it looks like a fine program, Mr. Rudling. I've heard these READ programs work in lots of schools," Ellen said, handing the clip back and rising from her chair. "What you need to see, though, is that you have to train a therapy dog. It's all one-to-one. You can't just drop a dog in a school and expect to reap blessings."

Cap appeared in the doorway behind Gracie.

The boy wasn't listening to his grandmother explain the Kozy Kennel program, words he had heard a thousand times before. Cap was looking from Gracie to his old teacher and back again. The pieces of a puzzle began to fit.

Who better to unload this little neurotic stray on? His grandmother was deluded if she thought the gimpy little mix would ever come to good as a therapy pet. Spacy Gracie was as twisted as the people she was supposed to chill out. Yet nothing Cap could say or do would shake his grandmother's misplaced belief.

And now, Rudling pops up like the cavalry. He's desperate. He thinks a dog can save his job. Who better to dump Gracie on? Here was rough justice for the taking: Cap could unload the little pup torturing his life on a teacher who had tortured his past.

"Mamaw, what about Gracie? She might work out for Mr. Rudling. She's had some training already."

Ellen Blair shook her head.

"That dog's not ready, Cap, and you know it. Maybe, maybe with another six weeks."

"I don't have six weeks," Rush said. The whine in his voice made Gracie pick up the sloppy tennis ball again.

"Mr. Rudling, I know the types of pressure you must be under at your school," Ellen said. "But you best understand, this takes time, and Gracie ain't just any dog."

"Mamaw, be reasonable. Gracie's got some training under her belt. She can feel her way through," the boy pressed.

"Cap, stop. I'm not going to risk it."

"Risk it? Mamaw, you're risking the whole business with all these stupid stray dogs—just feeding them alone, never mind the vet bills. Now, this nice Mr. Rudling from school wants to take one of those dogs and you—"

"When a dog walks out of here wearing one of our vests, with one of our badges attached, I want him to be flawless," Ellen said, tapping the desk for emphasis. "Gracie is gifted but she's rough, Cap. You know that better than anyone."

"Gracie will never walk out of here in a vest. You'd have to go to the state hospital for the type of vest *she* belongs in. And that's just fine with her. How's that for your flawless pet?"

The boy threw up his hands and left the room.

Ellen Blair drew a calming breath, folded her arms and swiveled back to Rush. "Mr. Rudling, we have classes here every Tuesday. Maybe you could come back and work with Gracie. And if it all works out in six weeks—"

"I don't have six weeks," Rush whined.

"You mind telling me why?"

"It's complicated," Rush muttered, rising from the metal chair and stepping over Gracie as he walked to the door.

"By the way, what's wrong with her?" he asked, nodding to the dog.

"Wrong?"

"She keeps staring at me. Gives me the willies!"

"No, Mr. Rudling, your willies were there before she showed up. That's why Gracie likes staying close to you."

"It's called *bonding*, Mamaw!" Cap yelled from the hallway. "Gracie is *bonding* with Mr. Rudling, and we ought to just give—"

"Mr. Rudling, good luck with your search," Ellen said, cutting off her grandson as she extended her hand.

Rudling looked down at the little black-and-copper dog that had never stopped staring at him. He reached down to scratch her ear, but the little statuette never moved.

The principal sighed. All he knew was six weeks was too long. The test scores would be out, and he wouldn't have his story in the paper to fight back. He was out of options.

Rush's panic was full blown now. A row of therapy dogs began to muster along the hall as he made his way out. It looked like a wedding procession or a funeral with canine pallbearers.

The Audi chirped hello as Rush hit the unlock button on his key fob. Behind him, the little copper-and-black dog was still staring out the hallway window, whimpering softly, the golden lamps of her eyes locked on the man and glowing.

"Funny how Gracie set to him from the start," Ellen said to her grandson as the two watched him drive off. "I've never seen her go after someone that hard."

Cap snorted and walked away.

"Gracie and Rudling are both nuts," he called over his shoulder. "They were made for each other, if you ask me."

Chapter Eight

The ribbon-cutting at Flattop Elementary took place in 1983, a year people would remember as both the beginning and the high-water mark for a school that fell so dismally, so consistently short of the slide-show promises made at the start of the big dig. Set on a sawed-off mountain in a dying coalfield community, the school was supposed to hold the line against poverty and ignorance. Year after year, armies arrived every morning in yellow buses and the kids poured over the ramparts—hungry and sick and socially stunted from the start. They were at least a grade level behind every other kid before they ever set foot inside a kindergarten. They wouldn't see a teacher until years after the wiring had been laid along the synapses of their undernourished brains.

For all its fancy landscaping and fine equipment, this school on the heights was no match for such a ruthless enemy. Every day the building was pulverized by need, leveled by grinding poverty—public education's Abbey of Monte Cassino.

"Don't think of the glass as nineteen-twentieths empty," the principal would mutter with a smile more bitter than wry.

The Flattop teachers learned to hunker down in their Monte Cassino fortress, taking the incoming rounds of crackpot reform and flimsy turnaround schemes with grim resolve. Most of the staff knew the truth: They weren't miracle workers, and most wouldn't describe themselves as "gifted" educators. But they were competent, hard-working professionals, and they knew it. They were locked in a school where competent and hard-working just weren't enough—and they knew that, too.

The churn was unrelenting. New teachers would show up, doe-eyed, with lesson plans about mock assemblies of the United Nations and cross-discipline units on the ecology of Appalachian mining. They would usually get pitched into filing cabinets after a couple of weeks. They were crowded out by fifth-grade refreshers on how to line up without talking and unending reviews of "there," "their," "they're." It was brain-dead work, for students and teachers alike, but at least it was worth five points on the big state test.

Michael Rose

Fatigue sent the teachers home from the school every night with a look that made their own kids scatter to other rooms, a look that made the bedroom lights go off without a kiss. It was a look so stressed and worn that your dog barely recognized you. One by one, it pried your fingers, stretched the tendons till your shoulders popped from the sockets, worked on you till you lost your grip on the ledges around the mountaintop school and tumbled helplessly to the valley below. You just held on as best you could, as long as you could.

Privately, most Flattop staff thought a transfer was their best chance of staying sane and employed. Publicly, they toed the line of wild imaginings, embraced their status as the shell-shocked mountain abbey of public education, and sang hosannas to make Flattop a school that guarantees opportunity for all . . . in the 20th century . . . the 21st century . . . whatever the next century happened to be.

*****

Thirty-five days. By Rush's reckoning, that's how much time stood between him and unemployment. By then, the test scores would tell the story. By then, and Chambers would storm through the doors, probably with someone from Human Resources in tow, demanding answers to questions that just couldn't be answered. There wasn't even a phys-ed job to dream about slinking back to anymore.

Eight hundred and forty hours. Rush did the calculations like a death row inmate while he picked at his crotch and stared through the office fishbowl glass. Lines of students were trickling through the corridors now, changing rooms for the next period. A couple of the kindergartners saw their principal, and they smiled and waved. Rush felt like his heart would break. How could they know? How could they know?

Rudling nodded and scurried back to his office, closing the door behind him. He pulled out his desk calculator and punched a few buttons. Fifty thousand, four hundred minutes. He wondered if a fourth Xanax for the day would put him in a ditch on the drive home. It felt like the least of his worries now. That evening, Rush paced the fake hardwood flooring while, behind him, the stainless-steel dishwasher was grinding away—an ungodly racket that filled his huge country kitchen. The appliance was supposed to be silky silent but had started to act up a couple days before. His wife wanted to get a repairman out fast, before family flocked to the big house for Easter, but Rush put her off. He'd put up with noise over new expenses right now.

The principal stopped the contraption midcycle and peered in, playing with the only component he understood, the soap dispenser. Satisfied, he latched it again, and the gear-on-gear fight resumed inside. Rush sighed and walked away. At some point, he would have to break down and call one of those handymen from the hills, the ones who tucked fliers into the doors of the fancy houses of Burnside Overlook. But right now he couldn't deal with it, not the money or the psychology of it. Hill folks regarded the McMansion owners as nothing more than pussies who couldn't handle basic plumbing, and they charged them as such.

The phone rang and Rush ripped it out of the cradle.

"Yes?" he snapped.

"Mr. Rudling?"

"Speaking."

"This is Cap—from the kennel?"

The kennel fiasco had been on Rush's mind all evening. It was his last chance to set things right at his school, and that bitch of an owner had screwed him.

"Mr. Rudling . . . you there? Are you still interested in a dog?" the boy on the line continued. He spoke softly and nervously, the way Eva did when she called him from home.

"Of course, I am," Rush said. "Why else would I go out there today?"

"Then, meet me outside the train gazebo on Main Street tomorrow morning at 10."

"You found another dog?"

"No, it's Gracie," the boy said.

"But what about your grandmother?"

"Leave that to me."

"Well, I've got school tomorrow, and I'm not set up for a dog yet. I don't have a leash or a bowl or—"

"You'll get everything—leash, food, bowl, vest, ID, all of it. Be there at 10."

"But I don't understand why it has to be—"

"Mr. Rudling, do you want the dog or not?" the voice said, louder and more demanding.

"Of course I want the dog," Rush repeated

"Then I'll see you at 10," Cap said, hanging up before the principal could reply.

Chapter Nine

Rush walked up the flagstones of Flattop with a bright little dog weaving between his legs. Gracie was executing an excited series of figure-eights, darting in and out of the principal's long strides, and the man had to stop every few feet to untangle his legs from the leash.

It was past 11, the last day of state testing at the school. Rush could see heads pop up in the school windows. The students were sneaking peeks at the dog in the courtyard. Adults came up behind them to play whack-a-mole with any bored head that wasn't bent to the test sheet.

Rush was holding Gracie with one hand and waving "settle down" to the kid-filled windows with the other. He thought he saw Mr. Banks in fourth grade. The teacher seemed to mouth something as he shot a dirty look at the principal and the rudderless mutt in the green therapy vest.

Rush unwound himself from the leash and scooped up the dog in one pirouetting motion. Without a word, he blew through the front door, past the secretaries and into the sanctuary of his private office—just a wild-eyed man toting a dog that was rapturously licking his face now. Eva slid from her station and followed him in, closing the door on the other gawkers.

"Look at this!" Rush yelled to Eva, dropping the dog and holding up his arms to display a toupee's-worth of black and copper hair static-clung to his navy suit. "I've got the end-of-testing celebration in the auditorium in just 15 minutes."

Eva silently walked over to his desk and retrieved a lint roller from the boss's top drawer. She swept the hair from his suit and sneaked in a few rubs and pats to his tight neck and shoulders. Gracie hopped up on the couch and watched them, panting and grinning.

"There—gone," soothed the secretary. She pet Rush's shoulder and then walked to the couch. "So this is our new comfort dog. What's your name, princess?"

"Her name is Gracie, and she is not a comfort dog," snapped

Rush. "She is a therapy dog! A neurotic therapy dog—probably the only neurotic therapy dog in the history of therapy dogs."

"Settle down, sugar."

"Eva, the dog is crazy. All she wants to do is stare—at me! She's a little four-legged stalker, and she gives me the willies."

"She's just fond of you, Rushmore."

"I don't *want* her to be fond of me. I want her to raise the friggin' test scores! Where's the number for that little bastard from Kozy Kennel."

Rush fumbled in his pocket for the Kozy Kennel business card. He picked up the phone and dialed. Eva settled onto the couch to watch the meltdown with Gracie, who was munching her shriveled paw and taking in Rush's every move.

"Cap? Rushmore Rudling. What the hell is wrong with the dog you gave me this morning?" Rush hissed into the phone.

The man's agitation was enough to set Gracie in motion. She picked up an autographed baseball sitting in a coffee-table display stand. The stand's brass plaque read "Regional Championship, 1986: Clarksville Pirates 8, Springfield Tigers, 4." Gracie's tail wagged as she offered it to the man, who was now snapping his fingers to get Eva's attention before drool erased the single greatest moment of his high school varsity life.

Rush was pacing the floor with the phone pressed to his head; whatever was said on the other end of the line was making him flail in anger.

"Uh huh . . . uh huh . . . Use my commands. Well how's this for a command—get your neurotic mutt out of my school," the principal screamed, slamming down the receiver. Rush slumped in his chair and tore through the desk, looking for Xanax. Gracie trotted over to the bottom drawer and offered him a necktie.

"Get her away!" Rush screamed.

The class-change bell rang. Today, it signaled the end of a week's worth of testing, and all students were supposed to assemble in the cafeteria for the annual post-test celebration. Every year—on the Friday before testing week—the students rallied in the big room for cheers and chants, and reminders to get enough sleep and to eat well. The faculty pressed high-fives and a few Jolly Ranchers into their hands. A week later, the students would muster again in the room. A couple of lucky ones would be selected to tear down the huge "Silence Please" banner posted there as classmates cheered them on and sucked on a second ration of Jolly Ranchers.

Rush could hear the kids filing down the hallway for the post-test ruckus. They were chattering and laughing, excited not to be shushed at the drop of a hat. File cabinets slammed in the front office—the last of the answer sheets and booklets placed under lock and key.

Thunder rumbled outside Flattop, building from a thin note to a throaty growl that rattled the windows. Suddenly, Gracie dropped the gray tie and scrambled back to the couch, wedging her head between the cushions.

"Oh my God. She's freaking out. Storms freak my therapy dog out!" Rush whimpered. "Eva, what am I going to do? I was going to introduce her to the kids at the rally. Now—"

"Rushmore, just be patient with her. Look . . . easy, sweetness," Eva said, stroking the small dog's head. "This is new for her, too. It's you stressing out that she's picking up on, honey. Didn't you have a dog when you were a boy?"

"Yeah, and someone ran him over! And I cried, OK? I cried like a baby. And I swore it would be the last time I'd ever own a dog. Until now," Rush said, casting a sharp look across the room at the woman who'd hooked him up with this scheme.

The sound of warm-up claps rolled down the hallway. The rally was under way.

Eva sighed, stood up and got the leash. She hooked up Gracie and walked her over to Rush, thrusting the leather into his hand with one testy motion.

Attached to him again, Gracie looked bright and happy. Rush's lip began to tremble.

"It'll be fine, Rushmore, just . . . expect more," was all Eva said.

The auditorium doors flew open and Rush walked down the aisle with Gracie. It was bedlam inside. The kids were yelling, squirming, bouncing, slapping, kicking, prodding and poking— everything but listening to the amended half-day bus schedule that Mr. Rooney, the assistant principal, was reading into a microphone at the front of the room. It was one squiggling, squirming mass of kids, determined to burn off a week's worth of energy in a 20-minute assembly.

"Hey, Mr. Rushmore! Who's that dog?" one of the students yelled.

For a second, the room stilled as everyone turned to watch the lanky principal striding to the front of the room with a green-vested Gracie in tow. A couple of students reached out into the aisle to offer the dog a Jolly Rancher, but she ignored them. Rush was all she saw.

The principal and the dog scrambled up the three steps to the podium. Rush stepped to the microphone, boxing out his assistant principal, tapping the contraption three times even though it was obviously warmed up and working.

"I want to congratulate all you kids for a great job this week. Our Flattop family is making huge strides, and I know the tests will show it," Rudling said, whipping around to eye the faculty members assembled behind him, ready to smack any face that smirked or rolled eyes.

"Mr. Rudling, why do you got your dog in a green coat?" one student yelled.

"She's gotta be in orange if you're fixin' to hunt," another student called out.

"Yes, the dog," Rush said, clearing his throat. "Students, I want you to meet Gracie. Gracie is a very special dog, a reading dog. She's been specially trained to work with students on their reading, and that's why she's wearing her special green vest."

"Your dog can't read!" a suspicious student called out, sparking a twitter in the room.

"No, Gracie can't read, but she's a therapy pet and that makes her a wonderful listener. She came to Flattop to listen to you read, children. She'll be in the media center with Ms. Merring, who hopes you'll come visit and read to our school's new dog soon!"

Rush's words were enough to stop a three-person procession that had formed in the center aisle. Leading it was Cynthia Parks, a first-grader whose nervous stomach had given out from the combination of Jolly Ranchers and assembly commotion. Janitor Joe took the end of the conga line, sweeping side to side with a wet mop that was soaking up puke.

In the middle, supporting the child, was a pretty woman in a purple dress that was now soaked dark at the lap. The woman's pale face was framed by hair the color of coal, parted in the middle and turned up at a jaw line that seemed naturally set and determined. She wore wire-rim spectacles, too mature for her years, and her gray eyes alternated looks of comfort for the child against her hip with steely don't-go-there glares at the worst offenders among the students who had now taken to taunting Cynthia. The woman was Kay Merring, the reading resource teacher in the school media room, the one Rush had seen in the hallway the day he took the job at Flattop.

Kay froze at Rush's announcement from the podium and swung back for a second to stare at the principal with a look of horror and amazement.

"Yes, children, Gracie is here! She'll be in the media room waiting for you with Ms. Merring, so come! Come quickly!" Rush continued, extending his arms, avoiding Kay's stare. He sounded like a deranged cross between Mr. Rogers and Jim Jones.

Kay shook her head at Rush. There was vomit running down the teacher's legs, and children on either side of the aisle were tossing insults freely now at Cynthia. Kay hugged the girl tighter and they walked together quickly to the girls' bathroom just outside the room.

"Does Superintendent Chambers know you're doing this?"

It was Rooney, the assistant principal, who had moved behind Rush's shoulder for the kill. Rush brushed him off with a wave. Gracie curled a protective lip and snarled at Rooney.

"Yes, children," Rush continued, "Gracie will be waiting. Come read to her!"

A few students tried to start a chant "Gra-cie! Gra-cie!" but it died in a growl of thunder. Gracie popped about two feet off the deck and then buried her head between Rush's ankles. The room erupted in laughter and tossed candy wrappers.

"That dog is *weird!*"

"Mr. Rudling, what's your dog a-scared of?"

"I ain't readin' to that dog. She's a pussy!"

The owner of the last comment was led out immediately, but other students were ready to step in. Their insults came thick and heavy, and the faculty instinctively filed off the stage to settle them down with finger snaps and clapped hands. Rush was left alone on the stage. He threw his arms wide, beseeching order, droning into the microphone as Gracie buried deeper into his socks.

67

"Gracie doesn't like thunder, children, but it doesn't matter. The sign-up sheet will be posted at the office. Come see her! Come read to her!"

The bell rang. The teachers dismissed the rows quickly, herding the students to the bus loading zones, shooting the principal dirty looks. Three-quarters of the room was out the door before Rush could formally dismiss the assembly.

Eva was standing beside the big auditorium doors when they closed for the last time. The secretary, the principal and the little dog were alone in the big room.

"How do you think it went?" Rush asked the woman.

Eva just smiled and shook her head. It was a sadder version of the look Kay Merring had given him moments before.

"I guess I'd better get that sign-up sheet posted outside the office," she said as she walked out the door.

Rush stared at Gracie. The little dog was beaming again, a playful pant in her throat.

"Could have been worse, I guess," Rush muttered.

*****

Kay Merring returned to the media center to find Gracie, a pile of shit, and another smelly mound just inches from the pile-of-shit's wingtip shoe.

"Kay, look, I know you're upset," Rush stammered, "but I promise everything is going to be just fine with the dog. You'll love her, you'll see."

The teacher blew a wisp of dark hair from her face as she studied Rudling, the dog and the unwelcome deposit on her classroom floor. Vomit from the assembly had soaked into her lap by now. The smell was competing with the fresh turds on her floor. She walked over, picked up the phone and called Janitor Joe.

Rush was forcing a crooked smile. In his hand was Gracie's leash and the Kozy Kennel therapy pet manual that Cap had given him hours before. The teacher pursed her lips and looked the principal up and down.

"Mr. Rudling, since this will be the first time 'dog' has ever come up in one of our conversations, I'm not sure why you seem so certain about how I'm feeling right now," the teacher said, dabbing the stain on her lap with a wet paper towel from the art station. "For all you know, I might feel like, oh . . . stabbing you with a pair of safety scissors."

Rush watched her walk over to grab the roll of paper towels and a spray bottle of disinfectant. She was young and pretty. There was early gray in her dark, straight hair, but it was a nice, unaffected touch that set off her broad, pale forehead. And it all worked together with those round granny glasses that looked smart (if a little too mature) on her smooth face.

Kay kneeled down to clean up the mess at his feet, and Rush reflexively took in the firm, athletic taper of legs that speed-walked the steep county hills for 45 minutes every morning.

She felt his eyes immediately.

"I'm covered in puke, picking up shit, and *that's* where his mind's at?" thought Kay. She knew from experience there was nothing to do but wait for the impulse to pass and the mind to clear. It happened with a lot of men like Rush. With the principal, however, those few seconds always felt like a lifetime.

"Kay, you know the state exam scores are going to be bad again this year, right? There's no way we make it, not in reading," Rush said.

"Listen, I'm not blaming you," he continued. "You're remedial reading, and it's your first year at Flattop, just like me. Nobody expects miracles. But we need a game changer at this school and we need it fast—something to keep people off our backs and buy us a little more time. This dog could be that X factor."

Kay said nothing. Cleaning dog shit on all fours seemed a less disgusting option right now than talking with this man.

The accident had embarrassed Gracie. The dog was munching on her small foot again, curled under a table in the corner of the media center. It was one of a half-dozen tables in the room, but the only one draped with a bed sheet. The fabric turned the table into a bright little pup tent. "Reading Fort" was expertly hand-stitched on the front of the fabric; and delicate borders of gold, silver and blue danced around the hem.

For now, though, it was just a holding pen, an asylum for a little dog chewing her foot while a principal droned on about how the pup was the best thing that ever happened to the teacher and to Flattop Elementary.

"Anyway, there is this school downstate that is making big gains with something called a therapy dog," Rush continued, fumbling in his pocket for the well-worn news clip.

"I know a little about therapy dogs in reading programs, Mr. Rudling. What I don't understand is why you'd just spring this on the school, without a word to anyone."

"Oh, come on, Ms. Merring, the tests are done and the numbers come out in twelve weeks. Do you really think the state and central office are going to give us time—after missing scores for five years straight? There was no time to meet and confer about this."

Gracie perked up as Rush began to pace.

"We've got to get out in front of this thing," Rush continued. "I want this therapy dog in the media center starting Monday. I want you to work with her for six weeks, get her settled in ASAP. I plan to call the paper before the year ends. With luck, we can get them to run a nice story about us before the scores come out," Rush said, flapping his news clip.

"I've got that, Miss Merring," a voice called from the door. It was Janitor Joe, mop and bucket in tow. He helped the woman to her feet and handed her a disinfectant wipe for her hands.

"Hey, Joe, whatcha—"

"Mr. Rudling, you might want to step away from that pile," Joe said, rolling his bucket to the dog turd and cutting the boss off midsentence.

The phone rang in the media center. Kay picked it up.

"Mr. Rudling," she said, pushing the handset to him.

Rush's eyes went wild when he discovered it was Superintendent Chambers' office. They'd had a call about some disturbance—a dog at the school assembly. Rush knew who, and he made a mental note to give Rooney, his assistant principal, permanent bus detail for this treachery.

"No, everything's just fine here," Rush stammered. "I was just introducing the kids to . . . Yes, I'll hold."

Rush crumpled, and only a nearby chair cushioned the fall. His face was goofy, otherworldly, fixed in a panicked smile, the same grin that was pasted on his face at the first meeting with Chambers. His eyes looked sick and vacant, and Kay could swear they were beginning to glisten.

"Superintendent Chambers, sir! Yes, good after . . . Yes, that's correct . . . A dog, yes . . . No, it's not my house pet, sir, it's a therapy dog . . . A therapy dog . . . A dog that helps kids read . . . Yes, sir, certified, licensed and vaccinated . . . No, sir, we haven't dropped your sister's Zen-based program—wonderful resource, expect big things from the scores . . . Of course! . . . Well, we'd love to have you here, sir. Have a goo..."

Rush stopped midword, cut off but still holding the phone to his head. He was gazing into space, stunned and groping his nuts again.

Gracie crept over and curled at his feet, offering her belly for him to pet.

"You know how I said you had six weeks to work with the dog?" Rush said at last. Kay nodded. "It's cut to two weeks—Chambers is coming here Friday after next, and he wants to see the dog in action."

Rush stood up and seemed to wobble for a second. He locked his hands behind his head, pulling his forearms tight around his ears, as if he were trying to block out some imaginary buzz in his skull. Then his feet shuffled vacantly for the door.

"Mr. Rudling?"

"Huh?"

Kay Merring had hooked up Gracie and was handing the leash to the principal. The dog's nails clicked on the linoleum, tap-dancing in excitement, and she smacked her lips and beamed at the man who still looked stunned.

"No . . . you . . . you better take her," Rush said, his voice flat and lifeless.

"Sir?"

"You've only got two weeks. Chambers is coming."

Rush shuffled out the door and down the hall. Gracie tugged and whined as he turned the corner.

Joe shook his head.

"A man wound that tight has no business owning a dog," he muttered.

71

Chapter Ten

Kay and Gracie just stared at each other once Joe left the room. The dog looked depressed with Rush gone and had taken up residence under the reading fort.

Making the reading fort was a nonstop weekend of work, even for Kay, who had spent 12 years finishing button holes in a textile mill before she became a teacher. The pay was good, and she would probably have stuck with the trade had a hook machine on the big factory floor not taken two of her fingers one day. Everything about the accident felt so casual to Kay: the sound of steel, metal-on-metal, ringing through the evening shift until the floor man dashed to slap the shut-down button. There was the smell and taste of metal-sweet blood, the bloody hand that wouldn't stop shaking as she held it up to her startled face for inspection. And, feet away, there were the last two fingers of her work glove rolling across the floor, still filled and soaked red.

The company settled, enough to pay for the night classes that brought her into teaching. But Kay never forgot how to fly across fabric with needle and thread, even after she moved into the classroom, even without the last two fingers on her hand.

Kay kept a sewing kit in her top drawer at school. At recess, when some of the children shivered in shirtsleeves outside rather than put on the humiliating thrift-shop rags they brought from home, Kay would steal off to the cloak room to mend a few. At the end of the day, she smiled but said nothing when a child put on a coat and took it off again, checking the pockets to make sure it didn't belong to one of the luckier kids.

One of those ratty coats belonged to Sue May Allen, "stuttering Sue," whose greatest fear was being called on in reading. Kay worked gently with the second-grader whenever she could. They sat side by side, Kay waiting patiently for the words to form, the little girl stumbling through basic nursery rhymes and leaning against her teacher for support. Only long spells of silence prompted the teacher to step in with mild, half-whispered coaxes and prods of "it's fine—go on."

If other children were nearby, Sue May wouldn't read at all. Not unless she sad cross-legged in front of Kay, draping her coat, the one that her teacher had mended, over both of their heads.

"I can only read in here," the girl whispered to her teacher in a voice too low for the others to hear.

Kay thought about this one night after dinner, sitting in her quiet apartment with only her cat Pharaoh for company. Suddenly, the teacher stood up, pulled a plain white sheet from her linen closet, and settled back into her easy chair. Beside her was a wicker basket filled with thread of every gauge and every color under heaven.

It was already 6 o'clock on a Friday evening. The sun was slipping behind the old mountain. On Monday morning, when the sun crested the eastern plains, Kay was still in the chair with the sheet in her lap. By now, however, the fabric was no longer white but blazing with color. The whole of the sheet was wrought with stitching as fast and as fine as Kay had ever done, fashioned through the night and light and half-light of precious days away from the school.

The radiant fabric was over the table in the media center when Sue May showed up that Monday morning. That day, the little girl and the teacher traded the threadbare coat for a real reading fort, a kingdom of golds and silvers and blues.

Now, a new face stared at the teacher from her reading fort— and this one was sucking on that little front paw!

"Come on, sweetie," Kay said at last, reaching in to gather Gracie in her arms for the walk to the faculty parking lot. "The asylum's closed for the day."

*****

Pharaoh lifted himself from the credenza with a heavy "mmmrrrhh," as if he had been working all day. The tabby padded to the mail stand in the small hallway of Kay's apartment. There were footsteps outside in the hallway, more than one set, which stirred the cat's curiosity, since no one visited anymore. The old tomcat sat on the rug and bathed his whiskers while he waited. Soon, the key would jiggle and trip the temperamental tumblers in the stubborn latch.

Michael Rose

The cat's hunch was right. There was something different. Kay was there, just like every other night, but something was with the teacher, or more precisely, around her. It was a blue nylon line, a leash wrapped more than once around her trim legs. Attached to it and tucked shyly in the space of the woman's ankles was a dog, a little dog wearing a thin green vest with white letters on it. The get-up made the gimpy pup look like a saddled miniature pony.

Pharaoh studied the runt. "For real?" his sour expression sang out.

Gracie saw the housecat immediately, and she dodged the disdainful stare of the old striped thing. Pharaoh seemed prickly, even hateful, certainly at odds with the bright silver bell strapped around his neck with a collar of purple ribbon. Gracie began to dodge the cat and the hard regard of his eyes, zigzagging between Kay's legs. The moves only pulled the blue nylon cord tighter, and Kay stumbled over the mail table.

"This leash—it's not going to work," she whispered to herself.

Any tether was unfortunate, but the leash that Rush Rudling had given Kay when he orphaned the dog to her care just made matters worse. It was a bulbous, blue contraption shaped like a cowbell: a fishing-line model that you set to random lengths with the squeeze of a trigger. In a heartbeat, the line arrested at any distance, for any reason. With Gracie, it only compounded the indignity and added to the confusion. How could an animal know the thinking behind the trigger? How could it fathom what froze the line at some invented point? The play in the line was sold for the animal's benefit. Kay knew immediately that it was just a torment—arbitrary, hard and cruel. Tomorrow, she would trade it for something finer: a standard leash made of cloth, perhaps, always five feet from loop to latch. It was a length that, if nothing else, made life certain.

The teacher bent down to free her legs and the pup. For Pharaoh, that was a cue. With a slow, casual roll of his shoulders, the old cat sauntered up to Gracie and swatted her on the nose— one shot, clean and hard. The little dog yipped and burrowed deeper between Kay's legs. Pharaoh looked on, bored already with the effort.

"Feel better now?" Kay said to the cat, the teacher's scold not quite masking a smile. "Is that what makes our little Pharaoh's day?"

The cat ignored her and retired to the credenza. With another world-weary "mmmrrrhh," Pharaoh slung himself up the old oak, spun precisely twice, and settled into the edge of wood and wall. He gathered his tail and smoothed it like a comforter before slowly turning back to the two interlopers, fixing them with cowl-eyed contempt.

Pharaoh was sorry he had moved at all. He would not move again, not until he heard the can opener sing from the kitchen counter. Or maybe the refrigerator door snapping open, since the woman had fried up oysters the night before.

Kay dropped her school papers on the mail stand and began to hunt for bowls in the kitchen. Gracie used the moment to study the apartment, steering clear of the dozing bully on the ledge.

In the corner of the living room was a cream-colored sewing machine, second-hand but sturdy, a commercial model with a floating foot. It sat next to a shelf of cheap pressboard, where generous space was reserved for the colorful bindings of children's books. Many were gilded and etched. Their glittering spines filled the stacks—a procession of bold knights, cunning wizards, and maidens in velvet with scepters and crowns. In the center was a wooden dollhouse, or something that might have made a good dollhouse had it not been stuffed with even more books.

It was a set, a children's anthology. The books nestled wall-to-wall and ceiling-to-floorboard in the little toy cottage, neatly arranged inside a three-sided house not much bigger than a toaster. The house's missing wall revealed 12 slim volumes, starting on the left with bindings that sported the playful greens of early May. These were the volumes of nursery rhymes, fables and light-hearted songs. Like a story of stories, they radiated to the right, into the deeper hues of blue, the thicker tales of adventure and the stoic courage of youth.

Gracie cautiously sniffed the old dollhouse, flecked with water spots. The fine hairs on her muzzle detected the slight warp of the wood, and her nostrils filled with must and time. At the base was written, "MY BOOK HOUSE," the name of the children's book set, a title that had been out of print for more than 50 years.

The decision must have been a reluctant one for the publisher: For years, "MY BOOK HOUSE" was a reliable staple and a cash cow of door-to-door marketing, at least in those parts of the country where people still opened their doors to salesmen.

Every month, men would provision fleets of station wagons and sedans with goods for the home, taking care not to sweat through the suits they'd need for the house calls in the weeks ahead. Their trunks were filled with everything from potato peelers to rug beaters, comforters to croup remedies, and always, always the latest volume of "MY BOOK HOUSE."

Gracie heard the splash of nuggets hitting a plastic bowl Kay had pulled from the kitchen cabinet. The can opener whirred, and the warm face of the woman appeared around the corner.

"Kibble! Get it while it's dry," the teacher called to the dog beside her book set. "You too, grumpy," she said with a smile to the cat.

Gracie gave Pharaoh his due, letting him trot in first. The cat stared at the dog with the new bowl in disgust. Then he sprang to the counter, where the proper wet goods were waiting in a saucer. The sight of two fried oysters garnishing his workaday tuna made the sullen cat coo softly.

"Thought that might cheer you up," Kay said with a smirk.

The pup limped in behind Pharaoh. The teacher tapped her foot as she studied her new charge. There was a tremble, a quiver of nerves in Gracie's legs. She stood at the bowl looking from cat to teacher. The pup nosed the feed and ate gingerly, casting worried looks at Kay and Pharaoh between bites.

"Train you . . . to be a reading dog . . . in one week," Kay said, boiling down her principal's command into his latest impossible task. The voice made Gracie peek over the rim of her bowl. Kay chewed her lower lip as she studied the small dog with the mangled paw and the timid ways. There wasn't much to her, this ball of copper and black with high foxy ears. She was so tiny that the edges of her green "Support Dog" vest almost cinched completely around her soft, white belly.

"Well, at least you're dressed for it," Kay said finally.

The teacher moved to the mail stand and picked up "Training Your Comfort Dog," the slim, self-published paperback from Kozy Kennel. Rush Rudling had handed her the book with the leash. The type was fuzzy and the paper was coarse. Pictured inside were setters, shepherds, beagles and even a few mixes like Gracie. All the dogs were clad in green vests as they nuzzled up to accept pats and strokes in nursing homes, oncology wards, and reading rooms. Most programs for comfort and support dogs opt for red and blue dog vests, the manual explained, but Kozy Kennel was different, opting for a renegade green. It was a cheerful, inviting color, Kay thought—not quite up to the rich purples that she had loved all her life, but, still, a color that lived up to the book's promise of "soothing and settling the mind with the promising emeralds of May."

"'Soothe and settle the mind.' Guess we've proven that dogs really are color blind," Kay said, glancing at Gracie, who had finished her bowl and was trying to pick a space on the living room rug to bunk down for the night. The dog circled in place and circled again, like a roulette wheel on a hard pull. It went on for at least two minutes—revolutions that ended with a hard flop on the carpet. The pup stuffed her withered paw into her mouth like a pacifier and settled in for the night. Her glowing eyes bounced back and forth across the room like a metronome. She reminded Kay of an old Felix-the-Cat clock, one of those black, plastic wall models from the '50s.

Pharaoh returned to his perch, performing his precise two turns before settling down. The teacher turned back to the training manual.

The Kozy Kennel paperback was filled with do's and don'ts. There were tips for dogs and handlers alike and step-by-step exercises to desensitize the dogs, coaxing them to ignore the externals, keeping their focus only on the trainer and the client. There was also a *Cosmo*-like checklist in the manual for both dogs and handlers. Kay took the trainer test and scored nine out of 10, missing only on previous experience. She gave the dog test to Gracie and stopped after six questions yielded five wrong answers.

"It's nine at night and I'm still giving tests . . . I'm spending my night giving another standardized test—to a dog. What's wrong with this picture?" Kay mused, stroking a small insurrection of dark tresses behind her ears.

She tossed the manual on the counter and walked to the bedroom to shower and change into her sweats.

There was hot water in the building for once and Kay lingered for a few minutes, bowing her head under the flow. Warm streams traced the drape of her breasts, full and dun, and rolled down her belly to find the creases of her thighs. She thought of touching herself, taking a humble offer of hot water and turning it into something sweet and dimly remembered.

The woman gathered inside herself, drifting through a collection of vetted memories and imaginings. So many of them from this spray, where passions past hid in the warmth of the droplets. The feel of nipples hardening against the cool press of tile. Warm water pooling in the small of a long back that pouts to invite, to demand. Forearms pinned to the wall, braced on the balls of the feet. Rocking to muscular thrusts that make the moment ache. The press of hips. The tip of the tongue, traced along the ear that burns. The rugged palm and thick thigh, manly and hard, striking the steadied feminine form, so eagerly offered. The sound, urgent, primal, echoing wet and sharp and sweet on the stones. And the feel of it, all of it, glowing like coal fired to crimson.

Kay lingered in the steam and heat, testing herself, discovering if the woman could fight through the fatigue. Not tonight. The warm spray on her shoulders already was giving out. The water heater in the basement was spent, and a clammy chill was beginning to build, slowly at first, then quickly.

She turned off the silver faucets with a sigh. Passion these days was like a forgotten key buried in the bottom of a drawer, useless for the moment but something you dare not throw out for good. She felt irritated, irritated over a small thing like not being able to find the woman inside when the water was hot, irritated that day so crowded into night, stealing everything. Fatigue ruled the earth. A factory machine took her fingers and she now slaved in a building of crazy demands and neurotic therapy pets for kids in a district that only cared about such things when the newspaper showed up. Her life, every bit of it, was stranded in a school on a flat-topped mountain—a school where the sign out front should say, "Our Mission: Fix Everything."

She checked the locks and turned in early, taking a few sips of wine to numb her mind, drifting away with a pale moon waxing through the bedroom window, wondering if the water would ever be warm again.

Chapter Eleven

Kay opened her eyes to see Pharaoh sitting on her pillow and staring at her through half-closed eyes. Sun was bursting through the blinds now. The cat was wearing that sweet-sour expression he got whenever the teacher slept in on the weekend. True, the bed stayed warmer longer on those days, but now Pharaoh's belly was beginning to gnaw and he needed to put a stop to it. He bopped Kay's nose with his, softly, just enough to get the woman moving.

Kay blinked. Pharaoh blinked back, and then the woman was up and about, stepping into the kitchen with the cat on her heels and Gracie trailing. The teacher picked up the manual again while the animals ate. A tired dog is a good dog. That's the secret when it comes to training a balky, high-strung animal, and the Kozy Kennel manual made no bones about it.

"Got a comfort-dog-in-training that's tight on the leash?" the manual asks in its FAQs. "Take it for a brisk walk or a run! Make its tongue mop the floor, and try the exercises again. You'll be amazed how a little fatigue leads to a major attitude adjustment in your animal."

Kay smirked as she leafed through the booklet, studying Gracie over her morning coffee.

"Nothing would amaze me about what a little fatigue can do," she said to the dog, who peeked over her morning bowl of kibble. Kay grabbed the leash and laced up her running shoes. "OK, sister, you heard what the doctor ordered. Let's see what you've got."

Pharaoh watched from the window, as the woman and the dog stepped out in the chilly mountain air. A narrow field separated them from an old service road beside the woods, and the two jogged for it. Every two strides, Kay would cut her gate a half-step so the gimpy little pup could keep up.

Beyond the road and the pines, Kay could see the rising green slopes of Burnside Mountain. The mountain had changed overnight, picking up a snow cap whiter than the frost that coated the lowlands. Curls of smoke rose up from cabins hidden by woods. They dissolved into a clear blue sky where a few hawks loitered, scouring the fresh snow for tracks.

"Hang in there, sweetie," Kay said, slowing a bit to slacken the leash. Gracie was running gamely beside her, eyes sparkling, tongue fluttering like a pink banner. The two fell into rhythm. Pine trees rolled by, trance-like, and Kay's thoughts drifted back with the drumbeat of her pace and her past.

Her lost fingers didn't bother her, at least not in the way most expected. She was still beautiful, women always know that, and when it came to the missing digits, the men it mattered to most were the ones who never mattered to her in the first place.

For the teacher, the classroom was another matter. Kay could always sense that one child at the beginning of the school year, the one transfixed, horrified, staring at the missing fingers while the teacher's words flew unnoticed over their heads. In their young eyes was fear, not malice or disgust that registered with some people when they saw the mangled hand. Kay always felt a stab of guilt at being the cause of their plight—the second-graders, that is, not the others.

Always, she drew these children aside during seatwork, behind the cloakroom partition. She would crouch down to eye level and slowly draw her hand from behind her back. In soothing tones, she would mention an assignment or note home—plain vanilla talk while she inched the hand forward, between them, the teacher's eyes gently fixed on the student's face all the while, waiting for the question.

"You know, it's OK if you want to ask me stuff," Kay would say to the shy ones after a pause.

"How did you do it?" one little girl asked, pulling away slightly.

"A machine in a sewing factory did it," the teacher said softly. "I used to work there."

"Did it hurt?"

"A lot."

"Did you cry?"

"Yes, I did," Kay said, "but I don't cry anymore."

"I would cry *all* the time," the little girl replied, staring in fear at the long, delicate taper of fingers that remained on the woman's hand, beauty that ended so abruptly.

"You don't have to cry. It's not going to happen to you," Kay said, her voice even softer, a caress, her eyes warm but carefully studying. "That's what I want you to remember. You're safe. We're here, and we keep you safe. It's never going to happen to you, so you don't have to be afraid. OK?"

A pause, then finally, "OK."

Kay was shaken from her thoughts when a truck rolled up the thin mountain road, unheard at first, breaking the quiet trance of her run. Kay tugged Gracie to the side of the road when it honked.

The two continued up and down the hills, silent in these early hours. The broad bowl of the dog's hanging tongue began to overflow with sweat. Gracie veered for a rut filled with dirty water, and Kay stopped her. They paused on the crest of a hill, and Kay pulled a water bottle from her waistband, pouring the liquid slowly into the cup of her hand, letting Gracie drink.

"That should do," Kay said to the dog, and the two doubled back for the apartment.

Pharaoh was watching as they came into view, the woman wiping her brow with a forearm and Gracie walking beside her on a slack leash, shaped like a perfect "J," the sign of a dog that is relaxed.

The stubborn apartment lock took its time to unlatch, Gracie went right for the water dish as soon as the door opened. Kay settled back in with the manual.

"Dogs won't do what you want if you don't have their attention," the book counseled. "Commands mean nothing if a dog doesn't see or hear you. Get on their level. Put a little music in your voice. Don't be boring!"

"Boring, huh?" Kay said, tossing the book to the cushion and looking at Gracie. "Is that what you think of me?"

The dog stopped lapping and looked up. Kay was standing in front of her dish now with hands on hips. The sly smile that she always gave Pharaoh was sneaking across her lips.

Kay moved to the stereo and pulled an old album belonging to the media center. With no extra money for new supplies, the school refused to give the records up, so Kay brought them home in batches to check for scratches. The needle dropped and a tenor offered a few melodramatic bars of Stephen Foster through the pops and crackles.

Beautiful dreamer, wake unto me

Michael Rose

Starlight and dewdrops are waiting for thee

Kay grabbed a dried purple mum from a living room vase while Gracie circled and settled on the cool linoleum, her jaw resting on her paw. The teacher kicked and pirouetted in a circle around the pup, stopping every few bars to tap Gracie's head gently with the flower. The primeval dance then continued anew—a few more circles and more anointing with the puffy wand.

"Arise, therapy dog!" Kate summoned dramatically, tapping the dog again. "Arise and soothe!"

The commotion was enough to roust the glaring cat. Pharaoh perched on the edge of his credenza, stealing swats at the purple tuft every time the woman circled.

Beautiful dreamer, queen of my song
List while I woo thee with soft melody

Kay stopped in front of the dog, arms akimbo, wand in hand. Gracie had barely moved. The only reaction was in the dog's gaze, which tracked the teacher until she fell from view. Then the dog's eyes swung back quickly, like the carriage on a well-oiled typewriter, to pick up the woman coming around the bend.

"Not doing it for you, huh?" Kay said to the dog at last. "OK, let's see how we do with Plan B."

She walked to the turntable and put on another album, a gift from an old lover, someone who drifted in from Shreveport one day and stayed on a few weeks hanging drywall. At night, he played fiddle in a zydeco band, and what Kay remembered best was that he got off on making love in public places, no matter the time of day, and his cock would muster eagerly from just the warmth of her breath.

"Eeeiiiiihooooooh!" the old Cajun on the record shouted, and Kay gathered damp strands of long black hair and pinned them to her head. She kicked her ass back just once, hard and bad as any biker chick in town, and began to move toward Gracie, rolling into a current of cowbells and jangles, washboards and fiddles, a sexy salsa with a demanding Cuban hip.

"Eeeiiiiihooooooh!" the teacher shouted, kicking her leg and arching her back. Her hands released the dark tresses to tumble down. She held. Then her long back snapped to, quick and clean. She was off again, strutting across the room toward Gracie, cranking to the hard Creole beat with a body still salted with the sweat of the morning run.

"Bet the folks at Kozy Kennel can't do this," the teacher called to the dog, who was mesmerized by the tribal incantation. From the credenza, the old tomcat also looked on, bored again. He knew this routine.

A broom handle popped against the floor of Kay's apartment. Muffled shouts came from below, something about it being "fucking Saturday morning, for Chrissakes."

"See all the trouble you get me in," Kay said, smirking at the dog and winding down the music. "Anyway, at least I've got your attention now," she added with a wink as she walked to the shower.

Gracie looked disappointed to see the show end but the gamble had worked: The focus was on Kay.

Chapter Twelve

For most of the week, Kay and Gracie practiced walking, sitting, staying and Gracie's favorite elective: avoiding Pharaoh. Much of the work took bribes—small doggie treats that Kay tucked between her palm and thumb, revealed whenever Gracie followed the command. That was fine with the manual, which advised trainers to bribe dogs till they puke in the early going.

By Wednesday, the routine was set. Kay settled cross-legged on her apartment floor, rawhide treats at the ready, a book from her stacks spread across her lap.

"Let's say I'm a seven-year-old . . . with head lice and no lunch money . . . tired, because daddy didn't stop beating on momma till 3 am . . . cold, because it's 15 degrees and I'm not wearing socks . . . still reading at a first-grade level," Kay posited, looking at the dog-in-training as she flipped through the book. "Let's just say . . . Got it?"

Gracie watched from the far side of the room, her eyes darting back and forth as she sucked the shriveled forepaw. Kay flipped to a favorite rhyme and began, embroidering the story with dramatic tones.

Miller! Miller! I've come to you.
My little gray pony has lost a shoe!

Gracie's ears perked up slightly, just like the merry gray pony in the story. She inched closer to the woman, to the bright rise and fall in her voice. From the corner of her eye, Kay watched the sly advance and read on.

I have wheels that go round and round
And stones to turn till the grain is ground.
But I've no coal the iron to heat,
That the blacksmith may shoe your pony's feet.

The pup slid closer, but she never closed the distance, not all the way. The dog refused to place her head close to the pages, refused to engage the teacher's eyes. Kay sighed, pulled out another treat and began to stroke the sleek, fine fur above Gracie's golden eyes—eyes that were always off the story. None of the words or treats or strokes seemed to work. They were never enough to close the deal and get the dog to favor the teacher with a tender, patient gaze that seemed to say, "Go on."

By Thursday afternoon Kay's tank was running dry, and she was hopelessly behind in her work. The building was clearing out for the day, and the teacher looked from the stack of files on her desk to Gracie and back again. There was no choice. That night's lesson would have to wait.

"Change of plans tonight, Sweetness," Kay said to the pup as the last buses pulled out of the parking lot. She fed, watered and walked Gracie as most of the faculty drove off, too, and settled back behind her desk as the dog dozed in the corner.

It was pushing six at night when Kay looked up from the interim reports on her desk to see Brice Jespers hovering outside the narrow window in her classroom door. The math teacher was standing there looking down at the floor like he was checking the shine of his shoes.

A stack of papers materialized just below his chest, and Kay quickly surmised what was going on. He was pulling together his own set of interims and exams, getting organized, preparing to talk to her about one of his students. She sighed slightly and put aside her own work. In the corner Gracie was now deep in sleep.

"How are you, Jespers?" Kay said as he walked through the door. It was a convention among faculty members at Flattop and at many other schools to call colleagues by their last names.

"Not too late, am I?" asked the man with a silver crew cut, one of the oldest instructors on staff. The tall math teacher was probably 58 with an angular build that seemed oddly befitting his discipline. He had a habit of tugging on his ear when he talked and forgetting, now that he was a "man of a certain age," that the time had come to trim the fuzz from the lobes. Jespers was pretty good about nostrils, though. Kay gave him that.

"Too late? Does Flattop come in that flavor?" Kay replied. "Have a seat. What's up?"

Jespers pulled a chair to Kay's desk and began to spread out, stacking and restacking a few sheets of school stationery. Kay began to read upside down and saw the name at the top of the papers across the table was Hunter Dibbs, a fourth-grader they had talked about before. It was six weeks earlier, give or take; and

Jespers was just talking shop that night. Kay remembered it, though, because Jespers seemed so animated, pacing in front of her desk and tugging that ear.

He barely looked at her as he recounted events—something about a problem he drew on his whiteboard that afternoon, something about a cannonball fired into the sky and the distance it would fly before it fell to earth. The math teacher had drawn the flight of the cannonball, just from the muzzle to the highest point, when he glanced at the students and saw a hand shoot up quickly. It was Hunter, one of the poorest kids in the school. There was a jittery stir in Hunter's fingers; and his hand traced little circles, the way kids get when they're excited and want to say something in class.

"You don't need no more, Mr. Jespers. Just double what you got so far; and that's where that ball is gonna hit," the boy had told his math teacher. "Long as the ground's flat and there ain't no wind, it's gotta be double."

Jespers repeated the boy's remark in the reading resource room that night and looked at Kay. He was no longer pacing. He was wondering if she had picked up the significance. Kay nodded, but the look in her eye must have told Jespers that explanation was in order.

"See, Merring? Parabolas, axis of symmetry—gravity as a uniform, steady force. Hunter was right about the problem, all you had to do was double the distance from the vertex, what I had drawn on the board. Inside his head, he's already got it. He's got it three years before he'll ever hear those words in a classroom. Merring, I really need to find a way to step it up with this kid."

Kay nodded again. The stress and fatigue seemed to ease from her mind, and she remembered how much she liked Jespers. He was one of those teachers who were just as likely to come to her about students ready to spring ahead as the ones struggling to keep pace.

Tonight, however, he was preparing to do both. The struggling student and the highflier were one and the same.

"Merring, it's Hunter Dibbs again. I've got a problem," the math teacher started, reshuffling the stack of papers he had just laid down. "We're doing division right now. Hunter is crushing every problem I throw at him—knows it cold. But I put the exact same equation in a word problem, and the kid crashes and burns. What's going on?" Jespers asked, pushing an exam across her desk.

She looked down to see Hunter's name at the top. A flurry of right-answer checks ran down the side of the first section, filled with number equations. The second part of the test, however, was littered with red x's. These were the answers tied to a word problem. The paragraph gave the cost of ingredients needed to make a holiday meal. It asked how much money the cook needed take out of an ATM with a debit card to buy those ingredients and feed her company. What if the meal was for 10 guests? What if four of them didn't show? What if half of them were on diets and wouldn't eat the dessert?

"The operations are really basic in the problem, Merring. Hunter can do them in his sleep. Why is he screwing this up?"

Kay nodded and chewed her lip, lost in thought now, staring at the sentences.

"Hunter knows his sight words and decodes just fine . . . that's not it," Kay said, thinking out loud. "But—debit cards at the ATM? You seriously think Hunter's folks use debit cards? His dad does odd jobs, and that's when he can get them. It's just money changing hands. Remember, we talked about this before? Background knowledge? Get rid of the debit card, and Hunter should be fine."

"Hmmm," Jespers said, pulling the paper back and studying it on his own. "Ok, so . . . if I decide to use the problem again next year, no debit cards at the ATM?"

"Come on, Jespers. Flattop kids have as much right to know about debit cards as anyone else. That's not my point. I'll speak to Taylor. She just did a 'how-they-print-money' unit in social studies. Her curriculum is too packed as it is, but I'll ask if she can sneak in something about electronic transfers, ATMs and debit cards and such, and put it in the lesson before they get to your unit," Kay said, scribbling a quick note on a pad beside her.

Jespers nodded and smiled. Then he stood up like he was going to pace, like the night long ago, the night he first brought up Hunter. Instead, the math teacher moved to a table in the back of the reading resource room, the one with the reading fort. He picked up the hem of the sheet and held it gently between thumb and forefinger, right where Kay's golden man-in-the-moon smiled down on a little gray pony stitched with a silver bridle. Kay watched him flip the fabric back and forth several times. He seemed amazed at how both sides looked so finished and neat. He seemed to be looking for loose threads, for shortcuts; but they just weren't there.

A quiet hum filled the empty building as the boilers kicked in downstairs, breathing a warm current through the baseboards. Kay remembered how one teacher, a man in his twenties, once tried to enlist her in a whisper campaign against Jespers, his math department chair. The younger man had said Jespers would be long gone by now if the state hadn't switched from regular pensions to the 401(k) types. He said the old man had blown out his retirement in the switch, and now he would probably be holding onto that department chair till grim death. Kay laughed when the young teacher said it. She knew Jespers. He would always teach, even if he sat on fortunes.

"Merring," the math teacher said at last, "you may not know it, being first year, but you're good at this. If you ever run from this school, I'll catch you and throw you back—toss you head first through those steel double doors."

Kay chuckled and, as always, her gray eyes glowed brightly at anything even resembling a challenge.

"Please, Jespers—I run that hill every morning," Kay said, nodding to the picture window that looked out on Burnside Mountain, now draped in darkness. "I'd dust you in the first quarter mile."

"Yeah, but I'm old and cagey. I know the paths and I'll sit in the brush. Jump out when you least expect it. I'll grab you by the collar and toss you right back in here. You'll never know what hit you."

"Think so, huh?" Kay said, smiling as she gathered her files, placing them in the heavy bag of work for the evening. "Time to go home. Them cold dinners ain't gonna eat themselves."

"Reckon?" Jespers said, teasing her whenever the hill twang sneaked back into her voice. He walked over to gather Hunter's work under his arm and headed for the door.

"Goodnight, Jespers," Kay said.

"Goodnight, Instructor," the man softly replied, leaving the door slightly ajar.

*****

Monday came, and Flattop Elementary creaked into action. Students and faculty drifted in later than normal, rubbing their eyes and wondering where the weekend went.

Kay welcomed the slower pace and used the quiet time to settle Gracie on a pillow in the corner of her classroom, not far from the reading fort draped with embroidered cloth. Even in the quiet building, however, Gracie was struggling. She did her roulette-wheel spin before settling down to munch her paw, her back always to the wall.

Students began to drift in. The dog's eyes bounced back and forth, tracking the children's movements. It was her Felix-the-wall-clock stare, the look that followed everything and focused on nothing. From time to time, students eased over to examine the dog, but Gracie refused to acknowledge them. Soon, the children grew tired of the pup in the green vest—the scared dog who would rather munch her paw than meet their eyes—and they retreated to old habits and friends.

It continued that way for three days.

Rush Rudling would appear in the classroom's little glass window every few hours to catch Kay's eye and test her reaction to his weak thumbs-up. She just shrugged and nodded to the dog, away from the students, fixed to the pillow in the corner of the room. By Wednesday afternoon, the principal of Flattop Elementary could take no more.

"What's wrong with her?" Rush hissed, bursting into the reading room at the day's final bell. Gracie sprang up at the sight of the principal and danced around his feet in giddy reunion.

"I think she just needs a bit more time," Kay said, looking at the dog.

"We don't *have* any more time. She's got to be ready next week," Rush snapped in a voice that was cracking. He grabbed a copy of *The Berenstain Bears* from Kay's desk.

"Gracie! Here, look—bookies!" Rush cooed.

The principal held the book in front of the dog and waggled it like a treat, inching back into a pack of kids seated on the floor. Gracie tap-danced around the linoleum, grinning like a raccoon,

89

but she refused to take the bait.

"Mr. Rudling, you're just getting her wound up," Kay said, gently tugging the book from the man's grip and half-pushing him to the classroom door. "You need to go to the principal's office. Now! Please, Mr. Rudling, let me deal with this. She'll be fine."

"You don't tell me where to go," Rush growled. "I tell you where to go, and—"

The spasm of anxiety and anger was enough to set Gracie off once again. She whimpered, yipped and lunged for Rush, who skittered out of the classroom in a flash.

Chapter Thirteen

Friday, third period, was always the cutoff at Flattop Elementary. That was when the Nutrition Club met. Classroom after classroom of students filed into the cafeteria wearing donated backpacks, empty and light. In a few minutes, the students would return to their rooms, their tucker bags now stuffed with enough canned goods and pasta to stave off weekend hunger.

It was the time of the week when students' minds drifted off, getting a head start on the weekend. Teachers fried from the last five days would often raise the white flag—shelving lesson plans, darkening the room and then feeding the videocassette player. Soon, soundtracks of *Nova* and *Babe* blended throughout the building. Students were told to stay in their seats while teachers bent over their desks, grinding out paperwork due by close of business.

"Filmstrip Friday," some still called it. Kay, along with some of the more stubborn staffers, couldn't bring themselves to give in. There was just so much to do and so little time to do it. The reading teacher drifted through her room, offering word puzzles and ice-breakers to students clustered over a few books.

A girl came up to tug the teacher's hem with a question. Kay, her arms full of books to be restacked and now refereeing a full-out hair pull by the Apple IIs, spun around.

"Wait!" she snapped. It was loud, and the first-grader's startled eyes filled quickly. Kay balanced books in one arm and reached out to touch her shoulder.

"Sorry," the teacher whispered to the child.

Keep it together, Kay thought, trying to make the orders stick by breathing deep from her belly. Not helping matters was the fact that she'd needed to take a leak for almost two hours and wouldn't be able to leave her room for another 35 minutes.

In the corner, unnoticed for days, Gracie curled on her pillow and worked on her paw, eyes darting around the media center. Kay drifted to the window, where the embroidered sheet was draped over the table. Inside the flaps, however, Sue May was nowhere to be found.

Kay glanced back to her desk and saw the girl, still wearing her Nutrition Club backpack, toying with the gilt edge of a book that peeked out of the teacher's tote bag. It was a volume of "MY BOOK HOUSE" that Kay had brought from home. The teacher was hoping for a little time that afternoon to work with the reading dog, but those plans blew up when her planning period blew out—again.

"Is this real gold?" Sue May said, stroking a finger across the gilt edge of the book.

"Just a touch, I think. Want to borrow it for a bit?" Kay asked.

"OK."

"First put your backpack in the cloakroom," Kay said, helping the small girl out of her straps.

Sue May took the book and settled back into the fort. Kay watched as the little girl studied the fancy cover. She flipped the book open and slowly turned the pages, glancing at all the line drawings. It wasn't reading, Kay knew, but at least the child was settled and surrounded by words, words that someday just might grab her. Sometimes, on a Friday, it was all you could really ask for.

Across the room, a boy spilled paste, and Kay walked over to clean it. By the time the teacher turned around again, Gracie had left the pillow and was edging along the wall, gliding unnoticed into Sue May's fort. The pup curled to the little blond girl under the embroidered sheet. Sue May sat cross-legged, and her little fingers began to trace the page.

Lucy Locket lost her p-p-pocket,
Kitty Fisher f-f-found it

Sue May stroked Gracie's soft fur as she read softly. The pup's distant gaze was suddenly warm, and Sue May's face seemed to bathe in it.

Not a p-p-penny was there in it,
only ribbon all around it.

Kay slumped in her chair, stunned. The bell rang and the students scrambled. Outside the media center, lockers banged in rat-a-tat haste. A couple of children came to the desk to ask questions, but the teacher never heard them and never moved.

Sue May closed the book, and, making sure no others were looking, the little girl kissed Gracie on the head. Then she bolted for her backpack in the cloakroom beside the door. The girl stopped suddenly and glanced back at Kay, who was staring at her all along. Slowly, Sue May walked back, laid the gilded book down.

"Thank you, ma'am," the girl said.

"You're welcome anytime, Sue May," Kay said, snapping to. "You know, I was listening, you with Gracie. You were wonderful."

The girl smiled a little. The look dissolved quickly, and Sue May began to stub the floor with her toe.

"I need to tell you something, Miz Merring. That book? Well... I took it yesterday," Sue May said, peering up. "It was at the end of class. You weren't looking, and I took it home."

"Why?" Kay asked softly.

"To practice the poem so that I could say it good. So that Gracie would want to come into my reading fort."

Kay smiled and leaned closer.

"Wanna know a secret, Sue May?" Kay whispered. "Gracie doesn't mind when you miss some words. She'll never mind. It's OK if you make some mistakes."

The little girl looked up and smiled. Then she dashed out the door without a word.

It was Friday. The whiteboard had to be cleaned and the chairs stacked before Kay's weekend could begin. The Apple II stations had to be powered down, and the overhead killed. Around the room, dozens of children's books lay open, ready to be sorted and stacked. And before she was allowed to flip the lights, Kay's tote bag still needed to be stuffed with tests and reports and old records to check for scratches.

There was a good hour's work to do before the room was tucked in for the weekend. Still, Kay didn't move a muscle. She could hear the children in the hall, crashing along the lockers, heading to the bus platform, but it seemed as faint as thunder beyond the hills.

The teacher's eyes began to drift . . . to the gilt-edge book . . . to the small dog staring back . . . to the embroidered fort . . . to something inside the folds that she couldn't make out.

Kay's eyes began to glisten, and she caught her reflection in the window.

"Busted!" she whispered. The woman in the window had obviously forgotten Rule 1 for rookie teachers. Never let them see you cry.

Chapter Fourteen

Education reporter Mark Delaney pulled up to Flattop Elementary with a back seat full of old Wendy's wrappers and Craig, the legally blind newspaper photographer, riding shotgun. Delaney was tired. He was always tired. You couldn't be the county council, business, zoning and education reporter for a piddly little mountain paper and be anything but tired. Night after night, Delaney would haunt the Main Street government complex, covering the most deadly meetings that public life had to offer. At breaks, he'd steal back to his car for bites off a fish sandwich, a smoke, and then shuffle back, often tardy, to endure more of the same. Usually the only other person in the room was the guy from local cable access. Local cable was the unwatched media of record for Hobbs County, which meant the guy was always chained to his camera.

"Did I miss anything?" Delaney asked him once after skulking in late.

"Yeah," the camera guy said. "The commissioner was laughing so hard at his own joke that he farted. Probably shit his pants, sounded so big and wet. Everyone's face got red, pretending it didn't happen. You better believe I'm going to YouTube that sucker tomorrow."

It was news in Hobbs County, too, Commissioner White and his on-the-record ass. The whole county complex was talking about it the next morning. The YouTube clip got posted and generated more than 70,000 hits in two weeks. It even landed on the Tosh.0 show—something the cable guy, who was soon canned for leaking the clip, could look back on with pride.

Sadly, the commissioner's ass was news that the *Hilltopper-Sentinel* couldn't handle. It was consigned to raunchy office gossip rather than print. The hearing had ended, and Delaney was back at the newspaper offices at 10 p.m., the only one in editorial at that late hour. He was trying to find a shred of drama in the evening's big event: a fight between two duplex owners over a property line that ran through an azalea bush. They hadn't had a decent story in

Hobbs County hearings since the council voted to put up the "No Hooker" signs on Main Street.

Delaney had to file at least seven stories a week. By Thursday he was fried. Thankfully, this morning's assignment was a no-brainer: a light feature about a new reading mutt at the hillbilly school on the mountain.

It would be the last story the reporter would have to generate before the weekend. Just a few hours more, and the 25-year-old could hole up in his apartment, smoke weed, watch baseball and scratch his nuts. There would be a well-balanced diet, including some floor food that didn't break the bachelors' five-second rule, and maybe, if the spirit moved, some pay-per-view porn on Saturday night. By Sunday, if he had any energy left, he might do a load of laundry or shovel a week's worth of Wendy's wrappers out of the '91 Escort, his home away from home. Work was always easier without the stink of old tartar sauce soaking into the cloth upholstery.

The reading mutt story would be easy. He could steal any background he needed from the news clip sent over by this Rush Rudling character, the principal who had cold-pitched the story 10 days ago. Cute photos of kids holding the puppy, that's all he really needed out of this assignment—that and a little text to wrap around it. With luck, the shots would be strong and Delaney would only have to write an extended caption.

The only problem today was Craig, the legally blind photographer and Mark's partner on the reading dog story.

A stick of a boy with bottle glasses and a full, black beard that always nested crumbs and scrambled eggs, Craig was the nephew of the guy who published the *Hilltopper-Sentinel*. The 23-year-old photographer had survived wave after wave of red ink and downsizing at the newspaper, buoyed only by family connections. Reporters and editors may have melted away with the readers, but Craig stayed on the payroll despite his crappy vision and a circulation that couldn't crack 10,000.

Unable to make out more than basic shapes, Craig worked his digital camera like it was filled with buckshot. He covered all the bases—firing off hundreds of shots at assignments both big and small. His shoots created hours of work and headaches for the editor, who cussed as he culled through dozens of shitty exposures for that one serviceable shot. By rights, whittling down the exposures was the photographer's responsibility but Craig couldn't do it, not with his eyesight.

The photographer's impairment added to Mark Delaney's work as well. The last time they worked a story together, it was at the cushy elementary school in the flatlands. The kids had planted a new school garden as part of a "food, fitness and fun" campaign. Easy enough, but the art was a nightmare. Mark had to break off interview after interview to grab his photographer and spin him around.

"Craig, over here! Shoot the kids!" the reporter hissed. "That's the fucking garden gnome."

A few fat drops of rain began to land on the pavement at Flattop Elementary, and thunder rolled behind the steel gray mist that clung to the school. Mark covered his head with a yellow legal pad and dashed inside the building, grabbing Craig by the strap of his photo gear to keep him close. The last thing he needed was for his legally blind photographer to stumble and fall off the frigging mountain.

"Look, that's Chambers' car," Mark said with a nudge, nodding to a black Mercedes that was double-parked in the back of the lot. "He must already be inside. We better get in before the dog-and-pony show begins.

"Listen, I've been in this school before. They're all fried out— zombies and crypt-keepers most of them. Watch what you shoot. I need kids and cute puppies not bags under eyes. And no gnomes!"

The school secretary, a well-built blonde in a smart charcoal suit, met them at the door. She led them over to Superintendent Chambers and Art Rooney, the school's assistant principal, who was whispering in the big man's ear. Chambers looked worried, but his face brightened at the sight of a camera crew on a commercial assignment.

"Ah, the fourth estate," he chirped, walking over to shake Craig's hand. The superintendent was smart enough to know there wasn't much reason to bother with the reporter today. The photo was the story.

"If you'll excuse me, gentlemen, I'll go get Principal Rudling and Gracie," Eva said.

She walked into Rush's office to find Gracie dashing back and forth with each rumble of thunder. She was yipping and climbing the walls, a canine Fred Astaire.

Across the room, Rush was bent over his desk. He was holding a Xanax between thumb and forefinger and whittling the little white pill with a disposable razor. The shavings were building up quickly, and Rush looked like a man trying to torch his office desk with flint and rock.

Beside the principal was a cheese cube from his Cobb salad. Rush stopped every few seconds to roll the cheddar in the Xanax scrapings.

"Rushmore!"

"Quiet!"

"You'll kill her!"

"It's just a doggy dose." the man snapped. "They give it to crazy dogs all the time. She needs it."

Eva lunged for the desk but Rush was too quick. He snatched the cheese cube and flipped it into the corner. The little dog in the green vest made short work of it.

"Honey! You have simply lost your miiind!" Eva cried.

"Just get her to the media center, and don't tell Merring anything. I'll stall them till the cheese kicks in," Rush snapped. He threw on his suit coat and dashed to the front hall of Flattop.

"Superintendent Chambers! Great to have you with us! And Mark! Thanks for coming out." Rush said. Then he turned to deliver an icy stare to Rooney. "Uh, Art. Want to check on those buses for me?"

Rooney sulked and walked into the fishbowl school office.

"Rush, son, I hear your work with the therapy dog is going gangbusters. It's gonna be a real shot in the arm for the reading program at this great school!" Chambers said, sneaking a peek to see if his positive spin was making it onto the reporter's pad. It wasn't.

"Uh, where's the dog?" asked Craig. He had two impressive cameras looped over his neck and was fiddling with the shutters.

"Gracie is getting settled into the media center with the kids and Ms. Merring, our reading specialist," Rush said. He figured he'd need 15 minutes at least for the Xanax to unfreak the dog.

"How 'bout coffee—anyone like some?" the principal asked. "Or maybe you all would like to take a look at the gym first.

We've got a new fitness program, part of our anti-bullying initiative. Exciting! There's a rock-climbing wall installed behind the risers, and we build trust by making the bullies hold the safety rope for a bunch of little wim—uh, the more sensitive children."

"That's gotta be a damn loose grip," the reporter mumbled to the photographer. Mark shuffled, checked a smartphone that wasn't pulling bars, and looked around the building. Class was in session, and the halls were dead. The reporter still hoped to get in and get out.

"Uh, Mr. Rudling, it's your tour but maybe we could focus on the media center . . . unless the dog climbs the walls, too," the reporter said. A chuckle spread through the group. Rush laughed, too, a weak, too-close-for-comfort laugh.

The walk to the media center was fewer than 50 steps and Rush milked every one. He stopped for a long drink at the water fountain. He stalled in front of a fourth-grade class and had the visitors peer through the plate glass. It was just a garden-variety lecture, and the only thing to see was a dreamy-eyed boy knuckle-deep in his nostril.

Snick, snick, snick went the shutter on Craig's camera. Mark waved him off.

The principal looked down the hallway for a bulletin board to linger at. Too many teachers had followed his orders and posted graphs of classroom achievement—lines that ran flat or, at best, feebly up. Finally, Rush found one where his orders hadn't been carried out, and he made big theatrical motions to draw his visitors' attention to it, as if it were on loan from the Louvre.

"Here, you can see how third-graders compared and contrasted our own beloved Burnside Mountain with Mt. Vesuvius . . . science and history . . . very interdisciplinary!" Rush said, pointing to the board. It showed cutaway diagrams of both hills, each in the process of having its top blown off. At the base of Vesuvius, stick-figure pagans were in full flight but there was nothing at the base of Burnside. The bulletin board banner read, MAGMA: MOTHER NATURE'S DYNAMITE.

Mark's eyes narrowed. The rocks flying out of Vesuvius looked suspiciously like the rabbit pellets from Daniel Boone's musket on that big city mural. Craig trained his camera on the principal and the bulletin board. *Snick, snick, snick* went the shutter. Mark pushed the camera down.

"Hey! Watch the lens," Craig muttered.

Thunder shook the corridor again, and Rudling peeked over his shoulder at the media center. Through the glass, he could see Gracie pulling another Fred Astaire on the walls.

"Uh, we should—this way!" Rush blurted, motioning for the men to stroll down the hall. Luck kicked in at that moment. Linda Blake's door flew open and her line of first-graders filed out for lunch.

"Well, who have we here?" Chambers cried, his voice filled with enough syrup to send the whole school into diabetic coma. He squatted to first-grade level, popping the button of his dress coat in the process, and prattled away with one kid after another—always keeping on the good side of Craig's snick, snick, snick. Most of the kids were stunned and bug-eyed, too hypnotized by the cool gear around the photographer's neck to pay any mind to the ooze of the stranger with the big belly and a fat arm around them, blocking their escape.

"They've only got 20 minutes for lunch," Linda Blake whispered to Rush. He brushed her off.

Down the hall, Eva was waving from the media center and flashing Rush the OK sign.

"Well, Superintendent Chambers, what say we let these youngsters get to their lunches and pay a visit to Gracie," Rush said, suddenly cheerful. The boss struggled to his feet and the group walked into the media center.

Eva and Kay were standing at the door, worried smiles welded to their faces. A few hand-picked students sat cross-legged on the floor, books in their laps. In the center of the room stood Gracie, glassy-eyed and grinning, her little green vest cocked to one side like a thugged-out cap.

The dog saw Rush and staggered to get to him—a sideways crab walk, like a miniature Lipizzan doing leg-yields in dressage. She almost made it across the floor before tripping and barrel-rolling the last few inches to Rudling's feet.

"Ha! Excellent! 'Sit,' 'shake' and now 'roll over.' Gracie is really coming along, Ms. Merring!" Rush blurted, grabbing the leash with a creepy, hysterical laugh.

Kay Merring stared, gape-jawed, but Rush ignored the teacher, not to mention the dog's stubborn refusal to abandon the phantom "roll-over" command. The principal tugged the leash, dragging Gracie like a pull toy over to the closest group of students.

The dog looked stunned but happy. The broad pink blade of her tongue was spilling over her jowls and wiping the floor. Her eyes were as golden as ever, but now they were locked into glassy bliss.

Rush draped Gracie across the students' laps and Craig flitted around the room in a frenzy of snick, snick, snicks.

"Children, I've told Superintendent Chambers and these men from the paper all about Gracie and how lucky our school is to have a special new dog—a reading dog," Rush continued. "I told them how Gracie loves to listen to stories so . . . so . . . "

Rush was nodding furiously at the two little girls, praying they'd pick up their cue. The students just stared, pinned under the flat-lining dog, the one just deposited in their laps like a fuzzy comforter.

"Uh, so . . . how about a story for Gracie?"

Kay Merring slipped across the room and kneeled between the two girls. She whispered softly in their ears as she stole worried glances at Gracie and reached over to stroke her. Finally, one of the girls lifted the book and started.

"*'A' is for anchor. 'Anchors aweigh!' calls Timmy the Tugboat!*"

"Good!" cried Rush.

Snick, snick, snick went Craig, the visually challenged photographer.

Pant, pant, pant went Gracie, the neurotic therapy dog Xanaxed out of her gourd.

Delaney and Chambers stood to the side watching the scene. The superintendent stole looks at the reporter, who wore a puzzled expression as he scribbled on his pad.

"So you see, Mark, the idea here is support—support for our struggling readers," the superintendent explained to the press. "The therapy dog is loving and caring. The therapy dog gives students the courage and support they need when they read to her."

"Yeah, the dog really looks like she's diggin' it," Mark said.

Chambers cocked an eyebrow, scanning for sarcasm. Eva slid beside the superintendent and whispered something to him.

"Oh, right. Thank you," Chambers said as he lumbered to the

dog and the girls. He hiked up the legs of his pants to buy some real estate for his fat ass and grunted as he flopped down to sit cross-legged beside the girls. Rush tugged on the leash, dragging the dead weight of Gracie across the girls even more, nestling the dog's head into the drum-tight fabric covering Chambers' crotch.

The photographer threw himself onto the linoleum to snick away.

"'B' is for Betty the barge. Betty is Timmy's friend."

The girls made it all the way to *"'F' is for Freddy foghorn"* before Chambers' knees gave out and he waved for Eva to help him to his feet.

"That was just wonderful, girls—great job!" the superintendent gushed. "And Gracie! What a fantastic reading partner you are. Girls, aren't you lucky to have Gracie as a reading partner?"

"Mmmmmm," the girls replied in unison, staring in revulsion at the spacy dog stuck in their laps.

The reporter checked the name spellings with Kay Merring, got the girls' ages and grade levels, and made sure the school had photo releases on file for both. He lobbed a few soft questions the teacher's way and got enough measured, qualified support for the reading-dog approach to cobble together a few fragments for the story. These shards of massaged and over-edited thoughts from the teacher could be tucked between gushes from Superintendent Shoot-My-Good-Side, thought Mark, determined to keep it easy.

"Any plans for taking this reading program to the next level?" asked Mark as he started to step away.

"Well, a dentist could help a lot," Kay replied.

"Dentist?"

"Yes," said Kay, turning to point to students in the room. "This student, and this one, and this one—it's hard for them to concentrate because their teeth hurt so much. Maybe Flattop could get a dentist up here a few times a year for some exams and basic care?"

"Hmmm, never thought of that. Might be a nice follow-up story," said Mark.

Kay shrugged. She could see the reporter's eyes had gone as dead as his pen.

Craig had *snicked* off at least 200 exposures in a 12-minute event. Something ought to work for the paper. The only thing left was a cute quote from the kids, so he ambled their way, ready to cast the line.

"Hi girls, good job," the reporter said. "Can you tell me the thing you like best about Gracie?"

The girls exchanged glances, each waiting for the other to deal with the man asking weird questions. Couldn't he see that they didn't like the dog at all? One of them finally gave in and took the bait.

"She don't bite," the girl muttered, twirling a strand of hair as she looked at the man who was scribbling again.

"Ah, that's a good thing, is it? You really like that the dog doesn't bite, huh?" Mark said, trying to tease out the quote.

"Mister, you're not sick are you?" the girl replied, crinkling her nose at the reporter.

"And . . . and . . . I like her vest," the other blurted out. "Miz Merring sewed it up for her."

"Yeah—that vest is really cool," the first one chimed in.

It was the first time that Mark had inspected the dog's vest close up. It was, in fact, not one vest but two fabrics stitched together. The top one was thin cloth—a green saddle with "Support Dog" and "Please pet me" printed on it large white letters. There was also some kind of doggy photo ID pinned to the side, and someone had stitched "Gracie" in script below it with gold thread. Underneath the green saddle, however, was a larger vest. It was a deeper green, and it was quilted. Someone had sewn them together so expertly that the two fabrics seemed to be one.

Mark recognized the vest underneath and knew all about it. He had seen this type of vest during one of his bouts of insomnia, parked in front of a late-night infomercial on basic cable. It was actually one of those Thunder Blankets, the ones they sold on TV to dog owners who can't get their mutts to shut up and chill out in storms.

Mark whipped around and cast a puzzled look at the teacher. Kay turned away to tidy a desk that didn't need it. Then the reporter felt a tug on his trousers and looked down to see the first girl, who was trying to get his attention.

"We love Gracie. She makes reading fun," the girl said in a flat tone, obviously reciting words that the blond secretary had fed her

103

ear a second earlier.

Good enough, thought Mark. He shrugged, scribbled, and motioned for Craig to pack up his gear.

"Get what you needed?" a smiling Chambers asked the photographer.

"Yeah, nice little story," Craig said. "They're holding space for tomorrow, so we'd better get back to the shop."

"Grrreat!" said Chambers, "Look forward to seeing it!"

The storm outside was picking up. Craig wrapped up his gear carefully, and the two started to head out. At the door, the reporter glanced back for a second. Chambers, Rudling and the secretary were huddled in one corner, while the teacher was on her knees with the two girls. In the center of the room was the dog, lying like a Sphinx, her eyes serene and her tongue slopped on the floor.

"Damn! Those Thunder Blankets must really work," Mark mumbled as he walked out.

*****

There may have been a thud when the paper hit the door, but Rush didn't hear it. It was Saturday, a time to sleep in and bank a few hours to help make up for 5:15 starts on school mornings. Every teacher tries to rise late, and Rush would have been a fool to do otherwise.

The principal was bleary-eyed and standing at his kitchen island when the phone rang. His wife handed it over with only a cool, worried "yes . . . yes, he's here" offered to the other end of the line.

"Rush! Rush, my boy!"

It was Chambers, more chipper than ever, so loud that the sleepy principal had to buy an inch of space between the earpiece and his skull.

"Have you *seen* the paper this morning?"

"No, sir. I've been running morning chores," Rush lied.

His wife watched him straighten up, tighten his bathrobe drawstring and comb out bed hair with his fingers. It was big news, whatever it was. Rush turned and mouthed a silent, exaggerated "Paper!" to her. The woman went to the door to retrieve it.

The front page hit him like a wake-up shot of coffee, a slap across the face. Half the space above the fold was a color photo of Gracie and the Flattop crowd. The little girls in the picture looked happy and engaged in their book. The bright, smiling image of *Timmy the Tugboat* nestled in their tiny hands. Beside them was the wise, old superintendent, clean shaven and every hair in place, a good egg who got down on the floor with the kids. His look carried an expression that mixed top-man confidence with enough soft, nurturing support to turn any mother green with envy.

Across their laps lay Gracie, resplendent in her green vest of two layers. The freeze of the frame had magically transformed the dog's nonstop pant—it was now a gorgeous, loving canine smile. The glassy glaze in her eyes was gone, Photoshopped into a golden look of friendship and joy. The dog's head tilted up, back and slightly to the right. It showered the girls with tender regard and also managed to hide the gargantuan rolls of fat spilling over Chambers' lap. "The paw that refreshes" read the headline.

It was beautiful, uplifting, iconic: the Mount Suribachi of school news photography.

"Inspired, Rush, inspired! There's no other word for it—you and this reading dog thing," Chambers gushed into the line. "My phone has been ringing nonstop all morning. Everyone! The school board, the county commissioner, head hunters looking for hot education prospects!"

"Great, sir," Rush said, fumbling through the paper for the story. There wasn't one, just a huge photo with a long caption: names, location and a glancing-blow mention of "research-proven" dogs partnering with struggling readers. Rush wondered what type of research was needed to prove they were dogs.

"This is big, Rush, big!" the superintendent continued. "An editor called my girl at central office to check name spellings. They're gonna put it on the newswire. And, Rush, get this, the school board wants you and me and the dog to come to the Tuesday night meeting. We're on the agenda. They're gonna give that dog a citation!"

"A citation? Sir, Gracie's only been with us a few days."

"Oh, that doesn't matter, Rush, don't you see? What matters is that *everyone*—you and me and the mutt—will be at that meeting. Cable access, Rush, and for once it won't be to get my ass chewed out for test scores!"

The superintendent was either giggling or sobbing, Rush couldn't quite make it out over the phone. Chambers was deliriously happy, whatever it was, and Rush decided to drop the other shoe rather than waste the ecstasy.

"Uh, Superintendent Chambers, sir, about the test scores . . . Well, as you know, we've done a lot of pre-testing at the school and . . . I'm not entirely certain . . . I mean, I'm not quite sure this is going to be Flattop's breakthrough year . . . for reading, anyway."

There was silence on the line.

"Bad, huh?" Chambers finally asked, his voice back to earth.

"Well, I wouldn't say 'bad' per se but—"

"Gotcha," Chambers said, his voice falling even harder.

More silence filled the line. Rush's wife was bobbing up and down on the balls of her feet, mouthing, "What is it?!" At last, the superintendent spoke again.

"You know your guy out there—Art Rudy?"

"That would be Rooney, sir."

"Yeah, that guy. What is it you've got him doing now?"

"Currently, Mr. Rooney's primary area of responsibility is, uh, transportation services," the principal replied. His heart sank when he thought of how a guy he was torturing with bus duty just might be sitting behind his desk next year.

"Well, move him to reading," the superintendent snapped.

"But why? I don't think Mr. Rooney, uh, fully appreciates the therapy dog approach at this moment in time and—"

"Don't you think I know that?" Chambers barked. "The guy was dripping poison in my ear nonstop when the reporter and I were waiting for you in the hall. Almost called the whole damn thing off, the guy had me so worried.

"Move Rooney to reading, Rush. Then, when the scores come out, I'll make sure he's the one who gets it."

"Gets it," Rush repeated.

"Everyone knows my position on test scores and measurable achievement. If a school scores bad, someone gets it. It's the only proven path to school excellence. Christ, public access TV must have about four hours of me on tape riffing about this very point to the school board."

"So—"

"So Flattop's test scores come out this year and Rooney gets it. Someone has to get it, Rush. And I can't have my most enlightened building leader worried about something like test scores. Not now! Reassign Rooney and I'll do the rest. You need to worry about Tuesday, my boy. Get that dog to the groomer—I want her smelling sweet! I want that copper fur shining like a new penny. Tell the dog shop to tack a cute ribbon to her ear, too. None of those badass bandanas, though."

"No badass bandana. Yes, sir."

"Rush, listen. Great job yesterday! Grrreat!" Chambers shouted and slammed down the phone.

Rush stood fixed, phone in hand, staring into space.

"What did he want?" his wife asked.

"He said he liked the picture."

"That's it? Just, 'I like the picture,'" his wife said, relieved but doubting a school superintendent would waste a Saturday call on something like that.

"Also, the school board is going to give the reading dog a citation on Tuesday," Rush said.

"For what?"

"For being in the paper?" Rush replied, doubting his own words.

"Well, what was all that about the reading scores?" she pressed.

"He said Art Rooney is out when Flattop's reading scores get released this year."

"Art Rooney? He doesn't do reading, does he?"

"He does now," Rudling said, walking away.

Chapter Fifteen

Gracie was in the lens for most of Tuesday night.

The new camera guy for local cable access had been on the job for two weeks. In that time, he had only been able to populate the airwaves with the usual stars of local government cable: frumpy matrons, beer-chugger officials in suits that won't button, and crazy-eyed sorts who show up at every hearing like barflies, the ones who always look like the Unabomber.

The cable guy needed something different, and Gracie fit the bill. The camera loved her. She was bright-eyed and lively. Her fluffy tail was upright and carefree, a soaring little spinnaker floating down the aisle of the hearing room. From the moment she entered the government complex, there was no doubt that hearts would melt for the cute pup in the green vest with the butterscotch ribbon clipped to her ear.

Superintendent Chambers led the procession of educators down the aisle into the hearing room. He was followed by the well-mannered therapy dog, walking on a loose, relaxed leash held by teacher Kay Merring. Every small foray Gracie made into the audience was quickly and gently corrected by Kay with just a few whispered commands and doggie treats palmed behind her index finger. Bringing up the rear, and nervously palming something much more personal, was Rush Rudling. The camera guy avoided him at all costs.

Rush had talked the superintendent into bringing the teacher along, despite the big man's reservations about "crowding the picture" with too many faces. Kay, too, needed convincing. Gracie was half-trained at best, a therapy dog with miles to go, and another dose of pointless publicity following the newspaper story left the teacher cold.

"Kay, I can't have Gracie bouncing off the walls at a school board meeting," Rush pleaded the day before the event. "Think of Flattop Elementary's reputation."

"I thought Flattop's reputation was how we got into this mess," Kay said. "The best thing is to call Superintendent Chambers and get him to postpone it."

Kay spoke to the principal matter-of-factly, as if Rush was just another voice asking for a second bathroom pass in 45 minutes. She began to walk away but stopped suddenly, her shoulders sagging, and turned back to Rush.

"Never mind," she muttered, "I'll go."

"Really? Fantastic!" Rush yelled, clapping his hands and bouncing on the balls of his feet.

"You know, Mr. Rudling, something happened to that dog on Friday when the reporter came out," Kay said in a flat tone that tamped down his enthusiasm. Accusation tinted her voice now. "I don't know what it was, but I know something happened. And I'm not sure I like it. I'm not going to let it happen to Gracie again. That's the only reason I'll be there."

The teacher walked down the corridor before Rush could reply. He wondered who besides Eva knew about the little matter of the spiked cheese, what his secretary had pointedly begun to refer to as Rushmore's "rover roofie."

Rush could see that Kay's suspicion was still very much alive when they arrived the following night at the county complex to retrieve Gracie's citation. The teacher had refused to let the dog out of her sight all day. She oversaw the grooming. She walked the dog. She monitored every scrap of food and every drop of water in Gracie's dish. And she insisted that Gracie ride with her in the caravan of cars from Flattop to the hearing.

Kay set the rules every time Rush and Gracie crossed paths that day. He was treated like a parent with supervised visitation rights, much to the dog's despair. Now, as the little delegation from Flattop walked down the aisle in the hearing room, Kay felt she could finally relax. They were in the homestretch.

"Chairman White," the prim public-testimony recorder squeaked into her microphone, "you and the other members of the commission have before you an article appearing in the *Hilltopper-Sentinel* on a pet reading program at Flattop Elementary School.

"The therapy pet at Flattop Elementary is named Gracie, and she appears before you this day, along with Superintendent of Schools, Dr. Dwayne Chambers; Flattop Elementary Principal Rushmore Rudling; and Flattop reading specialist Kay Merring."

Rush took his seat at the witness table and flinched at the full reading of his name. Gracie steadied him with a paw on his trousers. The TV camera panned from Gracie, who now sat under the table, to the commissioners on the platform. Chairman White began.

"I know I speak for everyone when I say how proud we are to have the community recognize our schools and the innovation inside their walls," the commissioner said.

Now it was Chambers' turn to flinch: "I speak for everyone" probably meant his camera time, as the voice of public education reform in Hobbs County, would be skimpy tonight. Gracie caught the big man's distress but ignored it.

"Usually innovation doesn't come in such a cute package, though," White continued, winking at the dog. "Superintendent Chambers, would you please introduce your guests?"

Chambers stood up. Magic time!

"Delighted to, Commissioner White, and thank you and the commission for your interest in our wonderful reading intervention program at Flattop Elementary, just one of the truly remarkable, inspirational and research-proven initiatives on the ground and running in . . . "

No one was listening. A chuckle spread across the room. The camera zoomed in. Gracie was now sitting in front of the podium, upstaging the school chief, and offering her dainty paw to shake. The only thing missing from the cable-access shot was a mournful whistle, mountain vistas, and the closing credits to Lassie.

The titter was enough to check Chambers. He pocketed his notes and changed course on the fly. "Uh, yes, well, joining me today are Flattop Principal Rush Rudling on my left, and teacher Kay Merring, on my right. And I think you might already have guessed who we have seated before me."

On cue, Gracie cheerfully barked, and the room erupted in a generous belly laugh.

Surprised and delighted to discover his inner Abbott to Gracie's well-timed Costello, the superintendent turned and nodded to Kay Merring. The teacher walked up to lead Gracie around the room so she could shake hands with each and every member of the commission. Meanwhile, Chambers droned on with his prepared remarks, ignored by panel and camera alike.

Rush relaxed in his chair. He was relieved to be away from the little dog who always tried to settle him but always had the opposite effect. Kay's order to stay away from the dog was the luckiest break he caught that day.

A finger tapped Rush's shoulder. It was Dr. Denton, sitting in the row behind him and smiling broadly. The next item on the commissioners' agenda was an update from the mental health department, and the psychiatrist was on deck.

"I am pleased to see the comfort dog is working so well for you, Mr. Rudling," whispered the shrink, patting the principal's shoulder.

"For me? No, you've got it wrong, doctor," Rush whispered back. "Like I told you before, I needed the dog for someone else."

"Ah, yes. The friend!" Dr. Denton said with a knowing chuckle. This wasn't the first smokescreen laid down by one of his clinic regulars.

"No, really. See?" Rush said, pointing to the commission's printed agenda and the line about Gracie's commendation. The superintendent turned briefly to glare at the two dog whisperers.

The ease that had settled into Rush's breast a moment before was flushed like a dove. The vibe reached the podium, and the leash began to strain. Rush's distress had registered on Gracie's fine-tuned radar.

"Tell me, Mr. Rushmore, how is your fiend sleeping since the dog arrived?" Dr. Denton continued, ignoring the agenda and the superintendent's stare.

"It's Mr. Rudling, not Mr. Rushmore. And I don't have a friend!" Rush snapped.

"Yes, isolation, so unhealthy!" Dr. Denton clucked, shaking his head slowly and sadly. "And how does this solitude make your friend feel?"

"What?"

"Let's try something. Complete this sentence. 'My friend feels happy and confident when his dog—'"

"What the fuck are you talking about, doctor?" Rush blurted out.

The recorder in cat's-eye frames turned to deliver a severe look at the two men. Chambers stopped midsentence and wheeled toward the principal, who squeaked like a schoolgirl. For Gracie, that was enough. She snatched her withered paw from a councilman's grip and began to scramble across the hardwood. Her leash snapped tight and danced back and forth like a trout on the line. The dog's nails, trimmed and manicured for the evening, were still long enough to tippy-tap and scrape along on the boards.

Cable access zoomed in and Kay tightened her grip. The teacher was nodding quickly at Rush, begging him to get to the front of the room so that Gracie would stay put.

"What the hell's wrong with her?" Chambers hissed over his shoulder, covering the microphone with his palm. Rush flew from his chair, bounding to Gracie's side. He leaned over to pet the pup, and Gracie showered the stressed-out principal's hand with kisses.

A big noise slopped over the audience. It went "awwwwww!"

Chambers saw his chances and moved in for the kill. Smiling like a car salesman, he walked to the front of the room and placed himself between Rush and the camera. Commissioner White joined the group and handed them paper. It had magically transformed that afternoon from draft-quality office stock into an ornate county citation for the dog.

Cable access zoomed in tighter, hunting for Gracie but just missing the mark. For a fleeting second, Hobbs County got an unsolicited close-up of Rush and his non-stop, nervous grope.

*****

"Wait, go back," said Ellen Blair.

She was sitting beside Cap, who was flipping through channels. The two were settled in for the night, and something caught the old woman's eye.

This had become a familiar routine, these evenings at Kozy Kennel, with Cap trying to find something on basic cable that would fix his grandmother to her old brown Barcalounger for the night. *Dancing with the Stars* and *Idol* usually worked. And, of course, Ellen Blair was always a sucker for the nature shows. The TV diversions were usually enough to keep the old woman and her drifting mind from melting away after dinner dishes, drifting into the kennel to check on dogs that Cap had already tended to.

"Go back," Ellen repeated.

Cap hit the down button on the remote control until the

television settled on the image of a little dog in a green vest, bright and cheerful, standing in front of elected officials on the government access channel.

"Gracie!" Ellen cried.

The old woman and the boy watched in stunned silence. The little dog was bounding across the screen—a cavalcade of cute close-ups interrupted briefly by workaday shots of the humans in the room.

"There! It's that man. See him?" Ellen yelled. "Who? The pot-bellied guy?" asked Cap, suddenly nervous and playing dumb.

"No. The lanky one grabbing his thing. See him? He's the one who came here that day to buy a therapy pet."

Ellen looked at her grandson, who was fidgeting with the remote. The old woman snatched it away. Her eyes grew narrow as she stared at the boy.

Cap refused to return the glance. His eyes darted around the room, buying time. He was getting tag-teamed: his grandmother staring from the Barcalounger and Gracie from the TV console. He needed a few seconds to come up with something to salvage the first story he'd sold her, the one about how the dog suddenly vanished.

"Cap . . . why does that man have Gracie?"

Cap sighed. There was nothing left to do but own up. Slowly and grudgingly, he traced the timeline of the lie, born weeks ago when Ellen woke one morning to find Gracie missing from Kozy Kennel. Cap was already up and at the kitchen table when his grandmother made the discovery. He wove a tale for the old woman, his tone soft and sympathetic, knowing how attached his grandmother was to the little stray who was now missing.

Cap said he'd walked out to check on the dogs the night before, during a thunderstorm, only to find that the neurotic little therapy dog must have flipped out and squeezed under the gate. It was all a lie, of course, and one that Cap tended with care in the days ahead.

Only hours after meeting Rush Rudling on the sly and handing Gracie's leash to him, Cap was driving his grandmother on the back roads of Hobbs County in a search for the missing dog. He rolled the kennel's truck slowly along the popping gravel, calling with conviction for a dog he knew wasn't in those thick woods.

In the days ahead, with his grandmother in earshot, Cap would call the surrounding shelters to inquire about the little pup. He even wasted an ink cartridge on "lost dog" fliers and tossed them in a dumpster when Ellen wasn't looking.

Most of all, Cap sat for hours and commiserated with his grandmother. The failing woman still held an iron grip on the notion that Gracie—the little doorstep stray who had been making Cap's life miserable since her arrival at Kozy Kennel—was somehow connected to that long-dead support dog named Lucky.

"So it was all a lie. You gave little Gracie to that man even after I said no," Ellen said at the end of her grandson's story.

Cap threw up his hands and began to pace the room. He looked from his grandmother to the television and back again. Finally, he spoke.

"Mamaw, I only lied because I didn't want to hurt you, but we can't keep doing this. Do you want to see the bills? We're getting skinned alive because we keep warehousing strays!"

"That dog was given to me, Cap—to me," Ellen said, patting her breast for emphasis.

"The note in the box just said to find her a decent home, Mamaw. That's all! It didn't say Gracie was some gifted animal or a reincarnation of ..."

Cap stopped. He could see his grandmother flinching because his next word would be "Lucky," the dog she just couldn't let go of. The grandson began to seethe—at his grandmother, at dogs in general and therapy dogs in particular, and the whole ridiculous proposition that had become his life at a joke business in the pokeweed hills, caring for a woman who could only get worse over time.

He wanted to go to college in Pittsburgh and stay if it suited him. He wanted to get work after school at a big engineering firm and rent a really cool loft in Lawrenceville, or maybe a condo on the Strip, one with a water view. He wanted to live in a place that, for once, had enough damn broadband to feed an iPhone!

All his life, Cap had been told to go as far as his dreams would take him. Now he was supposed to ditch that, after he had put in all those school hours, after he had kept his nose clean, after he had steered clear of the drugs and boredom and all the other crap that weighed so hard on this county. It was all bullshit! Now, he was expected to live and die in sight of that damn Burnside

Mountain, building bridges and apartments and roads and schools—all the things that should have been there for him growing up! And, until that time, he was supposed to be caretaker for a flea-bitten kennel and a doddering . . .

Cap paused. It wasn't in him to finish the thought. He rubbed a hand through his hair and decided to press the case for Rudling with his grandmother.

"That man is the principal of Flattop Elementary School, Mamaw. He promised he would take care of Gracie, trained or not." Cap said, stabbing a finger at the televised image of Rush and the pup.

"And you know what? Gracie looks great," the boy continued. "I mean, look at her. What does it matter if she didn't finish training? She's happy, Mamaw, look at her!"

"And what about the kids at that school?" Ellen muttered, shaking her head. "Don't they deserve a dog that's been properly trained to work in a READ program?"

"Would you please, please *look*," Cap cried, twisting the television until it was just a few inches from the old woman's face. "Look at where she is, right now. Right now! The damn dog is getting an award—a freaking award from the county, for the work she does at Flattop Elementary. Explain to me how those kids are getting hurt?"

The old woman turned away. Tears began to roll down her cheeks. The sharp look in her eyes was now in sad retreat, dissolving yet again into the fog.

"You had no right, Cap. That dog was given to me," Ellen said, her voice plaintive and childlike.

The grandson's anger melted at the sight of the woman, so pained and helpless and old. It was hard to remember the strong, woman she once was when he was little. That woman could do anything, even start a kennel in the hills, Cap remembered. He took a breath and softened his tone.

"Mamaw, I know how much Lucky meant to you—how much this new dog reminded you of him," Cap said, kneeling beside Ellen and taking her hands in his own. "There's no reason why we can't find another dog, just for you, a dog that isn't so nervous and high-strung. I could walk back into that kennel right now and find five dogs that you could raise just as special as Lucky."

115

Cap pointed to the TV and forced Ellen to look again.

"See, Mamaw? Look at Gracie. It wouldn't be right to take her back. That dog is happy and the kids must be happy, too, if they're giving her an award. Isn't that the way it's supposed to work? We tell people we're all about support dogs, so why would we ever take Gracie away from them? Let's find you another dog, just for you, OK?"

Ellen pulled her hands away.

"I never want another dog," was all she said.

Chapter Sixteen

Gracie was still in the limelight when the commissioners retired to the kitchen of the government complex for beer, chips and dip. It was a regular gathering after the Tuesday-night hearings, a chance to hobnob and horse-trade. Flush from his on-camera triumph, Superintendent Chambers demanded that Rush, Kay and the little pup attend the meet-and-greet as well.

"No need to waste the cuteness on an early exit," the super pointed out, adding that the dog might come in handy since the school budget was up for review at next week's meeting.

After a 16-hour work day, Gracie's extra-credit assignment was the last thing Kay wanted. Time spent here just meant she couldn't climb into a bath before attacking lesson plans that were sure to keep her busy until she dropped off to sleep. Rush, too, wanted to close these proceedings; Eva was idling in the parking lot.

The superintendent wouldn't take no for an answer. The little delegation from Flattop made the rounds, circling the Tuesday-night snacks with Chambers in the lead. Kay tended the leash while Gracie glued herself to Rush. The dog did her part, shaking hands again with the commissioners, accepting strokes and morsels, posing for smartphone pictures.

"Well, what have we got here?"

It was Lou Gash, the commissioner from the western district that included Burnside Mountain, a farmer who considered himself as good a judge of dog flesh as any man in Hobbs County. He was turning Kay into a maypole, winding the leash around her legs as he chased Gracie for closer inspection.

Gash threw off a checkered sports jacket, stripping down to a lime green, short-sleeve dress shirt. The old coot caught Gracie on the third turn around Kay and tugged back the lip of the dog, running a calloused finger over the gum line. He peeled back the triangles of her ears and squatted down close to peer in, grazing the dog's tender skin at times with a two-day stubble. Soon, Gash was squeezing Gracie's ribs like he was testing day-old bread and palming her tail, lifting it like a toilet seat to peer at her butt. The little dog yipped and sat on her haunches.

"Good stock somewhere in that mix. Looks like she'd be steady for huntin' dove and turkey," Gash said. "Too bad 'bout that runty paw, though. We coulda had a real flusher here."

That was enough for Kay Merring, who was unwinding herself from Gash's work.

"I'm out," she whispered to the principal, walking Gracie to the door, accepting a few smiles and waves goodbye while fending off a couple of pinches from one commissioner who had reached his five-beer limit.

The side parking lot was dark and vacant. Kay unlocked the door to her white Escort and coaxed Gracie to jump in—something the dog did with trepidation since the car, 6,000 miles past routine maintenance, freaked her out with abrupt rattles and knocks. Kay was about to turn the ignition when she remembered that her handbag was still on the kitchen counter at the commissioner's post-meeting social.

"Two shakes, Sweetie," the teacher said, cracking the window and walking quickly back into the complex. Gracie watched her until something else caught her eye, a glow between the rows of cars.

Gracie froze. The fur stood tall on her neck. Through the car window, she smelled the husky scent of tobacco. The glowing light disappeared and reappeared again, small and dark and red. Then, the full moon broke through heavy clouds and a form took shape: a man, standing in the shadows and drawing slowly on a cigarette.

Once Kay disappeared inside the building, the shadowy man ground the cigarette butt under his heal. Then he walked slowly and quietly to Gracie and the car.

It was Rooney, the assistant principal who tried to torpedo Rush. The one who had talked trash about Flattop's therapy pet—Flattop's newly decorated therapy pet—to Chambers. Gracie bristled at the sight of the man and slid to the passenger's seat as he approached the driver's window. A low growl began to well in her belly.

At the school, she had always kept her distance from the assistant principal and the hard, calculating regard in his eye. In recent days, however, Rooney's stare had turned from frosty to threatening. It was transformed by something the little pup would never know or understand: the news that Rooney was now the point man for the Flattop reading program. Rooney had worked there long enough. He knew that heads would roll once test scores came out, and the first to hit the basket would be the guy running the reading program.

Canine instinct took over. For the first time in her short life, Gracie bared teeth at another living thing. Rooney reached through the window. Gracie yipped and sprang at the hand, forcing it back through the glass.

"OK, we can do it that way, too," the shadowy man muttered.

He walked to the edge of the parking lot and grabbed a heavy branch. Again, Gracie lunged when the man returned to the window, but this time Rooney was ready for her. He stabbed the branch through the window crack. It found the dogs ribs and pinned her against the opposite door. The man reached in and sprang the latch.

"Get outta here!" he hissed, flinging the car door open.

Gracie bounded from front seat to back, dodging the stabs of the branch, but there was no place to hide in the tiny car. Her two-layer vest cushioned some blows. Then the spear found her neck, and the little dog yelped loudly.

There was nothing else left to do. Gracie scrambled over the seat and out the door. The tip of the man's shoe caught her ribs on the way out, and Gracie howled in pain. She scurried down the rows of cars, churning the gravel along the way.

Rooney slammed the door shut and flung the stick at the dog. It bounced near Gracie, and she sprinted down the road and into the brush.

Kay returned to the car and stood stunned, silent, not believing that the Escort was really empty. The teacher raced along the edge of the lot, looking between rows and along the weeds. Her stockings ripped and her knees began to bleed as she kneeled down to peer under the cars still in the lot.

"Gracie—here Sweetie!" she cried.

There was nothing. The little dog in the green vest had dissolved into darkness.

Part II

Chapter Seventeen

Thomas Tender only learned to love his eat-in kitchen after his wife left and the kids stopped spending time there. For now, the nicest room in the house was the stage for almost every ugly moment in his adult life. Or at least every ugly moment since his ouster from Wall Street. Or at least every ugly moment before Gracie, the neurotic therapy dog, made him briefly rich again.

The Tenders owned the worst house in the best neighborhood they could afford. It sat in a quiet community, one of the strip-mall suburbs corralling the capital city. For a couple with school-age kids, it was a good location, 20 respectable miles from the hellscape of the western hills, a priceless buffer from hard living even though the house was cramped and outdated from the moment they moved in. Still, the Tenders saw possibilities in the *Dick Van Dyke Show*-era split-level. It was just decent enough— the good Republican cloth coat of residential construction.

More than that, it was a chance for the family to claw back inside the margins of respectability after the debacle up North, the one that forced the Tenders to move back to the hills.

It happened after Thomas lost his job over a little kerfuffle at a Wall Street brokerage. Before that, the Tenders were living the Toll Brothers Estates life in a little gated community on a hill near Hoboken, New Jersey. Thomas was a Series 7 broker who caught the water taxi to work every day. The family lived in a Southern-inspired, 12-room estate on the banks of the Hudson. It was a crib with a copper roof, and it loomed impressively over the river, a beacon to all the little watercraft bouncing between the Jersey suburbs and Manhattan's financial district.

Thomas's wife, Louise, had plans for this house, too. They were abruptly shelved when her husband was wronged at work, dismissed over a little problem that, as Thomas explained it, could have been fixed with a couple of mouse clicks.

No one got hurt. No one went to jail. The problem was blown completely out of proportion, although, technically, if one were inclined to get a little nasty, it could be characterized as a little lapse into malfeasance. Just a niggling infraction of rules that those pencil-pushers at the U.S. Commodities Futures Trading Commission love to exploit.

It was a life-changing moment. Thomas Tender was sure he was supposed to draw some lesson from it, but for the life of him, he couldn't. Show a little imagination, a little enterprise, and the feds come out of the woodwork like the soulless, blood-sucking bastards they are. Was it any wonder the country was going to hell, the stockbroker thought.

Before he got fired, Tender worked the night trading desk for Commonweal Clearing Corp. in the financial district, shepherding a trickle of overnight orders through Wall Street while the A Team slept. It gave him a solid, six-figure base income just for scratching a quick "TT" on the sprinkle of approved buy and sell orders that came in at odd hours of the night to the three-man crew that Thomas headed.

There were lots of dead hours, and Thomas filled them by trading his own account. Commonweal was even generous enough to allow him to pull over a few accounts he'd managed in his last gig—a brokerage in Piscataway, an undistinguished retail storefront with a cheesy, red neon ticker in the window. The ticker hardly ever worked, although it was installed to reassure widows and pensioners in Piscataway that the shop was somehow wired into the pulse of Wall Street.

The clients that Thomas brought to Commonweal were the ones who never asked questions. They were the widows with mild dementia, the retirees on death's doorstep, the folks who had to be nagged to roll over their tax-free Metropolitan Transit Authority bonds when they matured. They were the last ones who would take notice if, say, a few dollars from their cash balances made a short excursion into Thomas's trading account at 11 p.m., just as long as it was home, safe and sound, by 4 a.m.

It was just a short intraday float—Thomas never used the clients' money to trade. It was parked in his account short term, a little trick to convince Commonweal's mainframe computer into thinking that Thomas had the scratch required to cover the big bets he was placing on margin in the overnight futures markets. No harm done, not as long as the money was slipped back in the clients' pockets before 4:30 a.m., when accounting showed up to reconcile overnight trades.

It worked great until the morning that Thomas, riding a great trade in the overnight futures market, tried to squeeze a few more pennies out of the position. He milked it for all it was worth, paying little attention to the clock. Then 3 a.m. came. Then 3:15. Then 3:30. Then 3:45.

Thomas was leaning in close to study the lime-green numbers on his screen when, down the hall, fluorescent lights begin to flicker in the front office. Accounting was showing up for work, and Thomas still had cash from 15 managed accounts sitting in his pocket. The numbers on the screen began to slow down. Accounting's computer run was sucking memory out of the mainframe.

Thomas watched a bead of sweat drip from his nose to his spacebar. His fingers flew across the keyboard, moving money back into the pockets of his 15 managed Muppets before the overnight computer run landed on his accounts. Everything was back in place by 4:29 a.m. Everything, save three managed accounts tagged "Not Sufficient Funds" by accounting's computer run that morning.

Thomas had missed by seconds. He got the "please see me" call from his boss, the daytime manager, at 8:30 a.m. He was given a choice that really wasn't: Resign and keep your Series 7 license, or lawyer up and deal with the regulators.

Commonweal normally would have turned a blind eye to Thomas's overnight float. The accounts involved were that meaningless. What the trading house couldn't afford, however, was any more publicity: They were already getting hassled by the Securities and Exchange Commission for a different scam, run by a couple of brokers on the day shift. These guys were front-running institutional orders, getting their personal buys and sells in a couple of seconds before the big boys. At Commonweal, you could pretty much screw around with the fry any time you wanted. They had pissed their rights away with the mediation agreements they signed but never read. The big fish, the institutional investors, were another story. Right or wrong, they still had the lawyers needed to bleed your bottom line. You had to fuck with them carefully.

Thomas had done nothing that awful. Not a single penny of institutional money was ever at risk. But the big public employee pension funds were calling in daily and asking questions now that the SEC was taking a look at Commonweal. Everyone was under orders to keep their noses clean until it all blew over. Thomas's big screwup was sticking his head out of the trench at just the wrong time. And timing is everything in trading.

Before the morning was out, Thomas was at the cab stand outside the office hugging a cardboard box flanked by two bored security guards. Nobody said a word.

Thomas avoided the glances of the guards. He stared blankly into the coffee shop next door. Staring back was a young cook turning orders of scrambled eggs on the griddle inside the front window. He was thin, greasy and, like Thomas, in his 30s. There were flecks of gray in the cook's stubble, and he had that rough look Thomas remembered from the hills, just another cowboy who had lost his hustle in the big city and, with it, his grip on anything better than a chance to scrape eggs for $7.50 an hour.

People on the sidewalk were looking from the cardboard box to the guards to Thomas. The trader began to feel shame. He grabbed the first black limo, a gypsy cab gliding by the taxi stand, rather than wait for a proper yellow-panel. The driver seemed to size up the situation and didn't say a word until he deposited Thomas at the ferry terminal.

"Here, keep it," said Thomas, tucking a $100 note into the Plexiglas pocket of the cab. The driver turned it over a couple of times before he said anything.

"Thanks. Take my card if you need a ride back."

Thomas took it, but he'd never need it. He lugged his cardboard box down the steps to the blue-and-white water taxi, bobbing on the gray water.

There was no one on the boat. It was a midday run, and everyone was already where they needed to be. Thomas stood alone at the rail as the boat pulled out, his gold tie and navy coat flapping in the harsh wind off the Hudson.

The cold made his eyes water as he scoured the bluffs on the shore. From the railing, he watched the mix of plants, homes and businesses unfurl like a ribbon. A small lump rose in his throat. A flash of copper roof, much like the roof of his Toll Brothers estate, came into view. Until he saw that glint of metal, Thomas didn't realize how much he needed to go home.

On the water—that was the way Thomas saw his house for the first time. He was standing on this same boat with Louise at his side. Two days before, he had landed the position at Commonweal and they went out to dinner that night to celebrate. They danced in Midtown, drank overpriced vodka in Tribeca and later fucked twice. The next morning, Louise was on the phone to the realtor while Thomas slept in, spent and happy.

"There. That's yours," the real estate agent had said from the rail of the water taxi. The man was taking Thomas and Louise house-hunting along the Palisades and was cagey enough to ferry them across the river. More sales were made that way than by crawling through tunnels or creeping across bridges. There was a girl on the ferry that day, Thomas remembered; a white dress she had on, and a white parasol, too. The fireplug of an agent muscled her aside so that Thomas and Louise could get a better look at the listed property.

"That one?" Thomas asked the agent.

"Nah, nah, nah . . . over," the man replied pointing up the Jersey shore.

"There?"

"Nah, Mr. Tender— over, the other side of that big savings and loan."

Thomas tried to follow the agent's hand and, for a second, he thought he saw it, the copper roof of the house they were hoping to buy, the roof that the agent had promised was visible from the water.

"There—see it?" the agent said, jabbing at the shore. "The one with the copper roof. That's what ya call a real Southern charmer!"

It was cold then, too, that afternoon they saw the house for the first time. The wind had sliced across Thomas's cheeks and whipped tears into his eyes. He looked sheepishly at the agent, making sure that the old man knew it was from the elements and not a wave of sentiment that would make him easy pickings.

Thomas's hands were stuffed into the pockets of a charcoal

Logan coat. He held Louise's arm in the crook of his elbow. Gusts of wind carried the notes of Creed, Louise's scent. It filled Thomas's chest and delighted him as the boat bucked along the river. The cutting breeze made his wife's dark hair dance across her pink cheeks. She traced back the long, fine wisps with hands cradled in soft kidskin gloves. Through the sturdy fabric of his coat, Thomas felt the squeeze of her arm when the house appeared on the bluffs. "I want it," she was telling him with sly pressure.

And she got it—that very day.

There was no reason not to have it, no reason even to quibble with the seller over the asking price, not after landing the position at Commonweal, not at a time when home prices ran nowhere but up. Thomas wrote a check that afternoon and slept like a baby that night.

Back then, it was just that good. It was just that easy.

*****

Now, as Thomas took the same boat home in disgrace, it was impossible to forget how happy he and Louise were that first day. The cardboard box was getting heavy, and Thomas rested it on the same railing that the couple once shared with the little agent. A tear rolled down his cheek, this one from the heart, and the cold wind flicked it off. There was nobody on deck to see, of course, but Thomas still felt compelled to check himself quickly—bracing for what was in store once he crossed over.

The house looked solid and stable when he pulled in the driveway, even in this moment of freefall, less than two hours after flushing all traces from his cubicle at Commonweal. Thomas knew this would be the last time he would ever see the house this way, a proud estate near the bluffs, one with a roof that was a brazen four feet higher than its neighbors. The lump in his throat grew larger as Thomas stood holding the box in the foyer, thinking about the scenes of domestic bliss this house had known. Sweet Joanne, the Australian triathlete turned au pair, fixing the after-school snack for the kids. Loyal Eduardo, the undocumented landscaper, dutifully taming the flash grass by Tender's artificial pond and scooping out any jumbo goldfish that had died overnight. And Louise, lovely Louise, his wife and high school sweetheart, the

125

woman he had rescued years ago from the rough hills back home, always looking so beautiful and intrepid after a spin class or a session on the $4,000 elliptical trainer in the basement.

To say goodbye to all of it seemed more than he could bear.

His wife always had good instincts, and she asked precious few questions after he told her what had happened. She may not know the particulars of Commodity Futures Trading Commission regulations, but she grew up in the mountains and always knew what shit-out-of-luck looked like. And now, it looked a lot like her husband.

The house on the Palisades sold quickly and for a decent profit. It was a Godsend. There was no severance. Wall Street was closed to Thomas Tender now. Even Louise knew it. There was no place to go now but back to the hills, where failure was just a footnote and a few relatives remained to give them a hand.

Thomas marveled at his wife's resolve. She learned it growing up poor in the hills, and it always came through in crisis. Louise handled the details. She turned off the power and stopped the paper. She cancelled the club membership and, with subtle pressure against a stranger's hand that had roamed to her hip, charmed a prorated refund out of the club manager. She pulled the kids' immunization cards and sold the preppy school uniforms, using the consignment store across town lest she bump into anyone asking questions.

Louise even helped tamp down objections from the kids, who were raised to protest any encroachment on comfort. Thomas watched as their mother spelled out the new rules of the game in tones that were measured and firm, if a little resigned, as if she were explaining why there would be no new bike at Christmas. She walked the children through the process of getting pulled out of school in the middle of a term and plunked down so far away from friends, to start again in a foreign place that their parents came from, a place that the adults had always insisted was only fit to leave.

But why? What happened?

"Your father and I just feel it's for the best," was all their mother would say. She led the discussions and didn't even shoot Thomas a sharp look of accusation, something that was certainly within her rights, something that he braced for whenever the family gathered. Still, even in her heroic stoicism, Louise had her lapses. Thomas often felt his wife staring at the back of his neck but keeping her thoughts to herself.

In three weeks, they were packed and ready to head out. It had all gone like clockwork. The only snag came on the morning of the move. The trailer rental was the only thing Louise had asked her husband to take care of, and he had screwed it up. She wanted something low-key, with flat paint and no markings, maybe even something that could be confused for a horse trailer. Thomas went to the cut-rate chain and came back with something garish. Painted on the side of the U-Haul was one of those Americana shout-outs: Davy Crockett tracking a bear in the woods with a coon dog at his ankles.

"They were the only ones who would rent one-way," Thomas sheepishly muttered when confronted about the trailer.

"Great. We'll look like the Clampetts," Louise said the first time she saw the artwork.

The day came, and Thomas circled the house, looking for Eduardo, hoping his lawn man could turn over the keys to the realtor who had handled the sale. Louise sat in the car, watching her husband roam the lost estate.

"Eduardo!" he called. "Eduardo! Where the fuck did he get off to?"

It was early, only a few joggers were on the tree-lined paths outside their house, the only one with a light on. From the corner of her eye, Louise saw the cheerful, pastel-colored playground of the day care center. Both of her children had attended it, all the decent children attended it. Beyond that was the beige awning of Trader Joe's, the store that stocked Tim Tams. Joanne, the Aussie au pair, had introduced the children to the rich chocolate biscuits she had grown up on. The kids loved them so much that Louise asked the store manager to stock them on special request. They did, of course. Now, the Tenders were going back to the place where buying Oreos instead of store brand was putting on airs.

"Eduardo!" Thomas called out again.

"Leave it. If we're going, then let's go," Louise said from the front seat of the family's Saab. For the first time, tears of anger welled in her eyes. She stared grimly out the front window, the two children curled up in back, the U-Haul strapped to the bumper.

Thomas slid in and turned the ignition. The gravel popped as they pulled out of their long circular driveway.

"Take the parkway," Louise muttered. "I don't want anyone to see our car, not with this damn hitch on it."

She looked down and studied the roadmap on her lap, even though she knew the directions to the hills by heart. Little tears went splat, splat, splat on the paper.

Around the corner of the house appeared a short man, brown from the sun. He leaned on a rake and blew snot into the cuff of his flannel shirt as he watched the packed-up car drive away. Then he tucked a card marked "Landscaping by Edgardo" into the front door after underlining his name twice in bright red ink. Maybe the next owner would bother to learn it right.

Chapter Eighteen

Gracie ran the highway at night, loping west to east.

It had only taken a few minutes for the pup to find the Route 23 bypass, and she hugged its weedy fringe. The section of county road lasted only six miles, and the two lanes of rural asphalt seemed to divide the county by field and by fortune.

To the east were the rich, chocolate-colored plots of huge corporate farms. The earth was damp and furrowed. Each crest sported a green ribbon, the early corn. Straight lines of moist, plowed soil marched down from the blue foothills. They made a graceful turn just inches from roadside wire fences—a bottom-line, maximum-yield, parabolic swoop—and then dashed back to the hills that bore them. Monster tillers sat cold at night on the horizon, ready to cut into more fat topsoil when morning arrived. Up close, they would be forest green or canary yellow. But distance and darkness reduced the behemoths to hard angles and shades of gray, colorless, like the flea-sized men who jumped on and off their diesel hosts every day.

This was the side of the road that Gracie had tried to avoid. A couple of close calls with Hobbs County Animal Control taught her to bolt the other way when the yellow panel truck came spilling into the gravel. There was nowhere to hide. She stood out in the antiseptic sameness of corporate farming, even under a new moon.

There was cover on the road's west side, where chaos and confusion ruled. This was the land of small-plot farms operating on the margin. It was crowded by thickets of pokeweed, their pulpy green and red berries blocking the light of late afternoon. Lush ferns claimed the rocky soil, reaching out with spiny arms to grab at passing tires. Filling in the gaps were the hemlocks and white pines, and nailed to them were the hand-lettered posts of "No Hunting," "Private Property," "No Trespassing," and sometimes, "If U Been Taking Shots at My Deres U Can Kiss My Ass!" The rule was always the same: the smaller the property, the bigger the sign.

One of the lots had no hand-painted sign, but there were dogs barking on the premises. Gracie's ears perked up at the sound, and she cut down the driveway to explore.

The gravel ran to a red farmhouse that was hundreds of yards from the main road. Behind it was a compound that looked a lot like Kozy Kennel. The brick building was fringed with steel, heavy-gauge fencing that was sectioned into pens. Inside were the dogs—not the Zen-like warriors of Kozy Kennel but squat, powerful beasts with huge necks and shoulders. They barked viciously with every step Gracie took. These dogs had red eyes, set deep inside skulls as solid as cinderblocks. Many had chewed ears, too, and cropped fur that was bone white and gouged with old bite marks.

The dogs scared Gracie, but something pulled her deeper inside. It was the scent of food, that dry kibble she remembered from Kozy Kennel, and it was coming from an old barn that sat beside the dog compound. Gracie made her way to the barn, creeping low and swinging well clear of the dogs. Their barking grew savage as she advanced. In a frenzy, some began to spring for the top of the fence and saliva poured from their jaws, framing a display of menacing teeth.

The door of the barn was open just a crack. Gracie poked her head inside, searching the dark room for the food. Her nose took her deeper, and she crept to the back of the building, toward a big plastic bin that sat in the darkness. There was food inside—she could smell it—but there was something else as well. Beside the bins were two lights, motionless, golden circles that bored into her like a laser.

A screen door slammed. There was the thud of footsteps. Suddenly, the golden circles lunged forward. Gracie was getting trampled by something that was anxious to get out of the barn, something that bowled her over and sent her into a barrel-roll across the floor. She looked back at the door to see a dog scampering out. It was not one of the bone-white fighters in the pens—this was something entirely different, a dog with copper fur and high foxy ears, a dog much like her.

"Fuck, he's back!" a voice called out in the yard. The thud of steps quickened to a run.

For a second, the dog in the door glanced back at Gracie, fixing

130

her in that stare. Then the dog took off running. Instinct kicked in. Gracie forgot about the smell of the feed. The dog at the door had been the trigger, and it sent Gracie flying, too. She sprinted out of the barn, hot on the heels of the other dog, and they made for the tree line.

"Get 'em, Davey, there's two!" someone shouted.

The dog in front sprinted faster and Gracie kept pace. They reached the woods in a flash, leaving the footsteps behind.

Gracie continued to follow the other dog along a ridge. It was her first good look at him, and a lot made her curious: the ears, the copper fur, even the small forepaw. She quickened her pace, seeking a few shy sniffs of this new companion, but he wanted no part of it. The new dog whipped around and flashed teeth whenever she moved too close, a small growl building in his throat.

Soon they were at the ridge's top. Gracie could hear the hiss of cars along the highway again. The other dog turned and stared at her for a long second, those golden eyes boring in once more. Then he turned and scampered back into the woods, following every break and twist in the brush as if he knew it by heart.

Gracie stood for a moment, listening to his escape, not sure if she should follow. Finally the little dog trotted back to the road and over a two-lane bridge that was the county line.

*****

Burs from mountain brush tallied her days on the road. They needled deep into Gracie's skin, locked under the thick copper-and-black fur. The pup's muzzle was stained gray with the dank, oily water she drank from roadside ruts. Her ribs sharpened and jutted with the passing of each hungry day.

Gracie slept along the highway in the daytime, avoiding the cars. At dark, she resumed her trek, always heading east, mile after mile, moving toward the capital.

Estates began to dot the landscape. She was moving into horsey land, all of it cordoned off with wood-rail fences that were more ornamental than functional. Each perfect square of rail corralled a few lush acres of rolling grassland. Behind the fences, steaming horses clustered in thermal capes to ward off the morning chill.

They paid little mind to what was beyond the fences, particularly a scruffy little pup that loped along the roadside in a miniature cape of her own.

It had been three days since Gracie last ate. Hunger grew from an occasional stitch to a regular stab in her side that gulps of water couldn't ease. The little dog's trot became shaky, unsteady and slow. She rested more than she ran, even during the safer evening hours. The dog became careless. Daylight would find Gracie curled up in open patches that were dangerously close to the highway.

A few cars noticed the small dog sleeping in the thickets but they all sped by. All except Thomas Tender, who, as luck would have it, found his bladder giving out on a stretch of Route 23 that was just a few paces from Gracie.

Tender forced his stream into the brown weeds, shielded by his own car from any passing cop, when a patch of green caught his eye. It was only a few feet away, nestled in a cluster of scrub on the south side of the highway. After a few moments, Tender could see it wasn't just abandoned furniture or a lawn bag pinned to the thickets. It was much too green for the season. It was slowly rising and falling—something underneath must be alive.

Thomas zipped his fly and crept over to investigate. Gracie heard the gravel under his feet and looked up, her hazy eyes falling dully on the tall, thin man. The dog tried to struggle to her feet but fatigue was just too great. The pup collapsed like a card table—a played-out stray too weak to make a run.

"I'll be damned," Thomas whispered as he studied the pup, drawing close enough to make out the lettering on the green vest.

"Support Dog," Thomas read aloud. "Is that a description or a command?"

The tall man walked over and scooped Gracie up gently. She whimpered slightly when his arms pressed burs deeper into her dry, broken skin. The pain was great but the energy to break free was gone. Gracie went limp as Thomas piled her into his car.

"What do you plan on doing with *that*?" Louise barked.

"You'll see," Thomas snapped back.

The dog was shivering as he carried her, so Thomas flicked the red console switch to warm the seat where she lay. As he sped off, the cabin fan kicked in with a soothing, warm breeze that feathered

Gracie's fur. She slept the entire 40-minute drive, rousting herself only once, to take greedy gulps of bottled water and a couple of bites of a drive-thru sandwich that Thomas had bought along the way.

"Yer dog sick'r somethin'," the fat woman in the drive-thru window asked, peering over Thomas's lap as she handed him the bag.

"She's just lost," Thomas said as he counted the change.

"Well you can be sick'n lost at the same time, mister. That dog don't look so hot," the woman pressed.

"Then give me a chicken nugget to give her," Thomas said, growing peevish at this pull-to-the-second-window interrogation.

"Can't. Manager counts every last one of 'em," she replied.

"He should check his math," snapped Thomas, brazenly studying her gut. The woman slid the window shut and gave Thomas the finger.

The U-Haul hitch was an ongoing hassle as the Tenders made their way home. The weight was skewed to the back of the two-wheeled trailer; by Pennsylvania, the fittings on the Class 2 hitch began to squeal metal-on-metal complaints every time the sedan banked along the twisty interstate funneling the family back into the hills.

Thomas pulled into rest stops only to find that the service stations were glorified, gas-pumping minimarts stocked with everything but a mechanic. A couple of times, he eased into the break-down lane, the spit of the gravel mixing with the blare of horns from impatient 18-wheelers. With the hazard lights clicking, Thomas walked around the car inspecting a coupling he couldn't understand. Louise just stayed in the car, stealing looks through the side-view mirror.

The interstate skirted the flank of Hobbs County, the childhood home that Thomas and his wife had managed to escape years ago, their family intact and prosperous and protected from this chapter in their lives. Until now.

The sawed-off outline of Burnside Mountain crouched in the half light of dusk, just an old, tired hill, colored sepia in the mist and the gloom. Droplets gathered on the windshield, a slow build that kept the wipers set on delay. The Tenders could see the mountain clearly every few seconds, when the swipe of rubber blades make Louise jump.

"You want me to pull over so the kids can see?" Thomas asked, nodding to a fat section of empty road marked Scenic Overlook. His children had never seen the hill or the slow rise of weathered land leading to it, the family's real home.

"Just drive," Louise said, her voice flat, tired and beaten. "It's late."

*****

The apartment was dark and empty when Thomas pulled into the driveway. Gracie barely woke when he lifted her from the car and walked her into the kitchen. There was a red note tacked to the refrigerator but Thomas didn't bother to read it. It would be from the landlord. It would say there was a three-strike rule on late rent payments and the Tender count was already two days away from going 0-1.

He cradled Gracie in one arm and grabbed a handful of dishtowels from one of the cardboard boxes the kids brought in. Then he tossed them into the corner.

"Might as well give her something else to bitch about when she walks in," he thought as he laid Gracie gently on his old lady's good rags.

Thomas smoked a Marlboro Light in the dim of the room, studying the sleeping dog as he waited for his wife to appear. The pup was matted and greasy, covered with burs from those shit-kicking hills. The stink of her dank fur competed with a moldy aroma that was waiting for them at the door.

The man walked over for a closer look. Gracie's breathing was slow, but it was deep and regular. The journey through the hills had ripped off Gracie's badge from Kozy Kennel. There were no tags or markings, except her green cape with "Support Dog" stitched into it. Thomas guessed the dog was trained to be someone's companion—maybe a dog for a blind pensioner or a deaf widow, someone who might pay to get her back.

A key fumbled in the door and Louise appeared, half-buried under boxes, her trim calf holding the door open. Gracie flinched, rousted slightly from sleep by the scent of the woman's Creed.

"God, it stinks in here," the wife snapped. "And why aren't you

134

smoking in the yard like you said you would? And what's that other smell? Jesus!"

Thomas nodded to the pile of rags with the dog on top.

Louise dropped the bags and stared, her mouth screwed in consternation.

"This is a joke, right?" she said at last. "I asked you for a Portuguese water dog last month, and you said no. Now, we're settling on some stray stinking up my kitchen, worse than your cigarettes, worse than whatever-the-hell that other smell is. And why is she wearing that green blanket? Why aren't you smoking outside? Why is that mutt squatting on my fucking good dishtowels?!"

Thomas smirked. Mission accomplished.

"Don't worry, we're not keeping her. She's some kind of specialized dog—a support dog, whatever that is. There should be a decent reward if I can figure out who she belongs to. The blanket has 'Gracie' stitched on it. That's something to work with."

"Well, do something fast with her or I will," his wife snapped. She gathered her boxes and walked out of the kitchen, ignoring the little dog who was staring up with wary eyes and a small paw stuffed in its mouth.

Louise slammed the bedroom door. A few seconds later, Thomas heard it open again.

"And get her off my fucking dishtowels!" she yelled before slamming the door harder.

Chapter Nineteen

Finding a new home had been the first order of business once the Tenders hit the hills. They set up base camp in a short-term rental, a high-rise complex in the heart of the capital, 20 miles to the east of Hobbs County. Cardboard moving boxes sat stacked and unpacked along every wall, under every bed and in every nook of the cramped apartment.

Outside the small apartment, the corridors seemed to be filled at all hours with strange smells and untended children. Most of them were young, rugrats who roamed the dark halls of the high-rise with bottles attached to small, vacant faces. Their naked bellies were barrel-shaped, protruding over ripe diapers or dingy underwear. They seemed to zone out everything except elevator buttons and wall sockets.

The Tenders were stuck in the rental for eight dismal weeks while the hunt for a new house continued. Louise, angry and humiliated by the family's shifting fortunes, would only put on clothes for real estate showings. Other days, she stayed in nightgown and robe.

Thomas and the kids began to give her wide berth. She began to drink heavily, something she hadn't done since her binging college days. The weakness ran in the family—both of her parents cut their morning coffee with liquor and died of bad livers in their 50s. Louise had vowed that the weakness would never catch up with her. She was determined to leave the hills and the hard living, determined to move up the social ladder, And she was well on her way to keeping that promise through most of the marriage. At parties, Thomas often noticed how nobody alternated low-calorie Chablis and skinnyritas with glasses of spring water better than his prim wife.

True, the kids had seen their beautiful mother glowing after a big night out, but never anything more than that. Now, back in the hills and spiraling down the social ladder, Mom always seemed to be lit up all the time. The Smirnoff bottle on the kitchen counter became her home base. By late afternoon, her face was as numb and expressionless as those toddlers in the halls.

The high-rise looked out onto a stadium-sized parking lot and nothing more. Louise would sit in the window every afternoon, four floors above the asphalt, and bang on the glass whenever the neighbors got within five feet of the Tenders' Saab, still the nicest car in the lot.

"Fucking lowlifes," she hissed. "Get a job!"

Thomas always wondered if that last line was directed at him, not the folks socializing on the pavement outside. He envied how easily the neighbors ignored Louise, turning their backs on the bathrobed woman with the dark, greasy hair, the one who liked to bang on the window whenever someone passed their fancy car, the LoJack lush of the fourth floor.

The new dog seemed to love these glass-pounding displays. Gracie's ears always perked up and she moved quickly to soak in Louise and her every yell and obscene gesture. The rest of the family steered clear as best they could. Trapped in the tight apartment, they breathed a collective sigh when the drunken woman passed out for the night.

Thomas sat down every evening to crank out applications and resumes for the handful of brokerages in the area. The manila folders he sent out included a letter from Commonweal, a one-sentence note on letterhead verifying dates of employment. The only thing these packages generated were a few disinterested calls, mostly branch managers probing for the particulars behind Thomas's forced exodus from the big leagues. Calls were short and ended abruptly, with promises to keep the application on file.

There was enough money from the sale of the Palisades house to keep them afloat for eight months at best. Louise was fading quickly and taking the children down with her. They were missing the bus to their new school and going to class in socks they had worn for three days straight. Some days, they smelled bad, as bad as the kids in the hall.

Something would have to change and fast.

Thomas blew half of his cash reserves on a no-documentation mortgage and deposit big enough to get the family the split-level with the tab of linoleum, the one Louise loved. Overnight, his cash cushion was reduced to four months. He was rolling the dice, looking to make a hard six, betting that Louise would shape up once he got her out of the high-rise—and betting he could land a job before the money ran out.

With Louise, at least, he bet right.

The sharp look in her blue eyes was back once the house papers were signed. Louise followed the moving men, tracking their work like a hawk, making sure that nothing was scuffed and sorting out the 40 percent of possessions that would have to go into storage now that the family had downsized from their Jersey square footage. She started the newspaper and hooked up the new phone. She found a private school decent enough for her two children and outfitted them with regimental ties and school blazers. She cooked and cleaned and charmed neighbors with casseroles.

Questions inevitably came up, and Louise was ready for them.

She explained how, despite her husband's meteoric and uninterrupted rise as a broker, there was still no place like home, how good it felt to be back in a place where you didn't have to lock your doors (although the Tenders always did).

She told the lie so well that her husband found himself wondering at times if she believed it. Thomas didn't have that luxury—not with the family finances in free fall and no relief in sight.

The lost-dog posters hadn't produced a nibble, much less a reward. For Thomas, that was a problem. He rescued Gracie for the bounty, and now the kids had taken to her. They wouldn't tend her, of course, but they loved to invite friends to the house after school and watch them freak out when their new dog extended her withered paw to shake hands. They wanted to keep her; but on this issue, Louise was of a single mind.

"I'm not mopping her shit off the floor all day," she told Thomas and walked away before her husband could reply.

That meant Thomas was toting his green-vested support dog everywhere he went. He did it grudgingly, unwilling to part with a potential reward. These days, $150 meant something. He was damaged goods in the financial services business—out of work and out of leads. The family was tightening up and cutting discretionary spending, which was pretty much anything besides the heavy new mortgage. He stopped the paper after the free trial subscription. He trimmed the fray on his ties with a disposable razor. He ate ramen when no one was looking.

Thomas still held his Series 7 license and believed he could make a living as an independent trader. The problem in this region was connectivity. Dial-up was still the default, and everything ran slow as molasses.

Thomas hooked up, logged on, and was treated to a trip down memory lane. A metronome autodial, few bongs and bings, an electro-Jews harp negotiating of data rates, and suddenly the online world was pumping into his Dell tower at a mind-numbing 9,600 bits per second—loading his trading software in just under 40 minutes.

The broker began to stalk the slow-rolling message boards, looking for new clients to replace the biddies from Commonweal. He discovered that the traders around him didn't lack for buy-and sell-tips. They'd buy and sell anything, no full-service broker required. Connectivity, that's what they bitched about.

The message boards were full of stories. It was always about some trader sitting with his cursor over the "sell" button, ready to tap the mouse and cash in. Then the link dropped. In the four minutes it took to sign back in, a two-grand profit had become a four-grand loss.

At least that's how they told it. The lamentations sounded pathetic to Thomas, who used to field these tales at his old Manhattan job, whether he wanted them or not. Traders would call up Commonweal at all hours. Sometimes they yelled, sometimes their voices cracked, but they always believed that the guy on the night desk was going to issue special dispensation—a magic "do-over" for whatever trade they had just screwed up because of a busted connection. Thomas had to explain that, while he believed every word they said, Commonweal wasn't going to adjust a trade based on what a customer said he was planning to do before the Internet connection dropped.

Now, Thomas was one of those voices, banished to the hinterlands here dial-up still reigned supreme, forced to trade with the masses. He had to admit that connection really was a problem for these parts, and it threatened any chance he had of scalping a few quick trades while he tried to rebuild a client base.

Thomas considered his tenuous position as he walked Gracie around the neighborhood one morning. They were roaming the path outside the local strip mall. And calling it a mall was generous: The whole thing was just a horseshoe of retail that seemed to have no rhyme or reason. There was a bakery, nail salon, tattoo parlor, barber shop and pawnshop—all anchored by a grocery store and huddled around a cracked, half-empty parking lot.

The store that caught Tender's eye, however, was different. Other businesses played country music on their intercoms, but this one was piping out cool, sophisticated jazz. Thomas stopped to peer at the sign.

"Luxor Trading Parlor & Pawnshop: T1! T1! T1!"

The yellow letters sat on a pitted window, painted over ancient words that had been scratched from the glass. Thomas squinted harder, filling in the ghost letters. "Mylen Learning Center," it once read.

"You got kids?"

Thomas looked up to see a fat man sitting on a stool beside the store. He had a buzz haircut and no neck. The top of the stool seemed to disappear under his flanks, layer after billowing layer. It reminded Thomas of one of those chocolate fountains, except this pasty man was in no way milk chocolate.

"Kids—you got 'em?" the man asked again. "I'm askin' because you look like you're studyin' our sign hard. Maybe wonderin' about Mylen?"

"Yeah, now that you mention it."

"Mylen ain't here no more, Tammy's neither. Tammy's was the tanning shop here before Mylen, and then Mylen took 'er down. And then Mylen went under, so I took 'em both."

"Uh huh," said Thomas, not sure he was keen on hearing the business history of the Mountainside Shopping Centre. Gracie ignored both men and started to strain for the door of the Luxor Trading Parlor & Pawnshop.

"My name's Finch, and that was mine first," the fat man said, jerking his head to the pawnshop over his shoulder. "Mylen lasted here . . . oh, 10 months, let's call it. They was gonna use computer programs to teach kids and get 'em all set for Harvard or Tech or wherever. Not much Harvard stock around here if you're askin' me."

Finch chuckled at his own joke, snorted and spat a wad. Thomas nodded grudgingly. The man had a point.

"Well, they went Chapter 7—Mylen, not Tammy, mind you—and they left all this hardware. Got 'em for a song! Their computers was OK, but, hell, I got a bunch more like 'em in the pawnshop. Don't need more. But them T1 lines Mylen installed—man, now they was somethin' worth buyin'!"

Finch squinted at Thomas, studying his face for a second. The lanky broker must have looked confused, and Finch started to launch into another explanation.

"Mister, did you know people are doin' the stocks these days on the computer?"

"So . . . Luxor is a trading room . . . a real trading room . . . stocks and futures and such?"

"Hell, yeah, it is!" said the man, folding his arms over his round belly. "These trader boys, they want speed, speed, speed! That shitty county dial-up ain't good for nothing, so I bought the Mylen's. Just scrape the education programs off the machines, and it was all good to go."

Thomas could see that Finch was also flashing a gold Rolex. He sat with his arms folded, twisting his hairy wrist until a glint of sunlight bounced off the chunky watch into Thomas's eyes. Finch and Gracie yawned at the same time, both growing tired of the exchange.

"So, like I said, the Mylen's ain't here no more, and if you was thinkin' about matriculatin' your kids—"

"No . . . I, uh. No! I *am* a trader!" Thomas blurted out. "Stocks and futures. You say you've got T1 lines?"

"Yep. Fast as shit. No drops."

"How much?"

"Mister, I ain't sellin' the Luxor, no sireee. Heh! Them boys is just getting' warmed up," Finch said, chuckling and jerking his head toward the Luxor's big glass window, the window that Gracie was straining for.

Inside, Thomas could see about a half-dozen men hunched over terminals on a long workbench. On the wall above them, a TV was strapped to the rafters with a plastic blue clothesline. The CNBC market ticker was spilling across the screen.

"No, not to buy," Thomas said, "how much is it to rent? To rent trading space at the Luxor?"

"Hmm," Finch said, stealing looks at Thomas's shoes. (Later,

141

Thomas would learn that Finch always priced his rent based on the condition of the customer's shoes.) "I'll take $200 a month for a seat. With that, you also get $20 in complimentary tokens for the video games in back of the shop. Lots of the traders love 'em—helps burn off steam when they get wound up. Come on in. Take a look-see."

Finch hoisted himself with a grunt, and the two men walked into the Luxor with Gracie leading the way. The men at the bench glanced at them briefly but said nothing, their gazes quickly homing back to their computer screens.

The whole operation looked like it could be boarded up and shut down in less than an hour. There wasn't much in the chilly room besides the tables, television, computer towers and monitors. The only thing that seemed out of place was an old whiteboard at the head of the room. It was obviously Mylen Learning surplus, and on it, someone had written in a large, confident hand, "Cut your losses and let your profits run."

"That's Piperson. He's the best we got," Finch said, nodding to the whiteboard.

"What?"

The fat man spat again in the trashcan by an office surplus bench. This stranger seemed slow on the uptake.

"Them words on the board. Piperson writes those things every morning—some saying. He wants to inspire the others, fire up the troops," Finch said, pointing to the men bent over their monitors. "That's him, back there."

Thomas looked beyond the row of hunched men trading in the front. There was one dark figure haunting the last row. Lanky and pale, the man sat with his fingers braided and hands locked behind his head, indifferent to what was happening on his screen.

The man seemed at odds with the other traders in the room, the ones who Gracie was scampering to get close to. Those men were glued to their positions, peering into the monitor, watching tick by tick as their stock trading software drew charts that tracked the rise and fall of the stocks, futures and options they were piled into. Their noses were never more than six inches from the monitor—and Gracie's nose was never more than six inches from them.

The only things that seemed to roust these front-benchers were the CNBC "Breaking News" announcements. It didn't matter what

142

the news was—a fresh GDP revision or the latest Lindsay Lohan arrest report—the traders looked every time CNBC flashed that fire-red "Breaking News" alert and sounded its gong of doom. They seemed powerless to ignore it, like cats stalking a flashlight beam.

The man in the back was different. Piperson wore a navy business suit and the fit was immaculate, so much so that he looked comfortable even when seated in his dress coat. The swivel chair issued a small creak as he continued to twist back and forth, his bony hands locked behind his balding head and his thin legs crossed elegantly at the knee.

He was older than the others, late 60s or early 70s, and his thin gray lips were bracketed with deep creases. There were dark circles, puffy and plum-colored, draped like bunting under his watery blue eyes.

A sleek Homburg hat, black and brushed, sat beside him. There was also what appeared to be a brass-handled walking stick. He looked like an upscale undertaker. Piperson was the only trader in the room that Gracie paid no mind to.

"Mr. Piperson, I got someone for you to meet," Finch said. He led Thomas over, and the two shook hands.

The man listened more than he talked. He seemed to like dogs, and petted Gracie's head often, watching the pup watch the other traders. Thomas tried to fill gaps in the conversation with comments about everything from the weather to computer connectivity to the CNBC anchors.

"So you used to work at Commonweal," said Piperson, his watery eyes dancing, stopping Thomas's monologue at the one point he was hoping to gloss over.

"Yes," the Luxor guest said, "do you know it?"

"Well, I used to work at Drake Securities in the same building," Piperson said. "Do they still have that great lunch counter across the street? You know, the one that serves those fried egg sandwiches?"

"I believe they do," Thomas said, remembering the egg cook in the window on his last day in the financial district. The old man's eyes sparkled even more.

"I don't miss a lot, but I do miss those sandwiches," Piperson said, stroking Gracie behind the ear as he talked. "So you decided to go independent and moved back here?"

"Yes, it seemed like the right move. We have family back here, and, hell, I guess you can trade anywhere these days with the right connectivity," Thomas replied.

"The right move or the only move?" Piperson said, his eyes sparkling even more.

Thomas reddened at the question and looked around the room as he gathered himself.

There was a huge aquarium bubbling on the back wall behind Piperson. Beside it, a young girl with orange fingers filing her nails. She paid the men no mind, and Thomas guessed she was the receptionist.

"The right move or the only move?" Piperson asked again, as if Thomas hadn't heard.

"I guess you could say it was a little of both," Thomas said with a crooked smile. Gracie broke off her concentration on the traders at the front of the room and swung around to regard Thomas Tender with her hard, golden stare.

Piperson cackled, triumphant, and turned to the owner of the Luxor.

"Mr. Finch, would you please set up a trading station for Mr. Tender, something next to mine? I hope to get to know this young man better."

"I can hook him up by tomorrow if he wants it," Finch replied. Thomas shook hands with Piperson, who also shook hands with Gracie. Then Finch led him out of the Luxor with Gracie, who had to be yanked hard to get away from the twitchy traders on the front bench.

"You said $200 a month gets me a seat?" Thomas repeated to Finch as the fat man settled back on his stool between the trading parlor and the pawnshop.

"Yep, that's your price . . . $200 a month and the seat's yours. I charge $10 extra if you want the porn rider, though."

"The porn rider."

"We don't filter what goes through that T1, so you can stay on if you like and download porn after trading ends for the day. Lots of them Luxor boys do it. Some can pull down pretty near 200 nudie shots or a half-dozen videos in less than an hour. Dang, try doing that on dial-up!"

"I think I'll pass," Thomas said. "Uh, how about Mr. Piperson? Does he get the rider?"

Finch looked up with a puzzled expression and then dug up a deep, wet laugh out of his lungs, a cackle that ended in another wad on the curb.

"Mr. Piperson don't need no porn," was all the fat man said.

Chapter Twenty

Piperson owned the aquarium at the back of the Luxor and stocked it with small fry. There must have been 200 of them, fingernail-sized neons that executed their safety-in-numbers choreography, swooping in tight formations among swaying fronds and pulsing bubbles with some fantasy nipping at their keels.

The aquarium dominated the back wall of the trading parlor, close enough to Thomas's chair that he could hear the filter bubbles. That's where Piperson put him on his first day, the day he became the new wingman for the old man at the Luxor Trading Parlor. Both of them sat well away from the plate-glass window and the TV hanging by a noose in the front of the room, the part of the room that the other traders hugged and haunted.

"So, Mr. Tender, ready for business?" Piperson said, flipping on his monitor and shooting his monogrammed cuffs through the dress coat he wore. Suited trading was a daily affair for the old man, Thomas observed.

Before Thomas could answer, he felt a tap on his shoulder. It was Finch.

"I see you got that dog again," the fat man said, staring at Gracie. "Is that supposed to be regular now?"

"Well, I didn't think it would be a problem since Gracie is a support dog," said Thomas, reaching down to adjust the green vest for emphasis.

"What's she supposed to be supportin'?" Finch asked, suspicion in his voice.

Thomas stumbled for words until Piperson stepped in.

"Mr. Finch, I can't see how this sweet little puppy could be a problem," the old man said. "Pets settle the mind. Why, you've never heard a complaint about my fish, have you?"

"I suppose," Finch said reluctantly, still staring at Gracie with a sour expression on his doughy face. "But I'll have to charge you the pet rider. It's $10 a month, same as porn."

Finch started for his stool outside. Before he got to the door, he turned and pointed again to Gracie.

"One more thing. She craps, you clean."

Thomas settled into the chair next to Piperson and nodded at the trading software that was loading smooth as glass on the old man's monitor, "Wow, you must be hitting 9,400 bits per minute. I remember at Commonweal, we were unhappy if our data stream slowed to—"

"Yes, technology is wonderful," Piperson said, cutting him off. The old man's watery blue eyes were focused on Gracie, who was watching the traders file into the Luxor. "Lots of our fellows here swear by technology, but I've never been able to make it work for me."

"Well, you must be doing something right, Mr. Piperson. That's not a buy-one-get-three-free suit," Thomas said with a smile, looking at the fine stitching on the shoulder of the old man's suit coat. Piperson chuckled.

"Well, I do have my discipline, but it has nothing to do with hook-ups and computer gizmos and such."

The old man's attention was only partly on the conversation. Most of his mind seemed to be on the traders at the front of the room, who were hunched over their monitors to enter their morning orders. The half-dozen men were a rough counterpart to Piperson. Most of them favored ball caps and fleece pullovers for trading, and they seemed twitchy. Their heads whipped up to stare at the screen every time the CNBC news gong went off. Then, in unison, they returned to their monitors to draw and redraw trend lines on the screens.

"They seem quite antsy today, don't they Mr. Tender?" Piperson said as he surveyed the room. "Usually they are chatting about Batman movies or playing Duty Call. Not so today. They're quiet today. I call that, 'trading with a puckered bottom.'"

Thomas got the meaning, even though the old man's phrasing threw him for a split second. "Duty Call" was obviously "Call of Duty," the wildly popular video game. And "trading with a puckered bottom" was cleaned up from Thomas's days at Commonweal, when discussions came up of any trader who was overleveraged or fighting the tape. These traders were always on edge and always making mistakes—closing out good positions too early, holding onto losses too long, always making poor choices because they were wound so tight. "Trading with their assholes crushing coal to diamonds" is how some at Commonweal described them.

"I wish I understood technology, but it's people I seem to understand best in this business," Piperson continued. "Back in New York, I hardly ever showed up for work before 10 in the morning. Why fight the ungodly traffic? And there was really nothing for a trader like me to do . . . not until mid-morning."

The noise at the front of the room stopped and a hush fell over the Luxor. The TV gong had sounded: Alyssa Milano had just delivered a baby. The traders swung back to their monitors, the news duly noted, and started to set up their screens for the trading day. All the while, Gracie's golden stare was upon them.

"As I was saying, once we hit 10 or 11 in the morning, then I had something to go on," Piperson continued. "You could clearly see it, Mr. Tender. One cluster of traders would be hunched over their monitors, following every little tick of the market. The other camp, the ones taking opposite positions, would just be milling around, sipping coffee and telling jokes. Guess which side I traded with that day?"

"So you entered a trade after the market had broken out?" Thomas said. "Don't chase the trade, at least that's what most people say."

"Yes they do, Mr. Tender," the old man said with a chuckle and a wink. "They also say, 'Being a little late in a trade is insurance that your opinion is correct.'"

Thomas nodded, impressed that Piperson was able to pull from memory what sounded like a direct quote from *Reminiscences of a Stock Operator*, a loose biography of Jesse Livermore that was the bible for many traders. Although it was written in 1923, the book still had legions of fanatic followers in the trading community.

The legendary Livermore, along with old Joe Kennedy and a handful of others, was one of the few traders who had made millions on Black Friday in 1929. Livermore's epic performance in the crash made him respected; but it was the book that made "the Great Bear of Wall Street" a saint. His observations about markets and human nature were still widely read and remembered. He was beloved, although Thomas never understood why so many wanted to pattern themselves after a trader who hit bottom in 1941 and blew his brains out in a public restroom.

"So you follow Jesse Livermore's rules," Thomas said.

"No, you've missed my point," the old man replied. "For every rule in trading, there is always an equally valid opposite rule. Try me, Mr. Tender. Give me a rule and I'll give you the opposite maxim."

Thomas cast a perplexed look, but Piperson seemed serious. The younger trader decided to take the bait.

"OK, let's see," Thomas said at last, "how about, 'Let your winners run.'?"

"'Bulls make money, bears make money, pigs get slaughtered,'" Piperson countered.

"'Trees don't grow to the sky.'"

"'Never too late to buy a stock going up or sell a dog going down,'" Piperson replied.

"'When you're yelling, you should be selling; when you're crying, you should be buying.'"

"'The hardest part isn't the buying and selling, it's the sitting and waiting.'"

Thomas pursed his lips, impressed.

"Which rule applies, and when, Mr. Tender? I can't tell and neither can they," Piperson said, nodding to the traders at the front of the room as he patted the head of the dog, who seemed transfixed by the one that the others called Big Ned.

Almost on cue, Big Ned slammed his fist on the bench. The man looked like a former high school wrestler. He wore a windbreaker, a blue shell that said "Ned's Plumbing and Heating" on the back. The career change seemed to be doing little for his peace of mind: All morning long, Big Ned had squinted into his screen and worked one of those spring-loaded wrist strengtheners. The *squeak, squeak, squeak* of the hand grip accelerated as the minutes of trading wore on.

Suddenly, Big Ned jumped up and flung the wrist contraption so hard it stuck in the drywall. Then he grabbed his monitor with two fists, shaking it loose from its moorings, throttling the box like he was locked onto someone's windpipe.

"Mutherfucker! Muuuuutherfucker!" he screamed while the other traders scattered to the sidelines. A black sheet over a bust-out wall was all that separated the Luxor from the pawnshop next door, and Finch flung it back and bounded into the trading parlor.

Michael Rose

"Ned! That's $1,500 to you—you hear?! Bust another one, and it's $1,500!" Finch yelled, trying to pry Big Ned's fingers from his monitor.

Piperson chuckled softly in back. Gracie whimpered slightly and pulled hard on the leash, angling for the man trying to strangle the monitor.

"I noticed that Big Ned sold quite a bit of the Standard & Poor's 500 this morning, right before the open. The chap seemed keen on getting a jump on the crowd. Now, Hank Dwyer—that's him over there, the serene one who appears to be reading an X-Men comic book right now—he *bought* the S&P futures not long after. They can't both be right, can they? In fact, it appears that our calm and collected Mr. Dwyer might be onto something this morning," the old man said.

Piperson clicked the "Buy" button. The line at the top of the screen read, "YOU BOT 20 /ES [Z2] @ 1967.00." Immediately, the profit/loss counter on the screen went to green as it rolled up the dollars.

Thomas turned back to the scuffle at the front of the room. Finch was now trying to put on a headlock but his huge belly was blocking the move. Big Ned countered with a leg snatch that put Finch on his ass with a loud thud. The traders cheered.

"The point is, I'm no better at interpreting old Jesse Livermore sayings or reading stock charts than the next man," Piperson continued. "But I can read people, and I've always found it more profitable to trade the man.

"Just find the stressed-out plunger, the one bent over his machine, following every little tick. His position is usually at death's door. Would it not be impolite not to open it for the man if he wants in that badly?" Piperson asked, directing Thomas's attention back to Big Ned, who was screaming and rolling on the floor with Finch wrapped around him.

Gracie needed no prompt from Piperson. She was locked on Big Ned from the start.

"You see, Mr. Tender, for every trading rule there is indeed a valid opposite rule. The important thing to remember is this: People, being what they are, will apply the rule that justifies what they're already doing, not the one that challenges the way they think and act. They will seek out the rule that leads them deeper into error, not the one that pulls them out and sets them right."

Piperson clicked the mouse again. The green stopped rolling and stuck on a number. Seven minutes had generated $7,000.

The old man flipped the switch on the computer to "off." He gathered his walking stick and Homburg, giving it a slight dust before adjusting the brim to the arch of his eyebrow. Finch and Big Ned were locked on the floor and wheezing mightily, but Piperson was no longer paying them any mind. Instead, he walked to the back and shook a few flakes into the aquarium, where the little neons bubbled to the surface.

"Don't tap the aquarium. It scares the fish," read the hand-printed sign above the tank.

Piperson gave Gracie one last pet and said goodbye to Thomas with a touch of his brim. The old man walked to the receptionist and gathered orange-tinted fingers that had been sneaking all morning into a bag of half-eaten Cheetos. She giggled a little as he bent over to kiss her hand, and then he began to sing softly.

I'd love to get you
on a slow boat to China
all to myself, alone

Piperson walked out of the Luxor, done for the day, and the receptionist turned to Thomas.

"He is an old charmer, I give you that," she said. "Can't say I care much for his music, though, especially that be-boppity thing he makes Finch play every dang morning. Don't know what it's called, but the old man says it helps fire up the boys."

"I know the tune," Thomas said. "It's the Dave Pell Octet. My college roommate was a jazz nut, and he had the album."

"Yeah, but what's that song called?" she pressed.

"'I Had the Craziest Dream.'"

*****

It only took four months for the new routine to set in. Every morning, Thomas slipped on his navy blazer and headed out the door, the end piece of a cinnamon roll sticking from his mouth as he walked to the Luxor. By his side was Gracie, still wearing her greasy green vest and tethered to a reel-style leash.

Thomas strolled from his modest split level, past the faux

Victorians and onto Washington Street, the main drag in town.

It was fall now, and the days were crisp with the mind-clearing air of approaching winter. There were 12 blocks to the Luxor, and Thomas preferred to walk. It was an easy way to combine the morning commute with his big family chore—bagging anything that came out of Gracie. Besides, there was no time to be gained by driving on Washington Street at rush hour. The overtaxed road was pinched with commuters, sprinkled with a few octogenarians making torturous, lane-clogging attempts at parallel parking and slow-rolling semis cutting through town to avoid the weigh stations.

Gracie stopped often, not just to poop but to peer. Every few blocks she would halt to study the front door of some cheap, prefab Victorian or a tony replica of an old townhouse. A surprising number of the townhomes were zoned residential-commercial, converted into low-overhead businesses like palm-reading rooms and tattoo parlors. It always amazed Thomas that a little suburb had enough clients to keep them afloat, although more people were getting inked these days, and pretty much everyone obsessed about where luck fit into their lives.

At the main intersection sat Weidenhut Realtors, a squat yellow clapboard house which would not have been mistaken for a business had Jane Weidenhut not seen fit to place a small, trailer-mounted billboard in her front yard. "SHORT-SALE SPECIALISTS!" and "STAY IN UR HOME—REVERSE THAT MORTGAGE!" the sign called out in alternating tweets of bouncing red neon.

Thomas crossed Tabard Avenue and slowed his step a bit. He was entering what he always considered to be the nicest part of Washington Avenue if not the entire town. It was a block of old Victorian mansions, real ones. Their wraparound porches were roomy and inviting; the rust-colored flashing along the high bevels always shone brightly in the morning sun.

The homes on this corner were owned by old families from the town. The gingerbread details were intact, the scalloped wood siding was always freshly painted, and the flashing along the soaring turrets was snugly attached. It was a far cry from the loose and flapping metalwork on the overmortgaged prefab Victorians, the ones that groaned with each gust of wind.

Gracie of Hobbs County

Thomas turned the corner on Talbot Street. Halfway down the block was the strip mall and the Luxor Trading Parlor & Pawnshop. Thomas led Gracie in and let her circle and settle on the pillow by his trading monitor. Originally, the pillow had been put near Piperson's aquarium but neither the dog nor the old man would have it.

"Your girl deserves better, young man. Keep her between us," Piperson said after Gracie's first few days.

He issued the friendly command like absolution, cautiously patting the head of a pup who paid little mind to the liver-spotted hand that was forever combing her fine fur.

It took a few days for Thomas to figure out what was going on. As always, Piperson sat in the back of the room studying the body language of the traders up front. He scanned for ticks and twitches until he found his mark. That was usually enough to get him to click off a countertrade that would flush out the wobbly plunger at the front. Once Gracie showed up, however, Thomas noticed that the old man paused a second, taking just a moment to look at the dog.

"That one?" the old man would seem to say, nodding at the mark, his watery eyes on the pup. If Gracie's gaze was fixed on the same man, the same puckered trader, Piperson fired off the order.

Together, the dog and the seasoned trader were triangulating stress in the room. Once they locked on the same mark, the green profit-counter on Piperson's terminal began to roll with a vengeance.

For weeks, Thomas had been tracking Piperson's trades from the corner of his eye. He figured that about six in every 10 trades worked—the old man was booking a solid income with big winners and small losers. Now, with Gracie as his hole card, Piperson was ringing the register on a staggering eight out of 10 trades, and his profits were soaring.

"Thomas, this dog is gifted—gifted!" Piperson would say, usually after booking more green on the screen while some trader melted down in the front.

"Gifted, huh. Well, the 'gifted' dog keeps making me late. She just stops in front of some random house and stares. At nothing. Costs me about 10 minutes every morning."

"Which house?"

"Different ones. Mostly the McMansions and the townhouses. Oh, and the old Victorians. She could stare at those all day."

"You see? Gifted!"

"Huh?"

Thomas only half-followed the story to follow, a long and strange lesson that flitted between economic history, Hollywood gothic horror, and random Wikipedia references.

What we know today as the Great Depression wasn't always the Great Depression, the old man explained. Use that phrase at the beginning of the 1930s, and most people thought of growing up poor in the 1880s and 1890s. First, there was a burst of economic growth—a span that spawned the bumper crop of confident, lattice-decked original Victorian houses, the McMansions of their day. Then a bank in Europe failed, and the world melted down.

In the years that followed, creditors hounded whole towns out of their proud new homes. There were grinding slowdowns interrupted, only briefly, by fleeting growth. It lasted for decades, and when it was all over, many of the Victorian mansions sat weed-choked and crumbling, and these abandoned houses were fixtures for generations to come.

"That, Thomas, was the real Great Depression. That's what the people called it. We don't remember it as such, but it's seeped into our memory nevertheless," Piperson continued as he stroked Gracie's head.

"Well, I sure don't remember anything about it."

"Yes, you do, Thomas. You just don't know that you know. Remember those old horror movies, the ones where someone has to risk going into a ghastly abandoned house if, say, they want to collect a reward?"

"Kind of."

"Do you think it's an accident that those old spooky homes are mansions from that era, a home where hands reach through the floorboards, or some young chap runs around in his dead mother's dress?"

"Hmmm."

"You see? The old mansions stood for something after people went bust and were forced to abandon them, Thomas. They stood for overconfidence leading to ruin. Just seeing them made people anxious. They averted their eyes and told their children never to play around their weed-choked lots. Those empty Victorians were viewed with fear—and Hollywood honed that fear by making them settings for their scariest stories."

"Interesting. What's this got to do with my dog?"

"Miss Gracie senses the stress hanging over the houses, stuck to them. Like a residue. Or an aura, perhaps. That's why she stops. She sees it in the houses just like she sees it in our esteemed Luxor colleagues."

"Uh, huh."

Thomas wasn't sure what to make of the old man, the one who believed that his stray mutt was either a Wharton School graduate or a Yucca spirit chaser. To Thomas, she was just an unintended headache, a gimpy pooch in a smelly vest that no one seemed interested in claiming for a reward.

"Well, Mr. Piperson, I can promise you that we won't be going into any house that Gracie singles out."

"Probably wise," Piperson replied, obviously disappointed in the young man's failure to grasp the import of his words.

"Mr. Piperson scarin' you with some of his spook stories, young man?"

Thomas looked up to see Finch's round face beaming at him.

"Yeah, well, don't take it to heart none," Finch continued. "Mr. Piperson goes off from time to time. Just listen with one ear. And wait till he gets to his excursions—hoowee! Now there's a bell-ringer if I ever heard one!"

"Excursions?" Thomas asked.

"That's what I said. Something about us all being on a favorable excursion, and—"

"Mr. Finch is referring to 'maximum favorable excursion,' I believe. That notion can wait for another day," Piperson said.

"Yeah, that's it!" Finch cried, clapping his hands together and chortling. "Maximally favorable excursions—we're all going on maximally favorable excursions! Every dang one of us, excurting away! Don't know how drunk I gotta be to buy that one."

Piperson smiled sadly and stood up to shake flakes into the aquarium, the last duty of his day, and began to softly sing.

I'd love to get you
on a slow boat to China

155

The old, thin man grabbed his hat and cane, dutifully kissed the receptionist's orange fingers, and was out of the Luxor in a heartbeat, but not before giving Gracie one last pat.

Chapter Twenty-One

After Piperson, the only one generating a steady income in the Luxor trading room-pawnshop was Finch, with his rent, his pinball machines and his second-hand watches.

Every morning, the fat owner would wipe down the smudges on the big case so that the traders drifting over from the Luxor Trading Parlor could see the gleaming Rolex Air Kings, Panerai Black Seals, and other expensive trinkets. It made no difference that the traders never used them to check the time.(Why waste the motion when the hour, minute and second are pasted to the bottom corner of your trading monitor?) That wasn't the point.

The traders wanted something to flash when they were having a good day, and Finch gave it to them.

For traders who were losing, the pawnshop worked just as well. They slipped through the tacked-up black sheet—the divider separating the trading parlor and the pawnshop in adult bookstore style—and sold back the watches after a bad day. Like 14-year-old boys stealing off to the bathroom with mom's lingerie catalog, they glanced sheepishly at Piperson as they passed, wondering if he was going to scold them about not following the rule posted on the whiteboard that morning. But the old man never looked at them. Finch, on the other side of the curtain, was another story. He was cheerful and bubbly and more than happy to shave $200 off what he paid for the same Mondavi sold from his glass case just two weeks before, when the trader was on a roll.

So it went, day after day. Flush traders on a roll would cruise into the pawnshop, ready to reward themselves for being market masters. Traders on the bubble, facing margin calls and meltdowns in their accounts, would skulk back to pawn their goods and survive.

It was a great business model, a real steady Eddie, and Finch also liked to reward himself with a new bangle every now and then. The first Friday of each month was usually good. The Labor Department released unemployment numbers that day and the markets usually went wild, shaking out one or two Luxor traders, often in a matter of minutes.

The path from bust to boom and back again was a real nut-wringer for the traders—and Finch had that covered, too.

In the pawnshop's back corner were the vintage pinball machines, Bally "Playboys" and the like. The boys from Luxor were habitual gamers and would often drift back to pour quarters into the machines when the stress became too much.

The Playboy machine was a crowd favorite. There was confidence in the backglass—Hef with his arms wrapped around two bunnies at once—and it reassured the traders. Everything was going to work out. They drifted to the back corner to drain their stacks of quarters and throw their hips against the sweet-sounding machine, the bunny bumpers making their steel balls dance inside the glass case. Then they slunk back to the Luxor to see if they would be trading the next day or asking for their old jobs back in plumbing and heating.

Piperson hated the pinball corner and hated it more once he saw Gracie pulled to it like metal to a magnet. The dog strained to follow each and every rattled trader to their Playboy sessions. The old man blocked her every time.

"That place, young lady, is much too rough for you!" Piperson scolded, hooking a finger through the pup's collar. There was another reason Piperson wanted Gracie to ignore the pinball players: Whatever had prompted these men to drift to the corner was, by now, ancient history. The old man and the dog had tapped into their twitches early, at the very moment they became make-or-break trades for the men at their monitors.

Thomas apprenticed in the old man's black magic. He learned to stay out of the way when it came to Gracie and Piperson. True, the young man deposited the dog in the trading parlor each morning and pulled her home every night. But in the hours between, anyone else would have thought Piperson owned the dog.

It became an unspoken bargain between the two traders. Thomas, and only Thomas, was allowed to sneak peeks at Piperson's trades a few seconds after they were entered and exited. The younger man's entries and exits lagged a bit, but he was able to grab the meat of most trades. For every five bucks that Piperson pulled down, Thomas was able to claim two or three. Even a minority share in Piperson was enough to boost Thomas's monthly gross to respectable levels by Commonweal standards: All for nothing more than bringing in a dog each day to keep an old man company.

The only time the Luxor's lights burned after hours was on poker night Thursdays, when Piperson sat down for some Texas hold'em with traders who were having a good week. Piperson loved the games and insisted that Thomas sit in on sessions, which meant Gracie attended as well.

The poker nights were the only time the TV on a noose played anything other than financial news. On those nights, Piperson stashed the remote control by his chips and cycled through a predictable series of shows. *American Pickers* was his favorite, although the old man would also flip over to rough-and-tumble shows like *Storage Wars* and *Baggage Battles* or even catch a bit of PBS's patrician *Antiques Roadshow*.

Piperson enjoyed them all, just as long as they involved the rough transfer of assets from the weak and unsuspecting to predators with an edge.

"Them boys could sell watches for me any day," Finch said, leaning back from the table to watch a segment of *American Pickers*.

"Indeed! Those gentlemen are on quite an excursion today," Piperson said with a smile. "Two mint-condition Samurai swords with supporting documents, bought in our nation's backwaters for $25 each. They'll sell for much more back in civilization, I'm sure."

Piperson chuckled, and punctuated the remark by splashing the poker table with a heavy bet, forcing half the players out of the pot.

"Aren't they? Aren't they on quite an excursion?" Piperson said in a singsong voice, reaching down to chuck Gracie under the jaw. The dog ignored him and scanned the other players.

"Oh, here we go again, crazy talk about the maximally favorable excursion," said Finch, leaning back in his chair.

"If you are going to use that term, please use it correctly, Mr. Finch," Piperson said, his voice flattening again. "Maximum favorable excursion, a concept developed by John Sweeney in 1985 and later applied as a trading strategy by Stendahl and Zamansky."

"That supposed to mean somethin'?" Doug Hill asked as he anted up.

"Put as simply as possible, a trade usually can only go so far before it turns down. It is that point, the point of maximum favorable excursion, when it's often wise to consider closing out and looking for new opportunities to trade."

"Hmm," Thomas said, "are you sure that's how to apply that principle?"

"Can we please watch Sports Center," whined Dan Lutz, rocking back in his chair.

"No, Mr. Lutz," Piperson said with a scowl. "The rule is that the biggest winner from the prior week's poker game is entitled to pick the channel. *American Pickers* will do quite nicely tonight."

"Yeah, but that rule means you always pick the channel," Lutz whined.

"And the point you're trying to make?" asked Piperson, looking at the hole cards fanned close against his chest.

"Yeah, but that ain't the half of it, is it, Mr. Piperson?" Finch chimed in. "About the maximum favorable excursion, I mean. You should tell 'em the rest."

"The rest, as Mr. Finch suggests, is simple extrapolation," the old man said, pitching his hole cards and standing to feed his fish while the other players tried to bluff and muscle each other out of a pathetic pot.

"Why should maximum favorable excursion apply just to trading? Why isn't it reasonable to assume that it applies to other things as well? Why not to a career? A marriage? The life of a car? A love affair or even to a country? Isn't it reasonable to think that each of these things also has a point where things are as good as they're going to get?"

"Bullshit! U-S-fuckin'-A, buddy!" said Deek Conrad, glaring at the old man who seemed to be lapsing into American smack talk. "We're still on top, and we always will be. Fuck your maximum excursions!"

"Perhaps," Piperson said, refusing to take the bait. He reached down under the table and stroked Gracie's head, ignoring Conrad's glare. Thomas was too curious to let it go, however.

"Let's say you're right. Why do you think maximum favorable excursion has anything to do with the country?" he asked.

"It's not what I think that matters. Why do most Americans think their children will have poorer, meaner lives than their parents did?"

"You don't have any kids, you old fart," growled Conrad.

"Easy," said Finch.

"If most Americans didn't believe that we, as a generation, have reached maximum favorable excursion, don't you think they'd expect better for their children?"

"That's only because Obama is trying to turn us into Egypt!" yelled Conrad.

"Mr. Conrad, I think Greece is the nation you're worried about turning into, thanks to our president. And both Greece and Egypt seem to support my point about maximum favorable excursion much better than your criticisms of Mr. Obama," Piperson said.

"If you boys done playin', I'm gonna power down for the night," said Finch, trying to choke off the conversation.

"We shouldn't be much longer, Mr. Finch," said Piperson, pushing a hard bet to the center of the table. It doubled the pile of chips in play, and everyone folded except Conrad. He was red-faced, glaring from his hole cards to Piperson, too proud to get out. Finally, he slapped his cards face-down on the table and re-raised the old man.

Piperson smiled and stroked Gracie's head. She was scanning the table as she had all night, and suddenly her eyes stuck on Conrad. The thick man's chest rose and fell heavily as he waited to see if Piperson would call, and the dog's golden gaze never left him. Gracie was saying Conrad was the one. Piperson called.

Cards were turned and the table was quiet when the old man with low two-pair scraped the chips to his side of the felt. Conrad watched, his jacks not good enough.

"This might be a good time to shut the lights, Mr. Finch," Piperson said with a chuckle. He bent over to offer a cheese curl to Gracie.

Conrad yelled and lunged across the table. Two of the boys grabbed his arms before he could get to the old man, who never flinched

"Cash him in and get him out of here!" Finch said to the men holding the cussing trader. "Hell, cash everyone in. I'm shuttin' down."

"Guess we'll be watching *American Pickers* next week, too," someone muttered as the Luxor boys shuffled into the night.

*****

The traders tended to show up late on Friday, the day after poker night. There wasn't much capital to throw around those mornings, after all. The ones who had it the day before ended up losing it to Piperson at the card table.

Finch hated poker night, and not because of the occasional ruckus. He just considered it a waste of good money that would otherwise find its way into his watches. But Finch put up with it, for the old man's sake. Truth was, Finch and Piperson were the best of friends, at least in normal hours.

The two often stood side by side, smirking at the room filled with traders. They whispered like schoolchildren passing notes. The old man helped Finch size up which trader was about to surrender the gaudy watch on his wrist back to the glass case in the pawnshop. Then they speculated about which trader was doing decently enough to drift over later and get their trinkets out of hock. Sometimes Gracie sat at the old man's feet to help inspect the carnage.

Traders are speculators, watchers in the truest sense of the word. They spend less than 2 percent of their day actually buying and selling. The other 98 percent is reserved for watching the markets and waiting—looking for that edge. This left Thomas and Piperson a lot of time to burn each day, sitting and chatting, ignoring their screens. They often filled the time by playing the game of their own invention, the game of old stock sayings.

The other traders paid them little mind. They were too busy bent over their own screens. They were concocting their own particular trading strategies and rules: the trend lines, channels and studies that covered their computer-generated stock charts by the end of each trading day. They drew them with reverence and assigned them magical powers, like the lines of their ancestors, posted on rough stone walls to seduce antelope and bison to the hunt.

Thomas looked at Earl Hagy, who was easily down $2,000 that morning. He was redrawing the lines on his screen, switching from a 10-minute simple moving average to a five-minute exponential moving average.

"He thinks that will change his fortunes," the old man said with a chuckle, nodding to Earl. "No, he *believes* it. All those little lines he's drawing right now, he believes they will change the flow of wealth, the trillions of dollars changing hands at this very minute from Chicago to Singapore."

Earl slammed his hand on the desk, down another grand, and added another moving average to his screen, this one a three-minute weighted moving average. He studied his chart as Gracie and the old man studied him.

"Mr. Hagy thinks that new line will deflect all that wealth like a great river back into his bank account, change its course; everything will happen because he redrew his little line correctly," Piperson grunted. "Interesting how people apply those computer studies in the same manner they apply old stock sayings. It's always to soothe and comfort their troubled minds."

Earl ran a hand through his hair and Gracie skittered forward across the hard floor, inching toward the man. Piperson laughed softly and patted her on the head. All the while, the old man was holding her leash tight.

"Gracie understands, Thomas. She has a talent," Piperson said. "This dog can find just the right person in the room, the one whose faith is breaking—at that very moment! She can find that one trader in the room even better than I can, and I've made it my life's work."

Earl slammed his fist on the counter again and clicked the computer mouse. Two seconds earlier, Piperson had clicked as well, and the green profit bar on the old man's screen was already rolling.

"So you're saying this doesn't work," Thomas replied, nodding to the little lines and studies that populated his own screen.

"I'm saying it doesn't work the way you think it works," Piperson said, his face deadpan now, his voice flat and unfeeling. Suddenly, the older man's expression brightened again. He stretched back in his swivel chair, fingers locked behind his head, bony elbows stabbing the air.

"Ready to play our game again?" Piperson asked.

Michael Rose

Thomas nodded halfheartedly, waiting for the old man to deliver a stock trading rule that the younger trader would have to counter.

"If you look around the room and can't figure out who the sucker is, then it's you," Piperson said.

Thomas propped his chin on his fist. It was the first time, the old man had tossed out an old rule that didn't seem to have a mirror image, a rule usually applied to poker, not trading. Gracie stopped studying Earl for a moment and turned to stare at Thomas.

Close to his ear, Thomas heard the old man chuckle.

"Well, there you have it. I think I've finally won," Piperson said, gathering his coat, putting on his brushed Homburg, and, as always, singing.

I'd love to get you
On a slow boat to China
All to myself, alone

Thomas watched the old man slide out the glass front and disappear behind the dirty brick wall, done for the day. Then he felt a nudge on his leg and looked down. It was Gracie. Those golden eyes!

*****

Life seemed to be running smoothly again. Thomas's depleted bank account began to fatten on winning trades he had purloined from Piperson's computer screen. Louise redid the kitchen in stainless steel. She began to offer her husband softer looks and blue-eyed votes of confidence, glances painted with a realization that, maybe, perhaps, she'd been wrong about her man after all. Perhaps this retreat to hill country was just a temporary setback, as Thomas had insisted all along.

In less than four months, the family had retired everything but the mortgage. The Tenders began to haunt more open houses—this time the new faux Victorians across the street.

Life at the Luxor, too, ran like clockwork. Piperson lavished big welcomes and smiles on Thomas and Gracie the moment they walked in the door each morning, and Finch was usually fawning at his side.

"Ya know, Mr. Tender, you seem to have the same good

164

breedin' as Mr. Piperson over here," Finch said, touching the young man's sleeve. "A man in your position has earned the right to somethin' fine. I got just the Rolex in the glass over yonder."

The routine only changed on Fridays. Those were the days Thomas drove up the highway to grab a few courses at the community college. He still had his Series 7 broker's license and had not abandoned his hopes of re-signing a few biddies from the Commonweal days, the ones who paid him just to stick tax-free bonds into a vault and didn't know about the unfortunate episode in New York. In his sights were college courses that would grease a career in wealth management—gaudy paper to hang in a new office.

"Honestly, Thomas, I can't see why you bother," Piperson scolded. "Everything you need to know is here, with Gracie and me, not with some $12,000-a-year adjunct professor."

Still, the old man was considerate, agreeing to tend Gracie on school days and freeing Thomas of the need to ask if his wife would sit the dog. Every Friday morning, Thomas would show up at the Luxor and hand the leash to Piperson before heading up the highway, covering the same road he had found Gracie on months before.

"Drive safely, young man," Piperson said with a smile every time the doggie exchange was made at the trading parlor. The old trader gently led Gracie to the table in back and settled her under the counter. Piperson had even begun to stock the Luxor's mini-fridge with steamed shrimp, Gracie's favorite, and the pup got a morsel after each winning trade.

It all ran smoothly until one Friday afternoon in late spring, a couple of weeks before the end of the term. Thomas returned to the Luxor late. Piperson and Gracie were missing.

"Oh, he said he had business and cleared out late morning," the orange-fingered receptionist told him.

Thomas drove to his own house, expecting that the old man had dropped off the dog early. There was nothing, not even a note.

He drove to Piperson's brownstone townhouse, the best rental in town, perfect for a man who distrusted real estate the way Piperson did. Thomas got out and stepped to the curb. He pulled a stalk of brown weed that had managed to snake through the concrete and chewed it, trying to get his bearings, lost in thought.

A dumpy old woman in a shapeless dress was outside the house, cleaning rooms that looked empty.

"Well, I didn't see Mr. Piperson long, but the movin' men was here a couple hours ago. They just packed everything up and left for the storage lockers across town," the woman said in a mountain drawl, talking so slowly that Thomas wanted to throttle her.

"Did he say where he was going?"

"No, can't say he did, except—"

"Except what?"

"Mentioned somethin' bout a cruise to China."

A sign from the leasing office was posted in the brownstone window. Thomas called the number. Moved, forwarding address to follow, the realtor said.

It was true. Piperson was gone. Gracie was gone.

Chapter Twenty-Two

Piperson and Gracie settled into a double-wide trailer 2,000 miles away. Housing was scarce in Keystone, North Dakota, just as it was in western Hobbs County, but for different reasons. Back in the rolling hills, the home of old coal, no contractor was going to build houses on spec for folks who couldn't afford them. On the plains, however, they still couldn't throw them up fast enough in 2013.

Everyone had money in Keystone, even the pimply counter boy at McDonald's who got a $300 signing bonus stuffed into his low-riding britches just for showing up the first day. The employer sweetened the pot because no one took that type of work anymore, not in Keystone, where getting screwed meant a starting salary below $70,000.

Here, stripper pole-dancing was a six-figure profession, and a humble bottle of Bell's beer was more expensive than a fruity cocktail in a Manhattan bar. Here, in hard, flat Dakota, the crust over the Bakken oil formation and its Devonian riches, everyone had money but no one had a place to call home.

Newly minted millionaires and transplants from construction startup firms joined the long waiting list of homebuyers, only half-believing the agent's promises of 18 months to pour the foundation. In the meantime, you took a double-wide trailer no matter the price—if you could get it. Sometimes the best thing available was nothing more than a pop-up trailer parked near a Walmart Supercenter.

It was rough, remote and, for the old man and his stolen dog, perfect.

A few well-timed questions at a local watering hole got him and Gracie a seat at a friendly game of Texas hold'em at the VFW hall. There were just a few drillers, derrick hands and tool pushers at the table, but Piperson walked out with $15,000 in his pocket. That led to more invites and leads on card games around town. Soon, Piperson was sitting in four nights a week—just a weird old man with some sort of helper dog in a green vest, a guy who rarely left the table without ringing the register for 10 grand or more.

Piperson was making more at poker than he did trading stocks and futures back East. And this game had an added charm that trading lacked. Piperson could stare straight into the eyes of these Dakota roughnecks—the fish marked by the infallible Gracie—as the old man raked their mountains of lost chips to his side of the table.

Keystone was perfect—off the grid but still on the tit of new energy riches, a place where too much money chased too few goods, a cash-and-carry town where drillers and builders were spreading the wealth and making hookers, barkeeps and card hustlers like Piperson rich overnight.

The only problem was the weather. On summer evenings, huge prairie boomers shook the flimsy walls of Keystone. And every time the thunder growled, Gracie pulled a Fred Astaire on the closest wall.

"Mister, that dog ain't right," one of the roughnecks said to Piperson one day. The greasy motorman was watching the dog in the green vest bounce off the firehouse cinderblock; and he was eyeing the old man suspiciously across the table, with $4,000 piled in the center and waiting for the flop. "What kind of support dog did'ja say she was?"

Piperson had only been in Keystone for five months, pulling down almost $200,000 in that time. Questions about the funny dude with the soft hands and the queer dog were beginning to bubble up. Some of the locals now cast a wary, calculating look whenever they saw the pair. The leader of this crowd was a lanky sheriff with acne scars and a suspicious disposition, a regular at the Thursday night VFW game in Keystone.

The lawman cocked an eyebrow every time the pup fixed her gaze on him. He knew something was up, but he never would have guessed that the dog was marking him as the fish in the game—the big loser in the $5,000 pot the old man was about to take down. Piperson watched the sheriff watch Gracie. The last thing the old man needed was for the sheriff to leave in a huff, heading for his plywood barracks, so sore about his losses that he spent the next morning online, surfing the law enforcement networks for leads about an Easterner with a gimpy therapy dog in a green vest.

The old man decided it might not be a bad time for another excursion.

He gave notice on his week-to-week rental trailer and booked a flight to Vegas. The only fly in the ointment was getting Gracie there. There was no way Piperson was going to ship her with regular dogs, crating her up for storage in the belly of a regional jet that lost almost as much passenger luggage as it delivered.

"Is there any way she could travel with me, in the cabin?" he asked the reservation agent on the phone.

"Is she covered under ADA?" the woman asked.

"Pardon?"

"That's the Americans with Disabilities Act. It covers support dogs, some of 'em anyway. We can let guide dogs and the like inside the cabin, but the dog has gotta be bona fide."

"Gracie is a support pet," Piperson said, eyeing the dog in the greasy green vest.

"Well, what's your affliction?"

"Pardon?"

"Why do you need the dog, if you don't mind my asking? I mean, what's wrong with you?"

"I'm sorry. What's wrong with me?"

"Mister, no offense but you don't seem to hear so good. Do you want me to give you the phone number for deaf folks?"

A broad crooked smile broke over Piperson's face. Two days later, he was at the gate with Gracie by his side in her freshly laundered cape. Looped behind Piperson's ears were two hearing aids— relics he had bought that morning at a local pawnshop. The tan hearing aids were vintage, big and chunky, making the old man's ears stick out. They were broken and tweeted every time Piperson touched them. The pawn store tried to sell him the pricier model, the in-ear design, but Piperson would have no part of it: Big, chunky and visible meant fewer questions about his disability, about why he needed Gracie on the plane.

He walked to the terminal counter to get his boarding pass and one for his support dog, a dog specially trained to assist the deaf. Every time the counter clerk tried to bore in with more questions, details about documentation and certificates from kennels, Piperson tugged his ear like Carol Burnett and made his hearing aids tweet. After a couple of minutes, the counter-man was printing out two boarding passes and keeping his questions to himself.

169

Piperson settled into first class, scotch in hand. He smiled as he thought about Vegas, the frying pan for the biggest fish so far. He daydreamed about taking down international players who dropped six and seven figures in one night and chalked it up with a shrug. Even Gracie seemed to enjoy the trip, gobbling a few morsels that Piperson handed her from a shrimp cocktail.

"My dear, if this goes well, perhaps you and I could someday be seated at the final table of the World Series of Poker," the old man said as he patted Gracie's head. The comment was strange enough to make the guy in 4A glance over. Gracie just stared at the last few shrimp on Piperson's fold-down tray.

They headed for a casino called The Outback, a new Australian-themed casino on the strip. It was done up to look like the real gambling hall near Australia's Gold Coast, a fortress that loomed over a bend in the Brisbane river. That casino, a plaque on the door of the Vegas knockoff explained, was a stately, colonnaded government building that was once the Queensland state treasury. And it was still called The Treasury, even after the action moved from collecting fines and taxes to raking in bets. Such was the Aussie affection for punting and games of chance.

Piperson and Gracie entered the casino just after dinner, the dog decked out in her green cape, the old man clad in the middle-age tourist uniform of khakis and a tucked-in polo shirt. Behind his ears, he sported the broken hearing aids that had worked so well at the airport. This time, however, the man who was supposed to be deaf added some insurance by putting cotton in his ears.

"The easier to not hear you, my dear," the old man said to Gracie as she watched him stuff the wads in his ears before the night began.

Piperson and Gracie were stopped at the door by two big Polynesians, probably ex-rugby players recruited as bouncers for the establishment. They stood beside velvet ropes in baggy pinstripe suits that broke too hard at the cuff. The syrup of their gold-tooth smiles was slathered on playboys, mostly trust-fund babies and spoiled brats, who strutted into the Vegas casino with trophy dates in tow.

Lowlifes also joined the stream of patrons. Most of them were Vegas locals, compulsive gamblers—punters in torn jeans and sweat-stained T-shirts who would have been at home in the pawnshop back in Hobbs County. For them, the rugby boys offered only dead stares and clenched jaws.

"Sorry, sir, no dogs," said one of the Polynesians, who shot out from the rope line to block Piperson at the marble entrance hall. Under the ill-fitting suit, the bouncer's chest looked big as an oak and just as hard.

"Sorry?" Piperson said, making a show as he studied the bouncer's lips.

"No dogs," the man repeated, louder, drawing a few stares from the crowd.

Piperson fumbled in his pocket for paperwork he didn't own and raised the bet by giving his hearing aids a tweet. Soon the floor boss walked over.

"Here you are, sir. No worries. Bit of confusion at the door is all," he said.

Gracie and the old man joined the patrons filing into the casino, past the unconvinced stares of the Polynesian gatekeepers.

Two big card rooms were on the right and, up ahead, Piperson could hear the frenzy of slot machines dumping tokens for a few lucky players. The two got lost briefly in a quarter-acre maze of slots. Then Gracie picked up the scent of steamed shrimp from the all-you-can-eat buffet and tugged on the leash.

"Ah, so it's that, is it?" Piperson said to Gracie with a chuckle. "Well, I never argue with my support dog."

It cost $17, and was billed as "authentic Aussie tucker." For Gracie, that meant only one thing: steamed shrimp, coral colored, comma-shaped, and big as a child's fist. They were laid out on the steam table marked "Prawns" at the end of the buffet. Piperson grabbed a tray, and the two made a beeline down the metal runners, grabbing a few pieces of overcooked ham and dry roast beef along the way. Gracie tugged harder and smacked her chops. Her gaze was fixed on the metal tray filled with goliath shellfish at the end of the line.

"Good lord, look at the size of them," Piperson said as he piled his tray high. Gracie smacked her chops again.

The two took a seat at the back and Piperson went to work, peeling the shrimp. They were obviously a crowd favorite: finger bowls filled with water and lemon slices were placed at every table.

171

Piperson popped one into his mouth, and a trace of disappointment shadowed his thin face when he bit down. A little rubbery and not much flavor, he thought. Kind of fishy, too. Gracie nudged the man's thigh for a turn, and Piperson flipped her a shrimp. She snatched it out of midair and gobbled it down in a flash. Immediately, she was nuzzling his leg for more of the oversized beasts.

Between bites of ham and beef, Piperson peeled a dozen more prawns, giving half to Gracie and tucking the rest into a Ziploc bag he was carrying. Then they headed for the card room.

The old man took a seat at the low-stakes Texas hold'em table, tossing $400 on the felt. The dealer smiled, said hello, and counted the line of bills for the security camera before pushing the chips across the felt. Gracie sat down beside Piperson and looked over the players around the table.

There were a couple of real Aussie businessmen, still in suits and possibly homesick, along with an old Chinese woman and a drunk young man in a white linen shirt with too many buttons undone.

The drunk was telling the other players a loud story about how he had redone the exhaust system on his car to squeeze 20 more horses out of the engine. Nobody seemed to be listening except his girlfriend, a cute blonde who stood behind the lout, rubbing his shoulders and grazing his back with big tits exposed generously by a scooped-neck red dress.

"They let you bring dog in here?" the Chinese woman barked at Piperson. With the cotton stuffed in his ears, most of what Piperson could make out was the thin-lipped scowl on the little woman, whose round face was hidden behind big dark sunglasses.

Piperson made her repeat the question, just for show, and then treated the table to the same story he gave the bouncers. The Chinese woman just scowled harder and muttered something under her breath.

Piperson folded his first five hands, giving Gracie a chance to study the players. The Aussie suits were clearly the fish at the table—"calling stations" who would see the big bets of other players and then fold after their flushes and full houses failed to materialize. They were tailor-made for the drunken lout, who was splashing the table with chips, muscling the Aussies out of their hopeless bets.

The game was developing quickly, and Piperson looked nervously at Gracie. The lout was raking in big pots without ever having to show cards. The suits were already short-stacked. Piperson would have to get into the game before they busted and left for the night. Gracie gazed from player to player, looking for something to lock on.

The sixth hand brought that chance. Piperson caught jacks at the open, a playable pair, and they turned into triplets when the dealer flopped the next three cards on the felt. Also on the table was an ace, and the lout fired off a $200 bet. The two Aussies called. The Chinese woman folded.

Piperson figured his three jacks were probably facing a pair of aces, but he wanted to slow-roll the hand to build up the pot. He looked down at Gracie for her blessing.

Until now, the dog had been more interested in the shrimp hidden in her owner's pocket than in the other players at the table. That changed with the lout's bet; the dog began to squirm and stare at the drunk.

The dealer turned another card, a garbage four of clubs. The lout fired off another $200 bet, and the Aussies called. All eyes were on Piperson—all except Gracie's, which were locked on the man making the bet.

The drunk was now smiling broadly and leaning back into his girlfriend's rubdown, but it didn't seem to be doing much good. Gracie, picking up a thick plume of stress, was tugging on her harness and straining to get to him.

Piperson smiled. This was textbook.

"That's $200 to you, sir," the dealer prompted.

"All in," Piperson said, pushing his remaining chips to the center of the table.

The lout brusquely shrugged off his back rub and began to study the two cards in his hand along with the four cards showing on the felt. The smile was gone. With Piperson committing all his chips to the hand, the lout's favorite strategy—muscling out opponents with big bets—was now off the table. He would have to win it outright or fold.

Now it was Piperson's turn to make a show of nerves, one that might keep his opponent in the game. After loudly clearing his throat, Piperson reached into his pocket for a handkerchief and dabbed his upper lip several times, covering his face for several seconds with the wipe of phantom perspiration. Gracie was distracted for just a second, thinking the stress might have shifted, but she quickly locked back onto the lout, whose smile had returned. He was sure Piperson's handkerchief display meant bluff.

"Call," the lout said, chuckling as he matched the bet and turned over an Ace of hearts and a three of diamonds.

A pair, facing the old man's three jacks. The lout had only one out to win the game, another ace on the final card. The dealer snapped the last card and a two of spades hit the felt.

Piperson reached out and raked in his winnings. Gracie smacked her chops; she knew a shrimp was on its way.

The Chinese lady huffed and shook her head.

"He all in! Why you call with that?" she asked the lout.

"Pull yer head in, old bitch. He knows what he's doing," the man's girlfriend snapped back.

"Easy, everyone—just a friendly game," the dealer said soothingly before turning to Piperson and whispering, "Well played, sir."

"Huh?" Piperson replied.

"Well. Played. Sir," the dealer repeated, mouthing the words elaborately, obviously embarrassed that he had forgotten the old man's infirmity.

"Baaa!" the Chinese woman said, shaking her head and glowering more at the lout. "Dog got more sense than you," the old hag added, nodding at Gracie.

"Madam, please. *Qing ni, bie rang yougang qing da,*" Piperson said. "*Zhe rang yu hen pa.*"

The woman huffed and scooped up her chips. She was gone in a flash.

"What'd you tell her, mate?" one of the Aussies asked.

"'Please don't tap the aquarium. It scares the fish,'" Piperson said, reaching into the Ziploc bag to hand Gracie another shrimp.

*****

One thousand miles away, on a sawed-off mountain in western Hobbs, in a school on that mountain, a girl with a kitchen-shears haircut sat under a table draped with a sheet.

It had been ages since Gracie had padded across the room to sit with Sue May, listening to the stories and poems from MY BOOK HOUSE, but the girl had not forgotten.

She sat with the book under the embroidered sheet, but rarely opened it. Instead, the gilded book bound in rich green sat closed in her lap. Sue May ignored it while she tugged anxiously at her kitchen-shears haircut and stared at her shoes.

Kay, her teacher, chewed her lip and watched.

"Would you like to read to me?" the woman softly asked, and crawled under the sheet, the reading fort she had embroidered, to join the second-grader inside. Sue May clicked her hard-bitten fingernails across the spine but didn't answer.

"Are you sure Gracie's not comin' back?" the girl asked at last.

"Sweetie, I don't think so. We've looked everywhere but…"

Kay paused for a second, giving her words time to soak in and weighing a big decision she didn't want to make.

"You know, I've been thinking," the teacher continued, "maybe our reading fort could use another dog—a special dog, just like Gracie. Do you think you would like another dog to read to, Sue May?"

The girl just picked at the binding with her finger, refusing to look up. Kay put her arm around her, listening to the small, hollow pat of teardrops rolling off young cheeks onto the rich leather binding of green and gold.

"I never want another dog again," Sue May whispered at last.

Later that night, down the mountain, Gracie also was dominating discussion at Kozy Kennel.

"I never want another dog again," Ellen Blair snapped as she flipped off the television and headed for bed. Cap, her grandson, sat in the stillness, thwarted yet again in his pitch to get a new dog. The boy promised that he'd help Ellen find one—one that would be even better than Gracie, the dog he'd given away without Ellen's permission, the dog that she still believed was some reincarnation of Lucky, her first therapy dog at Kozy Kennel.

The old woman was having none of it. She'd fallen into a black depression since losing Gracie, roaming the house most of the day in a bathrobe, rarely taking a hand in the day-to-day running of the kennel. Her slide was unrelenting, and Cap was powerless to stop it. The only thing he knew was that his dream—turning a scholarship at the University of Pittsburgh into a new life as a world-traveling engineer—would remain just that, a dream.

With Ellen like this, the best Cap was going to do was squeeze out a few classes at the community college just a few hours' drive from their home. It was close enough for him to keep an eye on Ellen and make sure that Kozy Kennel didn't go completely to hell.

Cap peered out the front window. In the driveway was a truck with an empty U-Haul attached, ready to be loaded for college. Cap made his way quietly out of the house, careful not to wake Ellen, and drove to the U-Haul dealer in town. The guy dozing on one elbow at the counter was surprised to see someone dropping off this late at night and requesting a partial refund.

"Around here, I can't remember the last time someone's actually dropped off a hitch," the man said as he opened the register and returned Cap's money. "We've had a helluva time just keeping 'em on the lot. Most folks are headin' out of Hobbs County, you know."

"Yeah, I know," Cap muttered, too low for the guy to hear. "Sucks to be me, I guess."

Chapter Twenty-Three

It sat on the water, on a finger of land jutting into Lake Erie and was packed to the gills with roller coasters. Along the fringe were boat slips, and Thomas Tender thought jealously about how people of means pulled up to Cedar Point Amusement park in $5 million yachts and pleasure craft. Like Elvis, they could purchase blocks of time and ride the coasters and the thrills, unencumbered by people like himself.

The trip was just something to do. It was a chance to fill the missing piece in that big, empty puzzle called time. Tender had too much of it these days, now that his marriage and business had busted out. It happened so fast it had made his head swim.

Hell, someone even stole his dog.

Louise didn't last long after her husband lost his seat at the Luxor Trading Parlor. And the seat at the Luxor didn't last long after Thomas went on an epic losing streak, most of it with old Finch glaring down on this trader with nary a watch to pawn. The big, green profits rolling across the monitor didn't last long—not after Piperson, the man obsessed with possessing the dog that used to lie at Thomas's feet, had suddenly vanished into thin air.

If Thomas had to pick a point, a point when things were as good as they ever were going to get, he'd have to pick that Friday afternoon at the Luxor when he lost Gracie, a dog he never much cared for. The downfall started with the old man, Piperson, who stole a dog and away he run. For want of a nail.

Tender had timed the visit to Cedar Point for an early day in fall. His parents used to take him to this amusement park when he was a child, and he knew it was a good time to show up. The lines would be shorter and the tickets would be cheaper. For a man with just $700 in the bank, the price of admission would never be just a detail.

He was at the gate early and had a shot at being first in line for at least one, maybe two, of the good roller coasters when the evening session started. The night before, Thomas holed up alone in an econobox motel affiliated with the amusement park. That would give him a 60-minute head start before the regulars were allowed into the gates. It was like the Oklahoma land rush—motel dwellers making a mad dash for the Dragon, the Condor or the Stampede. These were the coasters that mattered, the coasters that were world-class.

The heavy chain pinged as the staff pulled the iron gates wide. Young men were on their marks, pointed at the rides of choice, and they sprinted well ahead of the pack that followed. Thomas was in the second group, not as spry but still capable of outrunning a family with strollers and backpacks to lug. He made the line for the Millenium Force with only 20 people ahead of him, putting Thomas in the fourth car that would run.

The ride did not disappoint. The long, thin ribbon of steel climbed high enough to turn the yachts into toys. The altitude dissolved in a 40-degree drop and morphed into backbreaking banks, twists and loops—a feast of zero gravity. The brakes kicked in with a loud, rude explosion of gas, and the coaster stopped in a matter of yards. It was over before you knew it. Thomas held his hands over his head the entire ride, a keepsake of childhood bravado and trust that the restraints would do their job and stop the ride from flinging him into the icy waters of Lake Erie. Truth was, it didn't really matter either way.

He studied the park map at the ride exit. The Timberland Chase was the next-best ride, only a few feet away, but the line was already 50 minutes long. Thomas only lasted 10 of those before he had to beg off, and four college boys took two steps forward to fill his place.

It wasn't long before something else caught the trader's eye, the coaster set dead center in the park. It was the Top Thrill Dragster. To coaster aficionados and diehards, it was sometimes their first-pick ride. To Tender, it was one of the most beautiful sights he ever saw.

The track shot out in a straight line, propelling riders from zero to sixty in less than two seconds. It then reached straight up, almost a 90-degree angle. Up it went to a single point, just a single point in the sky, before rolling over to send screaming riders plummeting toward the blacktop. One hard turn of the track at the bottom, a straight line back to the exit gates, and that was it.

It was so clean and simple and beautiful. Set on the horizon, it looked like a miter, for a bishop or a Hessian on the battlefield—just a single, inevitable rise and fall. What had the old man called it? Maximum favorable excursion? Well, here it was in hydraulics and steel.

What Top Thrill Dragster lacked in turns, it made up for in speed. The hydraulic launch hissed with savage power as it heaved each car over the top, and a sign placed at the beginning of the ride warned passengers to keep their arms down to avoid injury. Most riders listened, but one husky boy, maybe 14-years old, stuck his arms up defiantly from the beginning. The car shot forward and Tender saw the boy's right arm shoot back, almost hitting the passengers in the seat behind him. Thirty seconds later, when the car pulled in from the ride, the boy was cradling his right arm like a baby, rocking and wincing in pain.

A fat woman in the same coaster car, helped the boy out as she scolded him.

"Why didn't you mind them rules—you're gonna ruin this trip for every damn one of us!" she yelled at the boy, who was rocking and holding his arm while the woman slapped his back. The kid's right shoulder dropped sharply, like it had been sawed off, obviously dislocated. A park hand walked up to the family, asking if the boy needed the first-aid station.

"Leave him," the fat woman said. "We done this before."

She pulled the boy over to the carneys and the milk-bottle toss on the midway. Softballs were laid out for paying customers, and the woman grabbed one from the stand.

"Hey! Two bucks to throw," the carney barked.

"Simmer down—you're gettin' it back," she snapped.

The woman wedged the ball under the boy's armpit, bent his arm into a chicken wing and wanged it down in one hard move. *Click, click!* The bone had found the socket. Thomas heard it from 10 yards away, over the noise of the amusement park, over the moan of the boy. The kid slowly rolled his arm in a circle, testing it, and then nodded to the woman.

Tender sat in the stands next to Top Thrill Dragster for the rest of the night, watching car after car take that single, giant hill. He was surprised to see the same kid boarding a car two hours later, ready to make another run. This time the boy kept his arms down.

The ride always ended with a hoop before the folks climbed

out. The louder they hooped, the quicker the line to board took a half step forward, so ready to be next. A gray-haired, toothless woman was seated beside Tender in the stands, watching the same amusement. They caught each other's eye for a second, but no words were exchanged. Finally, for no good reason, she decided to break the ice.

"Don't last long, do it?" the old woman said, nodding to the ride, nodding to the crowd. "You're done before you know it."

Two hours later, police were busy stringing yellow tape around the back parking lot. One cop was busy jotting down comments from a woman standing near the new "Do Not Cross" lattice. She said she had driven her camper and three kids all the way up from Georgia to sample this happy place and the world-class thrills. They were about to pull out when they heard a pop.

"I walked outside, and, good lord Jesus, this is what I seen," the woman said, pointing at the car beside hers.

The window was open on the driver's side. The blue-red pulse of cop lights revealed a man slumped in his seat with his arm draped out the window. Blood ran down the arm and balanced on the fingertips. Then it dropped and pooled in the parking lot, next to a pistol sitting in the gravel.

"That's it? Just one pop?" the cop asked.

"Hell yeah, just one! It was over before I knew it," said the woman, thumping hard on the side of the camper to scatter the faces of her nosy children back behind the thin curtains.

The cop nodded and scribbled some more on a pad. Then he squatted down to inspect the vanity plate on the car he'd just cordoned off. "I TRADE" was all it said.

Chapter Twenty-Four

"I told you so." It hung big and unspoken inside Kozy Kennel. It appeared soon after Ellen Blair saw little Gracie on cable access TV; and it stayed on for months, the unwelcome winter guest.

Cap waited and waited for pointed remarks to surface about his transgression, but Ellen never bit back. There was no reminder that the old woman was always against giving Gracie to the school. There were no pointed questions about who in their right mind would give Gracie up untrained, to a twitchy school principal who thought therapy pets dogs were commodities to be bought and sold.

Ellen's silence should have been a relief, but Cap learned to rue it. A little bitching would, at least, offer some insurance that his grandmother was still among the living.

Ellen's days as the drill master of Kozy Kennel were long gone. She spent much of her time swaddled in a comforter and parked on the living-room Barcalounger, washed in the blue glow of basic cable, watching only the nature programs on Animal Channel.

The burden of the business, from dog training classes to paying the vet, had fallen entirely on Cap now. Truth was, the grandson was taking on more of the business with every passing month, but the Gracie fiasco had hit the fast-forward button. Ellen stared expressionless at her nature documentaries while dinner cooled on the TV trays her grandson set before her. When she did talk, it was usually about Gracie or Lucky, the old woman's first pet.

There weren't many good days anymore.

"Want to go to Burnside Grove tomorrow and pick blueberries, Mamaw?" Cap asked, boxing out the flickering images from *Animal Planet*, looking into the woman's gauzy stare. Ellen shrugged off the question and turned up the volume on a commercial for Thunder Blankets.

Cap wanted to say something, but it was no use. His grandmother refused to let go. What little real estate was left in her mind was zoned for that freaky dog. The boy drew a hand tenderly across the old woman's brow, stroking away the wild, wisps of uncombed silver. There was nothing left to do; and one evening, Cap stole away to the kitchen telephone while his grandmother dozed in the easy chair.

"Dr. Denton, please," he whispered low. The receptionist on the other end said that Dr. Denton had left County Health for the day.

"Please have him call me, and tell him that he's to speak to me, just to me," Cap said. In his hand was a pamphlet about assisted living, something he picked up the last time he dropped business cards at the health department. He tucked it under the phone book and studied the glossy four panels whenever the grandmother was out of the room.

With the help of God, Medicaid, and the few relatives who still stayed in touch, there might just be enough to get the woman settled in a safe place—a chance for Cap to resume his regularly scheduled life, which was already in progress.

If it meant pulling the plug on Kozy Kennel, well, when you got right down to it, it was now just a hobby for a hobbled mind. It worked for a time, but the luck had run out.

Cap heard a shriek and went running into the living room. Ellen was standing in front of the TV, mouth agape, the remote control suspended in a hand still pointed at the screen.

"It's her!" Ellen yelled.

"Who?"

"I was searching my channels and . . . there! See her? Gracie! It's my Gracie!" Ellen screamed, looking at her grandson with wild eyes.

"Mamaw, they searched everywhere for that dog. She's just not . . . "

Cap's words trailed off as the show caught his eye. It was the opening screen of *Poker Studs*, the latest in a crop of card-game shows. Seated behind the scrolling neon credits were a half-dozen players in some swank Vegas casino. Beside one of the players was a little dog that was glancing hard around the table, a little pup with a green vest strapped to her back.

"Oh my God," said Cap, stumbling back into the sofa. "This is not happening."

"What's Gracie doing gambling? She's underage!"

"Mamaw, stop."

"They got her working in a dice joint!"

"Mamaw, for Chrissakes, she's not working. She's—"

Cap stopped midsentence. There was something going on. At the beginning of each poker hand, Gracie was her aimless, spacy old self, the rebellious pup that Cap had learned to despise in comfort-dog training classes long ago. She performed her signature roulette-wheel pirouettes, circling over and over in an effort to settle herself. Then, on camera, she curled up and gnawed that familiar shriveled paw while the players pitched their antes.

Almost as soon as she settled, however, Gracie was up again, staring at the table her golden eyes glowing in concentration and focused on one player. After the commercial break, cards were turned and one player was scowling and muttering—the one the dog was drilling into.

Shocked and speechless, Cap and his grandmother watched a few more hands. The winning player was never the one on Gracie's radar. It was usually some old guy in Model-T hearing aids, the one holding Gracie tight by his side and slipping her shrimp after each hand.

"How the hell did she get all the way to Vegas?" Cap whispered, stunned.

"I don't know, but I'm getting her out now," his grandmother hissed, a new fire in her voice and her eyes. "Next, they'll have her serving booze from a barrel under her neck."

She walked to the kitchen and picked up the phone.

"Get me the Las Vegas cops, and Las Vegas Animal Control, and the Gaming Commission, and . . . and . . . Siegfried and Roy!"

"Mamaw, sit," Cap barked as he snatched the phone.

He called information and got the toll-free number for the *Poker Studs* production staff.

"This," he said, stabbing hard at the dial pad, "had better be good."

*****

It all took place just outside the Luxor, the real one in Vegas.

Piperson had stopped to mop his brow in front of the diamond-tipped casino, the unmistakable onyx pyramid that cut the strip in two. The walk was part of a routine that had rarely changed since Piperson landed in Las Vegas. Every day, he would bide his time, holed up in the cool and shade of his extended-stay motel rental. He only ventured out when the hot desert sun fell behind the jagged tops of the Spring Mountains. Dusk settled into Vegas, and Piperson was on the prowl, heading for the casino, his green-vested dog at his side.

The first of those long, infernal blocks along the strip were the toughest, because Piperson now insisted on playing poker the same way he traded, in his dress jacket. He carried it over his arm at the beginning of the walk, unwilling to let the day's last burning rays bake perspiration into the expensive fabric. Only after the desert was sliding into the dim, cool balm of twilight did he slip it on.

The walk was an ordeal—particularly because Gracie insisted on winding the slack from the blue fishing-line leash around the old man's thin legs every few steps. Piperson put up with it all—the heat, the hearing aids, the neurotic therapy dog, everything. And why not? He was winning big in Vegas and earning considerable respect in the process: the sharp old guy with the guide dog. Even the bouncers at the casino offered to hold Gracie's leash while the old man put on and adjusted his dress coat.

That was blocks off, the sun had barely set, and Piperson stopped frequently to mop his brow as he walked his dog along the weedy fringes of the strip. Gracie was panting and her head hung low. Without bending, Piperson squeezed a warm stream of water from a runner's bottle into the dog's thirsty mouth.

"Yours, sir?"

The old man turned to look at his thin shoulder. A party of hairy knuckles had taken up residence there. Piperson spun around to see a man in a uniform, a cop nodding at the dog.

"Yours?" he asked again.

"Why, yes, I . . . yes," Piperson said.

He had assumed this was some parking lot rent-a-cop making sure the dog did her business in designated areas. Closer inspection proved him wrong. This one was in a mustard shirt and black shorts, a bike helmet strapped to his head and a radio microphone tacked to his breast. He was a regular cop working the Vegas strip.

"Where are you headed, sir?" the cop asked, unsmiling, straddling his bike, the black glint of light playing off his aviator sunglasses.

"The Fortuna. I'm registered for a tournament at the Fortuna tonight."

"OK, well, we got a call. Sit tight and we'll have you on your way in no time."

The cop said something into the radio microphone on his shoulder, but Piperson couldn't make it out. There was too much cotton stuffed in his ears. Three minutes later, a white panel truck showed up and a woman from Animal Control piled out. She took a broad, flat plastic stick and waved it over Gracie's shoulder. "Kozy Kennel" the stick's LED display announced in big, red letters.

"We're gonna need you for a few questions," said the cop. His hand was still on Piperson's shoulder, tighter now, and he nodded to Animal Control. The woman took the leash without a word and walked Gracie to her truck.

*****

"Aw, you're just jealous," Mark Delaney said to Marcus, the desk manager of the *Hilltopper-Sentinel*. "That dog is gonna get me on the wire again. Third time in a year! Hey, how many times you been on the AP wire, Marcus, hmm? I mean, back when you actually got your ass out of the chair and did some reporting."

"That first story doesn't count," the editor replied.

"Why not?"

"You didn't write shit, that's why," the editor said, tossing a wadded-up press release at the cocky reporter. "The AP only picked up that first one because our photographer, our esteemed, legally blind photographer, got a cute shot of the mutt draped over some kids at the hillbilly school."

"Just priming the pump, dude, just priming the pump," Mark said, batting the paper wad back with his pencil. "What about my follow-up? It was fantastic! The school board gives a medal to the mutt, and two hours later, Animal Control has an all-points-bulletin out on her. That's gold, and this one's even better: Poor stray puppy found six months later. Stolen. Turns up in Vegas. Heartbroken kids weep with joy, celebrate by reading *Pilgrim's Progress* to the mangy mutt! Who's not gonna want that story?"

Work was fun and exciting again. The kick-ass PR team at

Southeast Airways had picked up on the Gracie story with a vengeance.

The wheels had been in motion ever since Cap Blair called the corporate office, wondering if there was a discount for flying lost dogs back to their owners. Or maybe some professional discount since the owner in question was Kozy Kennel.

The answer was "no," of course, but Dawn Denkins, the ambitious Southeast intern handling the call, wasn't going to leave it at a canned corporate response. Only 23, she was sitting on a newly minted School of Communications degree and looking for that one project, the one that would launch her career.

Dawn took a few minutes to talk with Kozy Kennel and scratch some notes: A dog that had been either lost or stolen had turned up six months later—in Las Vegas, no less. The dog was named Gracie, and she had been working with some poor kids in an elementary school reading program deep in Appalachia. Problem: The kennel didn't have the cash to crate and ship the dog back 2,000 miles, and the owner wants Southeast to do it gratis.

The phone notes spawned a memo to her supervisor and the community relations department, which had funds for hardship cases. Dawn's memo about the lost dog quickly worked its way up corporate, and the young woman was assigned to be the point person for the project, responsible for getting the dog home and planting a few heartwarming human interest stories about a little lost dog, a school bereft and a New York Stock Exchange-listed airline with a heart of gold.

"Let's say I get this done. Uh, does it change my situation around here?" Dawn asked her supervisor when told of the assignment.

"Damn straight. Do it right and you can kiss the internship goodbye. You'll be full-time and career-track."

The first move was easy. Plant a bug in the ear of the hometown newspaper.

Mark Delaney took Dawn's call to the *Hilltopper-Sentinel*, and he pumped his fist in the air as she recited the new details of the story—his story. On Friday, at 10:30 a.m. in the train gazebo downtown, Southeast would be depositing Gracie back in Hobbs County. Representatives from the school and the kennel would be on hand to offer a few remarks.

Gracie of Hobbs County

"Take the photographer," the editor told Mark on the day of the event. "Tell him we're holding space on the front page for a decent shot of the mutt's homecoming. I just hope it's as good as the first one."

"Oh, come on! They say a blind pig finds an acorn if it roots long enough, but two in a row?"

"Your story, your problem," the editor said, peeking through the newsroom blinds. "And make sure he takes a rain cover for the camera lens. That sky doesn't look good."

The weather looked even worse by the time Mark's car crested the mountain, heading for the gazebo and the town's main drag.

The reporter and photographer were late, as usual, and dark clouds were thickening over Burnside Mountain. Fat raindrops began to pock the dirty windshield of the Corolla, producing a slurry of dust and grime that Marks cracked wipers couldn't quite clear. The car almost slid off the soft shoulders of the mountain; once, Mark came close to clipping a woman on a switchback.

It was Kay, the reading teacher at Flattop Elementary.

"Watchit!" she yelled when Mark's car chased her into a gully, the back wheels dousing her neck with rainwater.

Not that the extra water made much difference. Kay was already drenched to the bone, walking briskly along the road toward the depot, a thumb stuck out for anyone headed into town. She climbed back onto the fringe of the gravel and was almost sideswiped again—this time by a white passenger van with the chevrons of Southeast Airways on the side.

The last 12 hours had been a downhill race for Kay. It began with what seemed like a miracle: Rush Rudling's call.

The principal of Flattop Elementary rang early the night before to say that Gracie had been found. She had somehow made it all the way to Las Vegas, Rush said, and the police tracked her through the microchip under her skin.

"You say she's OK? How on earth—all the way to Las Vegas?"

"I don't know. All I got was a call from the superintendent's office five minutes ago, the secretary. Chambers says I have to be at the train depot tomorrow morning at 10:30. That's when the airlines is supposed to hand the dog back. I need you there, Kay."

"But why can't they just bring Gracie to my apartment? Look, just tell me where she is. I'll pick her up."

"It's not that easy, Kay!" Rush whined. "That guy from the *Hilltopper* was the one who told Chambers that Gracie was heading back to town. They're gonna do another dog story—photos and everything—and the superintendent is not missing out on that. You have to be there, Kay. You're the only one who can control that neurotic dog."

The line fell silent. Kay chewed her lip, thinking about Rush's words. She knew the night Gracie bolted from her car had almost cost him his job. And it had certainly cost Kay her peace of mind.

"I need you there, Kay. You're the only one who can work with that crazy mutt. Please."

It took 20 minutes of groveling, but Rush finally persuaded his reading teacher to attend.

She left early the next day, only to find that the battery in her car had died the night before. The sky was beginning to open but there was no choice—there wasn't enough time to call around for a lift into town. She'd have to start walking and maybe catch a ride along the way. Kay was wearing heels for the ceremony. They sank into the soft gravel after the first few steps, and she raced back to her apartment to lace up her running shoes. Then she started to trot down the long mountain road. After a few hundred yards, dark cords of hair clung to her forehead. The small hem of skirt peeking out from her trench coat was soaked and stuck to her legs. Her feet quickly turned cold and numb in the morning rain.

She had been walking for 15 minutes when the beat-up Corolla and the van from Southeast Airways blew by her. The teacher looked at her watch. Twenty minutes until the event, and seven miles to cover on foot. She'd never make it.

Superintendent Chambers was the first to show up at the train depot, or so he thought. The big man, decked out in his best suit, strutted across platform boards that creaked under his ample frame. The superintendent sighed dramatically and checked his gold Rolex every few seconds. This wasn't right. He was the superintendent, for crying out loud. He should never should be first at anything for anyone.

Chambers never saw the old gray woman and the boy standing in the corner, and he wouldn't have recognized them if he had. It was the delegation from Kozy Kennel. Ellen Blair's eyes were glued on the rails, looking for the train that would bring Gracie home. Her grandson stood beside her, smoking a nervous cigarette with one fist and gripping his grandmother's coat with the other. He tugged on the woman every time Ellen acted like she was going to make a break for it and shuffle down the tracks to fetch her dog.

Rush Rudling and Eva, the school secretary, arrived a few minutes later. The principal started to speak to the superintendent, but he was chased away with growls of "later!" Rush stood sullen and shamed, peering over Eva's shoulder at Chambers and the delegation from Kozy Kennel. Ellen saw and shot him a dirty look. Rush moved closer to Eva.

"Where's Kay?" he muttered.

"Settle down," Eva said.

He turned to say something to Cap, but Ellen jumped into his path.

"You had no right to take that dog, Mr. Rushmore. Gracie was not trained for the assignment. Unacceptable!" the old woman said, waggling her finger.

"Mamaw, it's Mr. Rudling, not Rushmore," Cap said, adding with a mumble, "and that dog won an award from the school system, you'll remember."

"Then why is she gambling in Vegas? Unacceptable!" Ellen repeated.

"You're damn right it's unacceptable!" Chambers yelled from the other end of the platform. "Where the hell's the pooch? And the press? And who the hell are you?"

On cue, Mark's vintage Corolla and the Southeast Airways van raced into the parking lot, a photo finish with both cars bouncing and bottoming out in the potholes.

Dawn Denkins stepped out and leaned into Mark's window.

"Hi. Who you with?" she asked.

"*Hilltopper*," Mark said, reaching into the glove box to find a pen that hadn't gone dry.

"Seen the dog?" Dawn asked, brushing a wisp from her furrowed forehead.

"Seen the dog? Me?" Mark repeated, more amused than shocked. "You're Southeast, aren't you, sweetie? You're supposed to have her."

"I'm advance," Dawn said, ignoring the "sweetie" shot taken by this reporter for a little mountain rag. "The visuals will be better if the dog comes off the train, not out of the van. We wanted to take her off our equipment, but you can't land anything within 70 miles of here."

Dawn did a quick circle.

"See any film crews?" she asked.

Mark and Craig shook their heads and moved to the platform to set up. The sky rumbled again, and the ground began to join the chorus. The train was approaching from the western hills.

Chambers was at the stairs as the passengers disembarked, and it was clear he had forgotten what Gracie looked like. The superintendent stopped a woman with a terrier in tow and groped for the leash. The woman slugged him with her bag and walked quickly away, while the camera shutter documented the PR misfire. Dawn stood a few feet away, shouting into her cellphone.

"Where is she?" the young woman was screaming. "I need that dog here on the platform *now*!"

Eva saw Rush's hand homing for his crotch, and she brushed it away. Then she leaned in and whispered to the principal.

"Rush, honey, maybe you better go over and help Dr. Chambers sort out those dogs."

"Me? He hates me! Where the hell is Kay?"

Wheels clacked across the boards of the platform. Everyone turned to look at the baggage handler who was making all the noise. He was pushing a dolly toward them. Perched on the front was a metal box, battleship gray, with punch-out holes and steel mesh on the front. Peering from inside was Gracie, her golden eyes glowing and her mouth clamped shut with a company-issue muzzle.

"Jesus! They've done her up like Hannibal Lecter," Cap whispered.

"There's my reading dog, my little sweet potater!" the relieved superintendent cried, thudding down the platform with his belly rumbling, his tie flapping, and the camera snick, snick, snicking at his heels. Chambers lunged for the leash, but the sight of the birdcage over Gracie's muzzle stopped him short.

"Uh, what's wrong with her? I mean, she got something I should know about?" the big man muttered to the baggage handler.

"Just policy," said the man, whipping off the restraint and

holding out his hand for a tip that never came.

Snick, snick, snick!

Dawn and Mark raced down the platform after the superintendent. Mark pulled out his pad while the young intern stepped forward and unfolded a piece of paper.

"Schools are the key to our children's future, and we, at Southeast Airways, are delighted to play some small role in reuniting this wonderful, talented dog with the students who love her so," Dawn said. "When it comes to excellence in education, no school reading dog should ever be left behind, and Southeast—"

"Get off my dog, mister!"

Everyone turned to see Ellen marching toward them, with her grandson in tow.

"I said get off!" the old woman shouted as she snatched the leash from the superintendent's hand.

"There must be some mistake," Chambers said, trying to hold his forced smile and muscle the leash back.

"There sure as hell is! Gracie belongs to Kozy Kennel," hissed Ellen, pulling back harder.

Gracie had been watching the back-and-forth with interest. The small pup would shuffle a little this way, a little that way—it all depended on which combatant seemed to be freaking out more. Then the little dog saw Rush—her beloved, long-lost, nut-fidgeting principal who was standing in back—and she sprang for him with a yip of glee. She only got a couple of feet, since her leash was wrapped around the superintendent's ankle. Gracie began to whine.

Mark nudged the photographer.

"What's that, Gracie? Trouble at the ol' Title I school?" he snickered. Dawn heard the crack and sneered at him.

"Let her go!" Ellen screamed, grabbing the leash back. Gracie lunged again, and the nylon line executed a perfect leg sweep on Chambers. Craig *snicked* away as the school superintendent rolled down the depot's muddy embankment.

Gracie bounded over to Rush, whimpering and weaving through his legs while the principal tried to make his escape.

"This never would have happened if you'd let me bring my cheese chunk!" Rush yelled at Eva, who rolled her eyes and walked away.

Chapter Twenty-Five

Three hours later, Mark Delaney was back at the *Hilltopper-Sentinel*, filing a 750-word story that would never run.

"But why?" he yelled to the editor, who had spiked the piece without a word. The move surprised everyone in the office, particularly since Marcus had put almost two hours into culling that day's shots from the legally blind photographer.

"Because nobody wants to read a story about how our superintendent of schools went down to the depot to strong-arm an old lady out of her dog—that's why."

"*Everybody* would read that," Mark yelled.

"Maybe. But I sure as shit am not going to be the asshole who runs it," the editor barked back. "This is a community newspaper. You want to rock the boat, sell it to a grocery store rag. I'll even give you the photos to pitch. How about the shot that looks like Chambers strangling the old biddy with her own leash. That one kills me. Looks like it damn near killed her, too."

"Such a wuss," Mark said, grabbing his coat and heading for the door.

"Yeah, but an employed one," the editor shot back. "By the way, you spell 'melee' with two e's."

*****

Kay dialed the number five times before Rush picked up without hanging up. The principal was angry with her, with everyone.

The principal was now convinced that Gracie was the bane of both his professional and personal existence. He blamed the reading-room mongrel for the reprimands and memos that were fattening his file at central office. He knew these seedlings-with-subject-lines would sprout into a mighty oak: grounds for dismissal after school let out for the year.

"Mr. Rudling, Gracie isn't to blame for everything. How is the dog to blame . . . " Kay swallowed hard and stopped. She couldn't believe she was going here. "I mean, that time you were written up for, uh, allegedly enjoying familiarities in your office after hours. How is that Gracie's fault?"

"If Eva hadn't tripped over that mutt's old chew toy, there wouldn't have been a thud, and that snitch Rooney wouldn't have been gawking in my office window at 8 p.m. That's how! He's never gotten over me putting him on reading like the superintendent told me to. Think about that!" Rush snapped.

"I'd rather not," Kay said, pinching her eyes shut and rubbing her forehead.

"Look, let me bottom-line this for you," Rush said, borrowing business jargon. He did it when he wanted to sound decisive, but it usually made him indecipherable, like the time he wasted an entire faculty meeting on "expect more, pay less" mumbo jumbo. "I say the dog goes. Chambers says the dog goes. That means the dog goes. End of story."

The principal hung up. The phone rang again before Kay even had time to remove her hand from the receiver. The boy on the other end started like the conversation had been going on for hours.

"Yeah, well you don't know me but I'm the guy whose grandmother owns Kozy Kennel . . . the one at the depot," Cap Blair said.

"The woman who's got Gracie, you mean."

"That's the one. Listen, what's with Rudling? I keep calling your principal about the dog and he keeps hanging up."

"I just spoke to him," Kay replied. "He's not going to let Gracie back in the building."

"Yeah, well Mamaw's not too crazy about that idea, either," the boy said. Kay heard the phone bang against the wall and then Cap's voice, more distant, snapping off "look-settle-stay" commands on the other side of the room. The boy returned and picked up the handset.

"We need to sit down and talk," Cap said. "Meet me at Darrell's Cafe Saturday morning?"

"But what about Principal Rudling? Superintendent Chambers? Your grandmother?"

"I'm working on it. Just meet me."

Cap was already seated in a booth when Kay arrived at the cafe. The teacher was disappointed to see that Gracie wasn't beside him. Instead, Eva, the school's secretary, was at the table.

It was 10 in the morning and the place was all but empty, the Saturday morning tradesmen having grabbed their coffees and fried egg sandwiches hours before. Cap and Eva were in a corner, hunched over the flyspecked linoleum table and engaged in serious deliberations. The leather seatbacks hid them from the sprinkling of regulars still in the cafe.

Cap saw the teacher and waved her over.

Kay slid in beside Eva and they nodded cautiously to each other. Then they turned to the young man who had called the meeting.

"I guess I'll just get right down to it then," Cap said. "My Mamaw's got this delusion about Gracie being some reincarnation of . . . My grandmother's just deluded."

The boy from Kozy Kennel shook his head and lit a cigarette with one burning in the tray. His foot was bouncing nonstop, like the cup of coffee in front of him was number eight for the day. Everyone was edgy and quiet when the waitress came for orders, and Cap only continued when she was out of earshot.

"Here's the thing. My Mamaw thinks she's capable of keeping Gracie, but she's not. I'm not. The whole freaking world is not, as far as I've seen. Except maybe you—you got the dog on TV, after all, and picked up some award for it. Why don't you want Gracie back at school?"

"Sweetie, this isn't coming from us," Eva said.

"Where's it coming from?"

There was a pause.

"Rush," secretary and teacher said on cue, in unison. Surprised, they both doubled over and snickered. Eva was the first to collect herself, but it took a few tries.

"Now, now. Let's not be cruel here," Eva said, dabbing her mouth lightly with a napkin. "There's also Superintendent Chambers. And your grandmother, too, don't forget."

"How could I?" Cap muttered.

"Mr. Rudling has it in his head that, somehow, Gracie has it in for him," Kay told Cap.

"Oh, how silly—that dog just adores Rush!" Eva said, the

Southern lilt rising with indignation at such a ridiculous thought.

"I know. It is silly. But he thinks that night when you slipped on a dog toy in his office and got caught . . . "

Kay stopped and her pale cheeks turned scarlet. She took a forced sip of coffee and tried to think of a way to end the thought without getting Eva's water glass dumped in her lap.

"Oh, he should hush up! That's not why I slipped," Eva said. "I slipped because whenever we spend time together . . . "

Now it was the secretary's turn to pause. Her sharp blue eyes darted to Cap for a moment. She sized him up quickly, almost as adept at detecting malice as Gracie was at flushing out stress. Eva decided to risk it, sending Cap to the counter for extra cream and leaning over to whisper to Kay.

"Well, I happened to mention to Rush that I liked that bestseller with, you know, the paddles and blindfolds and ties and such. Just mentioned it, mind you! But now he's taken a notion that's the only way I want things. He even stole a sleep mask out of his wife's nightstand. Thought it made a good blindfold. That's why I tripped. That woman soaks those things in Dolce & Gabbana and I was getting woozy from it. I swear, where he gets these notions—feeling like he's gotta be the full-out dom to get me in the mood. He's more Dom DeLuise, if you want to know the truth."

"Who's Dom DeLuise?" Cap asked as he sat back down.

Kay and Eva looked at each other. Their eyes started to glisten and they both twitched, trying to hold it in. Kay broke first—the curl forcing its way onto her lips and Eva raise the stakes with a stifled, throaty chuckle. Then they both exploded in laughter. Other customers turned to look.

"Sorry, did I say something?" Cap asked.

"Don't know why you're sorry, sugar. It's 'Mr. Christian' who should be sorry."

"Who's Mr. Christian?" Cap pressed, more confused than ever.

Another round of laughter, this one with spilled coffee and warnings of pants about to be pissed. The story loosened the table, and the three settled in to set things right.

The easiest obstacle was Rush. Kay promised that she would make sure that Gracie stayed in the media center, away from the principal.

"Do you think that'll be enough for him," Cap asked his secretary.

"He'll listen to me. He always does," Eva said. "Besides, I can always threaten to start calling him 'Rushmore' again. He hates that so much. It'll be fun to bring it back from time to time."

"So, Cap, that only leaves your grandmother and Dr. Chambers," Kay said.

"One thing you should know about my Mamaw is that she loves these therapy dogs—she really does," Cap said. "And she believes in what they do. Or at least she did before her mind started to slip."

The young caretaker of Kozy Kennel paused to take another sip of coffee and light another cigarette.

"If she could just see the dog working with kids, if Gracie is any good, I *know* she'd change her mind."

The women sat silently, playing with packets of sweetener and mulling the problem. Finally Kay spoke.

"Can you get your grandmother and Gracie in the car with you?"

"Sure," Cap said, "but what good will that do?"

"Drive them past the school and let Gracie out to pee. Do it within 50 yards of the school. You'll get your reading demonstration," Kay said.

"I don't see how—"

"Trust me. You'll get it," the teacher said, cutting off the topic.

"So that only leaves Dr. Chambers."

"Dwayne don't like the dog?"

The three turned around to see a young blonde in the next booth. She was dressed for the evening in the middle of the day, and she was nursing a coffee with her back to the group.

"Dr. Chambers, you mean?" Kay finally asked.

"Yeah, Dwayne. I know him through work. I'm an . . . entertainment coordinator."

"Lord! This town could use some coordination," Eva said, dabbing her lip when Kay gently shushed her.

The woman in the next booth asked if she could slide in, and the three made room. Kay noticed that the woman's fingers were bright orange. She said her name was Retha. She not only knew Chambers but also Gracie and even the dog's father—a stray that used to hang out in town at night.

"This Gracie is the dog from the paper, right? Sure, I know her," Retha told the group. "There was a guy downstate who used to bring her into a stock-trading business. Don't know how she got there, but some other guy ended up swiping her. Sweet old guy, too. Big hand-kisser."

Kay glanced again at Retha's orange fingers.

"Anyways, this is my second go-around here in Hobbs," Retha continued. "The first time I was an entertainment coordinator up here, I used to see an old stray that looked just like Gracie only older. In fact, the first time I saw Gracie I thought she was the Hobbs County dog. That boy must'a been her daddy."

She paused to chuckle a moment as the memory surfaced.

"You want her at school? Leave Dwayne to me. I think he'll put up with a dog in school faster than he'll put up with word circulating about his goings-on. Most of 'em don't want the missus to know when their entertainment's gettin' coordinated."

Chapter Twenty-Six

The doors to the Flattop Elementary media center were open when Gracie bounded in, bright-eyed and searching, with Ellen and Cap in hot pursuit.

The boy had done just what Kay had instructed. With his grandmother in the passenger seat, Cap pulled off next to the school and put on his flashers.

"Gracie needs to go, Mamaw. Be right back," he said as he hopped out and walked the pup to the grass beside the fountain at the entrance.

Gracie circled for a spot to go, then her ears perked up. She could hear the chants of the drill squad in the big auditorium. She could hear the squeals of play from the blacktop and the intercom announcements in that soft voice that belonged to the woman in the principal's office. The dog lifted her head and filled her nostrils, sniffing for more details. Cap followed the final plan, dropping the leash by his foot, and Gracie took off for the building.

Cap and Ellen both watched as the little dog bolted into the media center, through the rows of chairs, her head down, peering, her eyes filled with familiar sights.

Kay was cleaning the whiteboard, when Gracie spotted her legs between the rows of chairs. The woman was straightening the room at the end of the day, and soft music played from the room's old record player, more old records getting checked for scratches. Gracie sprinted forward, her leash still attached and trailing. She bounded for the woman with a yip and a squeal.

"Gracie!" Kay cried, scooping up the dog in her arms. The teacher dropped to her knees to stroke the soft fur, and the dog spun in place and licked the teacher with delight at each turn. There was a look in Gracie's eyes, a look that Ellen had never really seen from this dog, a look of love and trust.

Something rustled in the back of the room and Gracie glanced over. It was coming from the fort, the embroidered tent. Inside it was the little girl, the one who read to her so long ago.

Gracie bounced to her feet and scrambled for the girl, who buried her face in the dog's neck. Beside them was the gold leaf book, unopened, and Gracie nudged it. Sue May smiled, letting Gracie settle into her lap, and she flipped the book open. Then, as if nothing had changed, Sue May began to read to the dog.

"Mamaw, you see? Gracie is safe here," Cap said softly to Ellen, who was watching closely. Kay walked over and offered her hand to the owner of Kozy Kennel.

"Hi, I'm Kay Merring. You must be Cap's grandmother. It's a pleasure to meet you at last."

Ellen shook hands but didn't reply. Her eyes were locked on the little girl petting the dog and reading in a soft whisper under the tent of many colors. Cap looked nervously at his grandmother. It was hard to tell what she was thinking.

"I trained that dog at my kennel," Ellen said at last. "Half-trained her, really. She wasn't ready for this. She still hasn't completed the course."

A new album dropped on the record player. It was badly scratched, but you could still make out the music. Sue May stood up and held Gracie's paws as the two box-stepped across the room. The little girl smiled as she looked at her feet. She kept her steps small, careful not to step on the pup by mistake. Gracie seemed unconcerned—the dog stole quick, greedy kisses that make the girl giggle as they danced.

After a minute, Gracie jumped down. Kay smiled and walked over to take the girl's hands in her own. She had big feet for a woman, and she let Sue May stand on them as they laughed and waltzed around the room. That only coaxed Gracie on. She circled round and round the student and teacher, winding the leash tighter.

"Gracie, heaven's sakes!" Kay called out, laughing. "Enough with the Disney moment!"

The pup obviously disagreed. She lassoed them tighter and spilled them to the floor. They were pinned, suspended in giggles, and the dog blessed the moment with another round of sloppy kisses that just made them laugh harder.

"That leash," Ellen said, smiling across the room. "Have to do something about that leash—before the school takes her."

"Well, maybe we can bend the leash rule just once," Cap said, standing close to his grandmother.

The two walked back to their car and were startled to find someone loitering in the lot, a young blonde in a tight skirt and man-killer heels.

"Just figured I'd come up to see how it went," she said to Cap and Ellen. It was the girl from the coffee shop.

"Uh, Mamaw, this is Retha," Cap stuttered. "She's an entertainment coordinator and, uh, she knows Gracie!"

"I know Gracie and her daddy, too," Retha said. "They's both real good dogs. Is she settlin' in OK with that school."

"I think so, Miss Retha," Ellen said. "You say you know Gracie's father?"

"Oh sure. He's always roaming around town, but I can't say I've seen him lately. I'd love to give him some type of home but he's skittish," Retha said, shifting from foot to foot. "Truth is, I wouldn't mind having Gracie, too. I love 'em all—dogs that is. But it's hard to take care of one proper when you work irregular hours."

Retha nodded to the Blairs' truck, the Ford with "Kozy Kennel and Comfort Dog Training Academy" painted on the door.

"Lady, I gotta say, you are one lucky woman, doing what you do. That's gotta be the best job in the whole wide world, least as far as I'm concerned."

Cap's eyes sharpened at the comment. He seized the moment."

"Hey, Retha, we could give you a lift. Maybe you'd like to see Kozy Kennel on the way back? You could meet our dogs and we could explain how they get trained. OK, Mamaw?"

Ellen watched Retha, the way the girl looked at the lettering on the truck. And she knew her grandson well enough to know what he had in mind. At last, she spoke.

"Sure, Cap. This young lady can tell me about that daddy dog, and we can tell her a bit about the kennel. Mind you, Retha, things are changing at Kozy Kennel these days, what with Cap heading off for his studies and all. I can't offer much to someone filling in at the kennel, but we do have that spare bedroom—at least as long as Cap's up in Pittsburgh."

The three piled into the truck and headed down the mountain, oblivious to the tall man in the suit who was pacing the basketball court with his hands locked behind his head.

"Hey, Mr. Rudling, whatcha know!" Joe the janitor called out as he walked to the court.

"Uh, hey Joe, whatcha . . . "

Rush's words trained off when he realized that Joe had beat him to the punch.

"So looks like we get the dog back after all," Joe said.

"Yeah, great."

"You seem kinda cool to that, Mr. Rudling," Joe said, closely studying Rush, the principal who was always wound too tight.

"Don't think anyone would be surprised if that dog stays and I go," Rush said.

"No, maybe not," Joe replied, "but mind if I ask something?"

"How about later."

"No, sir. Now is probably the right time to ask," Joe said. He walked over to the side of the court and picked up a basketball, studying it, trying to spin it on his finger as he talked. "Hope you don't mind the question, but it's been dogging me for a while. Your best day here as a principal—was it even half as good as your worst day back when you were just teaching PE?"

Rush stopped pacing, startled at the question, and looked at the janitor.

"Well, Joe that's hard to say because," Rush started. His words faded as he watched Joe spin the ball. "No, not even close. You may not know it, Joe, but I was a damn good PE instructor."

"Oh, I knew that, sir. My daughter, Jane, had you when you were coaching youth league. She always went on about how you were the best."

Rush thought hard.

"Jane Delmar," he said at last. "I remember her. Power forward. Strong. Soft hands for a big kid. Not the quickest feet on the court but worked like hell in practice. Sure, I remember."

Joe smiled at Rush.

"That's Jane! She thought a lot of you, Mr. Rudling, back when you were teaching, doing what you do best. So if this principal deal at Flattop doesn't cut your way, well—"

"Well, what?" Rush asked, swallowing hard.

"I'm thinking it leaves you in better shape than most, Mr. Rudling, if you don't mind my saying so. I mean, you love what you do . . . what did before they made you come over here. And you're damn good at it, too. Not everyone can say that. There's gotta some place out there that still needs that. I mean, my daughter ain't the only kid who stands to benefit from a great PE instructor."

Joe slid to the top of the key and shot. It bricked hard off the rim.

"Damn, thought I had that," the janitor said. He trotted over to pick up the ball and popped it to Rush with a crisp chest pass.

Rush stared at the ball. The coarse leather grain felt natural in his big hands. He looked from Joe to the ball and back again.

The janitor chuckled.

"Relax, sir. The game's called HORSE, not dog."

Slowly, naturally, the tight, crooked line vanished on the principal's worried mouth, replaced by a schoolyard grin.

"Yeah, that's it. HORSE!" Rush said. He dribbled left, faded to the top of the key and drained his first shot with an easy flick.

Chapter Twenty-Seven

Sam and Derrick Wainwright crouched near the riverbank under the shade of a leafy fig tree. The boys exchanged confused looks as they watched a commotion unfold on the footpath by the river. Something was roiling the stream of Queenslanders out for a bike ride, run, or twilight stroll along a lush and manicured ribbon of Australia parkland that hugged the Brisbane River at West End.

Every few feet, the joggers, cyclists and pram-pushing couples would part, revealing a tall old gent wearing sunglasses and a black Homburg. That was mildly curious. Most of the hats on the footpath this day were Yank-style caps worn by Brisbane bogans and toughs. Their brims were razor straight and cocked thuggishly to one side. This gent, the one in the black felt hat, must have been in his 70s.

What was really strange, though, was the dog he had on the leash.

The man was half-walking and half-dragging a copper-and-black dog with high, foxy ears and a shrunken paw. It kept bolting to the right, pulling the pair into a line of pedestrians going the other way. Each time, the man yanked back and snapped off a few testy words, although all Sam and Derrick could make out was "Caesar, no!"

The dog was done up in a vest and bracketed into a stiff, U-shaped leash, the kind that guide dogs wear. Every few yards, it happened again: the dog veering hard right, the man pulling back just as hard to the left, both hands glued to the stiff stirrup of the leash.

An ibis strutted by. The pushy bird looked like a miniature stork, and it was scouring the grass for any crumbs, oblivious to the crowd. The dog saw it and hunkered low. When the bird was only 10 yards away, the dog sprang, pulling the harness so sharply that it sent the man's dark sunglasses flying. The man and the dog tumbled off the path, narrowly escaping the wheels of a mountain bike barreling straight for them.

"He looks like Dad, that time the push mower went crazy and

dragged him through the hedge," Sam said, sitting up for a better look.

"I think he's blind," offered his brother, a small crease now marking his forehead. "Why is the guide dog trying to kill him?"

The man in the black hat was now on his hands and knees, fishing for his lost sunglasses. One hand combed the thick grass under a Moreton Bay fig tree near the river. The other hand kept a tight grip on the dog, still scampering for the right side of the path and another shot at the bird. Pedestrians eyed the two suspiciously and gave them ample berth as they passed.

"Caesar, no!" the old man yelled again.

"I'm getting this on YouTube," said Derrick, fumbling through the pockets of his school uniform for a phone and flicking the video capture button. "'Guide dog goes troppo; kills poor blind bugga.' I'll get 5,000 views in an hour, no worries."

The boys raced down the hill, their navy-gold regimental ties flapping in the charge.

"You right, sir?" Sam called out.

"Did your dog go crazy?" added Derrick, never one to beat around the bush.

Piperson looked up to see the two boys running his way, framed by the Brisbane River's graceful bend at Kangaroo Point. They looked to be about 11 or 12 years old and had yet to shed their school ties and blazers. One of the boys was holding up a cell phone as he ran, pointing it stiffly forward.

The dog saw the boys, too, and he froze, soaking in their agitation. A woman scolding a toddler passed by and the dog whipped around to laser on them. His paws scraped the asphalt, looking for traction as he strained to break free of the leash, running in place like a cartoon character.

"Easy, Caesar," Piperson snapped, pulling back hard. "Gracie never behaved like this."

The dog turned in his harness to sneer at the man.

"Here, sir, your sunnies," Sam said, holding out the sunglasses that the man had been fishing for.

"That's not how you do it—it frightens blind people," his brother chided. He snatched the sunglasses away from Sam and cleared his throat, as if he were about to recite a few verses of "The Man from Snowy River" in an Aussie primary class.

"Sir . . . mmmmm . . . we are Derrick and Sam, brothers from West End and we both go to Saint Bart's," Derrick said, taking slow, even steps toward the man and his dog. "I am walking to you on your left side, sir, and I have your glasses in my hand. I am handing them to you just now. They are right at your chest."

"So I see. Thank you," Piperson replied, snatching the glasses in one quick motion and holding tight to the leash. "May I ask why are you talking like that, son?"

Sam and Derrick exchanged confused glances. The man was a Yank—and this Seppo could definitely see.

"We thought you was blind," Sam said.

"Sightless! Blinds like to be called sightless," Derrick corrected.

"He doesn't like to be called anything. He's not blind."

Derrick flipped off the video capture button, disgusted at losing both a good YouTube clip and an argument.

Piperson sat by the side of the path, fanning himself with his Homburg and catching his breath. Reluctantly, the dog settled down next to him and scanned for people and prey.

"Sir, how come you have a guide dog if you're not blind?" Sam asked.

"Why'd you think I was blind?"

Sam nodded to Caesar's heavy harness and the "Service Dog" lettering on his green cape.

"Oh, well Caesar isn't a dog for blind people, that's only some service dogs," Piperson explained. "Some dogs are for deaf people or other things. Autism and post-traumatic stress disorder and such."

"Tim's brother was a digger. I heard Mum say that he came back from Afghanistan batshit crazy," Sam muttered to his brother. The two boys took a couple steps back.

A cyclist whizzed by the group, making the return trip from Kangaroo Point to Brisbane's city center. He had on racing gear and he chirped the bell on the handlebars as he passed. "Mind yer dog or get him off the path, mate!"

"We're on the left," Piperson called back, although the rider was already 20 yards down the path.

"Were you an American soldier? Is that why you have a service dog?" Sam pressed.

Michael Rose

"Yah, and why is she acting crazy?" Derrick added.

"It's a male. Caesar. I had another dog, Gracie, a superb dog, trained back in the States. I'm training Caesar now to be a support dog. A long process, as you can see."

"But why do you have Caesar?" Derrick asked.

"I'm deaf," George said.

"But you hear us," Derrick continued, a cloud of suspicion covering his face.

"I can read lips."

The old man and the boys were standing by the side of the path, eyeing each other suspiciously as the stream of pedestrians continued on the footpath behind them. Caesar spun around to eye the boys and the old man as the tension built between them.

"Are you in Brizzy on holiday?" Sam asked. "What happened to your good dog? Gradie was it?"

"Gracie," Piperson corrected, his watery blue eyes softening.

"I lost Gracie back in the States. Later, I traveled back to, uh, reacquire her. It was a difficult proposition, given the awkward circumstances surrounding her loss."

Derrick started to ask another question, but Piperson waved him off.

"I was driving into town to get Gracie back, and I a saw a dog trotting on the side of the road. It was late afternoon and getting dim, but I was sure this was my Gracie! It looked so much like her, right down to that short forepaw. And that's how I came by Caesar here."

The boys had coaxed the dog to roll over for a belly scratch, and Derrick cast a worried look at his brother. Both were wondering how a mutt named Gracie could be confused with a male clearly sporting "meat and two veg."

"Uh, sir," Sam said weakly. "Why would you reckon some bloke dog—"

"It wouldn't have been a good idea for me to hang around," the man continued. "I managed to coax this dog into the back seat with a bag of chips, and I drove off quickly. Didn't realize I had the wrong beast until I was 20 miles down the road.

"It became obvious when I stopped for gasoline, but I noticed something else—something even more amazing. Caesar here had the same keen eye as Gracie, perhaps even more so. He was

206

watching the customers at the filling station, and I was watching him. The more agitated they were, the more interested he grew. There is obviously a shared blood line, I'm certain of it! And rather than risk another run into town, the situation being what it was, I determined the best course of action would be to train Caesar properly."

"Train him to do what?" Sam asked.

The boys listened as the old man explained how Gracie had an amazing talent for sizing up people, the ones about to buckle under pressure. Together, Gracie and Piperson had invented something new: dog-assisted stock trading.

Piperson said he was on a layover in Brisbane, brushing up on his Mandarin and honing Caesar's people skills at the poker table. Soon, they would set out for the stock exchange in Shanghai, a city at the center of global finance, a market about to open its doors to foreign traders. When it did, Shanghai would be "ripe for the introduction of dog-assisted trading."

"I only hope that my Caesar here can shine at Gracie's level," the old man said, tugging hard as the dog again tried to slip the harness. "We're off for Shanghai just as soon as he masters that look—that Gracie look."

Piperson nodded across the river to a great stone fortress on the banks of the Brisbane, the real Treasury Casino.

"That's where we're headed now, boys," he said, "The poker rooms await—great practice for Caesar."

"Sir," Sam said, "how did you know what that man on the bike yelled a while back? You couldn't read his lips—he was going too fast. Are you really deaf?"

Piperson swallowed hard and made a mental note. Two Aussie schoolboys had called him out in less than five minutes. He would have to do better.

The old man scanned the terraced bluffs nearby. Houses peered down on the Brisbane River, big homes with fringes of gingerbread and lattice. They looked a bit like Victorians, but many stood on stilts, a testament to the river's predilection to flood and kill by the hundreds. To Piperson's delight, Caesar was eyeing the houses, too—just as fixed on them as Gracie had been on the ill-fated Victorian mansions back home.

"Stout fellow! Gracie would have done just so," Piperson said, patting the dog's chest. "What do you call those, boys?"

Sam and Derrick glanced at each other.

"Houses, sir," Sam said. "What do Yanks call 'em?"

"No, the style. What's that style called?"

"Oh, right. Queenslanders. Those houses are Queenslanders all right," Sam said.

"Sir, are you really deaf?" Derrick repeated.

"It comes and goes," Piperson replied in a low tone. Then he turned on his heels, dragging Caesar down the path. The boys stood their ground, watching the man and dog walk away, and Piperson could hear them debating his story.

Calls of "Sir!" and "Sir, wait!" tapped Piperson on the shoulder, but he ignored them. Deaf means deaf.

The boys followed the man in the Homburg hat as he plunged his dog back into the stream of pedestrians. Together, they walked to a path leading to a row of two-story Queenslanders that teetered on the bluffs. Then the old man and the old Hobbs County rover broke from the crowd and walked up the hill toward the houses.

"Comes and goes," Derrick repeated to his brother. "Reckon he was lying?"

"Dunno," Sam replied. "Does seem keen on houses, though."

Michael Rose writes for a labor union in Washington, D.C., and he has reported on issues in K-12 education since 1986. Prior to that, he covered a variety of beats for several newspapers and news services in the Washington area. His articles and profiles have won awards from the Maryland-Delaware-DC Press Association, the Education Writers Association and other organizations. To research this story, he took Rocky, the family German shepherd, through therapy pet training classes. This is his first novel.